THE
VIEW
FROM
HERE

THE
VIEW
FROM
HERE

DEBORAH McKINLAY

Published by
Soho Press, Inc.
853 Broadway
New York, NY 10003

Library of Congress Cataloging-in-Publication Data

McKinlay, Deborah.
The view from here / by Deborah McKinlay.
p. cm.
ISBN 978-1-56947-871-4
1. Marriage—Fiction. 2. Family secrets—Fiction. I. Title.
PR6113.C4897V54 2011
823'.92—dc22
2010032518

10 9 8 7 6 5 4 3 2 1

For Marcus and Frazer, our beautiful boys

PROLOGUE

I WAS A BLONDE eating an avocado, in a country where avocados were plentiful and blondes were rare, on a hot night over half my lifetime ago. Outside it was nearly dark, the sea in the curve of the bay was flat and shadowy, and somewhere across the street music played.

I have been told that there are hamburger chains and hotels with strip-lit lobbies in that part of Mexico now, but then it was mostly blue-walled places where you could eat chicken and yellow-walled places where you could drink beer and, once in a while, dusty tourists passing through.

That evening the restaurant was busy, but I heard American voices and I looked up. They were a dozen or so, adults and children, and people watched as they sat at several tables pushed together, on the open side of the room. One of the women fanned herself with a menu.

The children, who had been noisy, settled suddenly, and it was just as the gabble dipped and a quick, engulfing quiet fell that a voice, still party-pitched, announced: "Sally, I have never slept with your husband."

A measured, cooler tone answered, "I couldn't care less, darling. Everybody else has."

O N E

THE MIDWINTERS HERE are never pale. Paleness suggests translucence, and our winters are swampy, no hint of crisp blue overhead. Just now, near Christmas, there is gray rain and a slip of mud at every doorway, and I am thinking a great deal about death.

The season, its associations with joy and birth, denies me the opportunity to speak of such a smothering topic, despite the circumstances, despite my hope, which is to die, softly and soon. Of course even once the fresh twelve months is upon us, I will not express this wish, not in words, at least not to Phillip or Chloe. I suspect, anyway, that they know and that it is this knowledge that hushes them sometimes and hurries them from my presence, though they never confront me with it, or anything else. I am fragile now, as glass, in their eyes. No matter the rage of my thoughts.

I remember the pain, the first that signaled this ending. I remember it quite vividly; it came not long after last Christmas on a day as dull as this one. Evidently we remember things because they are anchored in some way, but anchoring is a weighty concept, and I was, just then, in the grip of something shrill . . . panic. I was reading a letter.

The letter was signed *Josee*, like that, with an *ee*. I knew who Josee was, but the *ee* fixated me, since it signaled so clearly the age of the signer, until the pain interrupted and shook my concentration for a half beat. Nobody over forty is called Josee with an *ee*, are they? Though of course, soon enough, that must change. As I said, I knew who Josee was, so her youth was already familiar to me, and had seemed, in that different context, unremarkable, but at that moment it glared, suddenly scarlet. I stared at her signature—fat and a little wild—for a few more unwinding moments, though it was the line above it that held the real clout, and then left off the slow distracted pat that my left hand had set up at my midline, the pain having receded into what doctors call "discomfort."

I folded the letter and put it back in its envelope. And I put the envelope back into the drawer of my husband's desk, Phillip's desk, where I had found it. Where I had gone looking for it, or something like it—something that would tell me what it had told me.

I will be forty-six years old next July, if I live until then, which I doubt. Almost no age at all if you look at it from a mathematical perspective. To me, though, forty-six seems fairly aged, perhaps because my forty-plus years have afforded me so many lives, this last the most content and therefore the least notable of all. That is, until Josee's letter came, and the discomfort came, and with those things the story and, worse, the reminders of stories past.

. . .

Richard Luke was a scrubbed-looking man, athletic and good-schoolish. His coloring was fair, the kind that tends to redden slightly with sunlight, and his features, though handsome enough, were so even that they rendered him not commonplace exactly, but unexceptional. He looked as though he should be advertising something wholesome. When he asked what had brought me there he dropped the *x* in Mexico.

"A boyfriend," I replied, shrugging to complete the explanation.

"Mexican?"

"At heart," I answered.

It was the woman to my left who laughed in response. She was Richard's wife, Patsy, and her magazine-cover lips were tilted into a suggestive curve.

I laughed too.

It was a cocktail party, delicately backlit pink, the temperature clement enough to encourage bare shoulders among the women, and the sounds of ice cubes against glass and water against the stone of a courtyard fountain wove in and out of the easy small talk. The year was 1976, and Mexico was a place where people went looking for a good time.

Six carefree, attractive Americans to whom I had recently been introduced were strung along the happy balcony. Watching them exercising their practiced charm on a few of the better-heeled locals, I decided that they were probably always having a good time.

Patsy Luke quit laughing and drifted toward a woman called Bee Bee Newson. I had caught Bee Bee's eye a little earlier and had felt, just slightly, appraised by her. She was a thin woman with a thin face, though the thinness was offset by the thickness of her hair, which was that ash blonde color that is only ever achieved with professional help. It hung straight and grazed her collarbones and her eyebrows and emphasized the shaded quality of her eyes. They had caught mine only momentarily before she had swung away, leaving me with the rear view of her expensive-looking outfit, white trousers and bright silk top, and a large gold bracelet that evidently annoyed her. She kept raising her arm and shaking her hand to adjust its position on her wrist.

Cornered then by the juxtaposition of a stone pillar and Richard's elbow, I began, a little headily, to flirt with him. I was almost two months out of a dreary breakup from the boyfriend I had mentioned and I was young, and conscious that my white dress showed off my tan.

The flirtation, though, rewarded by too bland an attractiveness, didn't command my energy for long and my happy mood might have faltered had Richard not, with the clamp of an innocently sporty hand on my upper arm, twisted me toward the beaming moon-face of Maria Rodriguez, our hostess.

"Lovely party," he said.

Two high points of thrilled color were set burning in Maria's plump cheeks. She nodded shyly.

At the other end of the balcony Bee Bee's husband, Ned, raised his voice, uniting the gathering. "Nice place you have here, Señor Rodriguez."

Arturo Rodriguez lifted his hand in a dismissive thank-you

and looked pleased. There wasn't a nicer house for five hundred miles, except one, which he knew, as he knew everything about that region. There was, some twenty minutes' drive distant, a butter-colored palace, set in high-walled, glamour-tinged privacy above a crystal sand beach. Anyone who ever walked on that beach pointed and looked up.

Arturo liked to know people who spent time in houses like that, so when he had heard that an American couple called the Severances, who now stood not three feet from him, were vacationing there, he had wasted no time in advising Maria that she must give a little party. I was Maria's English teacher, one of the few English speakers she knew. And that was how I had come to be standing among the well-tended foliage and black wrought iron with Richard and Patsy Luke and Ned and Bee Bee Newson, who were in turn guests of the Severances, Mason and Sally. They all looked as if they breakfasted habitually beneath orange trees.

Mason Severance had been slipped to my side by the subtle repositioning that interruptions create at parties. He was a striking man whose silver brown hair had been cropped a little shorter than was fashionable then. In profile he could have graced a gold coin, or a poster for some sort of epic movie. He was thumbing the paper napkin wrapping his empty glass absently. There was something terribly intense about him, apparent in even so slight a gesture.

"Is there much work here," he asked, "for an English teacher?" He made "English teacher" sound exotic.

"Enough," I said. It was a lie. I almost never worked.

"And you like living here?"

"Yes, I do."

"Well, if you find yourself out in our neck of the woods

any time feel free to come in and say something charming." Ned said joining us. He was grinning.

I grinned back. He had that quality that children and women warm to, an avuncular combination of humor and kindness. He was thin like his wife, but in him it was rangy. He looked as though he could tap dance, and whistle in tune, and make corned beef hash from a secret recipe. I already liked him.

"Have you seen the house?" Mason asked. It was the kind of house you could refer to in that way, simply. It was famous and had warranted, I'd heard, a five-page spread in *House & Garden*.

"Only from the beach," I answered, meeting his gaze.

"Come for lunch on Sunday," Sally Severance cut in.

I looked at her directly then, drawn by the command in her voice, but in fact I had been half watching her for much of the evening. She was the most beautiful woman I had ever seen.

"Yes," her husband confirmed, "you should."

"Thank you," I replied.

My glass was empty now too. I handed it to Maria's maid and saw, from the corner of my eye, Maria gesturing with a flappy one-handed motion for her employee to circulate with more drinks. But the maid didn't seem to notice, and anyway, the party was fading. In the west the sky's mauve tint had deepened.

Sally shut her eyes briefly, concentrating it seemed on the ice she had taken with the last mouthful of her drink. Then she looked up and, with very little disturbance of her flawless face, shot a glance at her husband. He, immediately catching the message in it, set his own glass down and said in a farewell tone, "Sunday, then."

They left, the six of them, amid much fluttering from Maria and a great deal of hand pumping from Arturo. I stood on the curved steps and watched them go. At the gate Bee Bee tottered slightly in her delicate shoes and almost tripped. Ned steadied her and, turning, waved his free arm and called, "See ya, Frankie."

I smiled. It was the first time anyone had ever called me anything but Frances.

· · ·

Many years later, in a rearranged world where I am once again known by the name my parents selected, twenty-seven days elapsed between my discovery of the letter signed *Josee* and the afternoon that I went to Doctor Griffith's dun-colored office in Barnham with my husband. She had asked us to come together, telephoning me after a routine visit the week before. The pain, though no worse, had been constant, and I had mentioned it to her. You don't think, do you, in those moments that they will change your life? She had sent me for tests.

Even our joint summons did not alert me to what was to come. I was preoccupied with other things, other concerns. Phillip parked the car neatly between the two white lines nearest to the medical center's automated glass doors and then, in the busy waiting area, we sat for a few minutes, side by side on blue vinyl, thinking our own thoughts. Then we were called, and told what we were told. You don't really take it in. Or I didn't, not then.

I have wondered sometimes since what went through Phillip's mind as we listened to those words, smoothly delivered in Dr. Griffith's even tone—a considered weld of concern and reassurance and professionalism—whether perhaps, like me, he felt that he was being punished, though for a recent transgression rather than one long past, as in my case.

Anyway, she said what she said and asked for our questions and then, with clean efficiency, set the great train rolling, the great thundering train that takes over your life when you have the sort of tumor that I have.

In the twilight time between the first set of investigations and the scheduled longer hospital stay for the initial attempt at treatment, cure even, we went to Italy and stayed in a pretty hotel on a pretty lake, its blue blurred to dove at the edges by fog because of the time of year.

On the second morning of our stay I wanted my green scarf. It is the scarf that goes with my cream coat, and I wanted it very much, but I couldn't find it. I turned out all the drawers, neat and organized and almost empty, as they only ever are on holidays, and then I hauled our suitcases out from the back of the wardrobe and searched those. Eventually I realized that I had forgotten the scarf and I sat on the edge of the bed and shook, and then I began to sob.

Phillip said, sitting beside me, "We'll get you a new scarf, darling, a beautiful new scarf." His tears began then too, stifling mine. "Everything will be all right," he said through them.

And I thought, *It will. We'll make it all all right.* It was not my illness that was uppermost in my mind at the time.

I had told no one about Josee's letter, not even Catherine or Sonia, my closest friends, which is strange I suppose given the amount of talk, and all the rest that marriage and children and life throws up to women, that has passed between us over the years. But I had not been able to face any sort of telling out loud. That would have elicited advice, and judgment, and discussion, until the thing had grown to the point that I'd have had to unload it, confront Phillip, and I did not have the energy. That sort of confrontation demands passion and blood and youth, and mine had been draining from me.

Of course the fact that I had buried the knowledge, and worse the gradual understanding, that my husband was unfaithful did not alter the fact of it. The thing did not disappear, or reform into some new easier-to-handle shape, or even lie dormant, but festered instead, emerging in that kind of sharpness that women have so much more readily at their tongue-tips than men.

Verbally, I had always been mercury to Phillip's molasses and it had been impossible, with what I knew coiled tense inside me, with Josee's letter repeating itself in my head, not to spring at him from time to time, not to sting him a little when the opportunity presented itself, as inevitably it did. We are a man and a woman married twenty years, after all, and finely tuned to each other's failings, no matter how slight. But then, more than once, in the middle of some petty, terrier-tongued attack I was struck by the possibility that my malice would be reported to another with whom novelty and unavailability were still oiling the way for constant, soothing affection. And so I attempted to wrap my razors in cotton wool, alternating my small meannesses with anxious gushes of geniality. It is unfair, isn't it, the way that the betrayed are so often wrenched into behavior that makes them ridiculous, behavior that helps to justify the betrayal?

Phillip was no more evenhanded with me, switching bouts of criticism with displays of affection that smacked of trying too hard, settling often into long, distracted silences. Things had been that way for several months. A sort of electrified space had grown up between us, primed to spark into some ghastly, goalless argument. The kind that leads to nothing but exhaustion and waste.

But then, unexpectedly, there we were, hand in hand on that big bed in the honey-lit Italian hotel room, husband and wife again, a new tie binding us. A new challenge had been added to the bonds that living together and sleeping together and losing people and crying and raising a child together had already wrought. And I decided that it would be possible to banish this other woman, an outsider, a trespasser, both from my mind and from our lives, and to start over.

It was very easy during the soft days that followed to settle on this resolution. They were so pleasant. Full of wine and long lunches and meandering walks along pastel alleyways to the lakeside, all designed not to tax me. We went on ferry rides, Phillip winding my new scarf—the color of the lake beneath—carefully around my neck. A gauzy tenderness descended between us, blunting the edges of our talk and turning our lovemaking gossamer. I believed us to be in one of those fresh-start phases that characterizes long marriages, the links a little delicate, but the purpose shared.

I thought that way until, arriving back in England, I queued to buy tissues in the airport and, turning from the kiosk, saw Phillip speaking on the telephone. He was at one of a quartet of those curved plastic booths that shield only the upper half of the body. He was leaning against the molded exterior and I could see his face. What was it about him, about his manner, that warned me, even across the acres of strangers and hospital-lit serviceable surfaces? His eyes were dipped, almost closed, and his expression was intense, urgent even, utterly engrossed. Suddenly, sensing my gaze perhaps, he lifted his head and hung up, and then he roved his eyes, scanning for mine. On catching them, he sent me a cheerful, childish wave that I felt myself hate him for and he lumbered toward me, battling with the luggage trolley. Then we left together, he leading the way to the taxi stand.

That night we stayed in a hotel in London and ate supper in our room at one of those tables that waiters wheel in and prop up and dress with white linen and vases of candy-colored blooms and foliage that do not belong. As we began Phillip said, "The books are doing very well," and smiled, as if he were awarding me some sort of prize. He has always smiled like that.

Phillip is an attractive man, but his looks are quiet—long legs and a sprinkle of gray at the temples—so the smile takes you by surprise because there is so much self-confidence in it. Just then, aware of its attractiveness and the effect that that surprising smile could have, even on me, even after all these years, I felt a bit sick. All the more sick because I wanted to ask, and yet desperately did not want to, whether this news about the books was based on some fresh information gleaned during a hushed and passionately vital telephone call to his editor. That's who Josee was, is—Phillip's editor. Well, Phillip's and Tom Creel's.

Phillip and Tom are partners in a small, but very successful, advertising agency—Creel & Grace. There are two other partners now, but their names only feature on the letterhead. Phillip and Tom, on the back of some ideas that were boozily sketched out over a long Sunday lunch at the Creels' house at which I was present along with Tom's wife, Alice, have written two books about marketing together. The reviewer for the *Times' Weekend Supplement* called these books the "rare sort that change the way you think" and a lot of other people said similar things. Phillip and Tom have been on the radio and on the television and are quoted now in all sorts of places. They have had their photographs in the papers.

Josee has one of those photographs in a frame on the bookcase behind her desk. I saw it there when, joining Phillip for lunch once, I met him at his publisher. I have wondered since whether it was already happening then. Whether they stood in the same room as me, a pair, smiling. Knowing.

"So I thought I might do another one," Phillip went on, "only without Tom. I've spoken to him and he agrees. In fact, it would work out well because then he'd be in the office while I was at home." Another smile was awarded here. "What I mean is that I could stay at home for the next few months, with you."

I had too many conflicting thoughts to reply straightaway. Phillip lifted his soup spoon again from the side plate where he had rested it while he spoke and held it in midair for a moment, waiting.

"In case you needed me," he explained, unnecessarily.

Phillip and Tom had, for several years now, shared a two-bedroom, two-bathroom flat at the less expensive end of one of the more expensive areas of London. Alice and I never went there, preferring to stay in hotels, or with friends, when we were in town. We spoke of "the flat" as if it were "the dorm";

it had that sort of association for us, studenty. But Phillip and Tom each spent about three nights a week there, more or less happily, not making the journey in from home on the other days, their seniority having afforded them this luxury, and a bevy of keen young assistants. Reflecting on this arrangement I thought, surprisingly for the first time, that Phillip might have confided in Tom about Josee. If he had, would Tom have told Alice? The idea appalled me. The humiliation. Strange, isn't it, the sense of shame that someone else's misdeeds can engender?

But now here was Phillip suggesting that he should give that up, the weekly trip to London, to the office. To his lover. He would be with me all the time, and even if I'd miss the small freedoms that I had come to enjoy in his absences—the mistimed meals, the unstructured days, the long evening conversations with friends—I took this suggestion as a sign that I might have misread the airport telephone call, that the well of warm feeling that had been refilled during the past few days had not been poisoned after all.

"I'd like that," I said as the waiter reappeared at the door. He had forgotten our water.

The next morning we met Chloe at the station. It was Friday, and she had taken the day off work so as to spend a long weekend with us. It was her third trip home since my news, which is what people called it—*I was so sorry to hear your news*—and she had spoken to me every day. She greeted us on the busy concourse with a young person's shout and flagrant affection. Chloe is twenty-five years old and very pretty. She looks just like her mother.

"Let's see," I said, peering at her feet.

She twisted a slim leg toward me to show off a new knee-length black boot and said, "Maggie gave them to me," a little shyly, as if this gift were illicit rather than something naturally passed between blood-tied people, between a woman and her daughter.

She still feels, I think, a need to protect me, not from Maggie in particular, but from her relationship with her. She wants to stress that I am "mother." It is what she introduces me as. She calls me "Ma" these days, while reserving an unadorned "Maggie" for the woman who gave birth to her. I need her reassurance much less than she thinks, but I appreciate her efforts anyway. And, it's true, I was once much thinner-skinned on the subject. The day when Chloe was ten, when Maggie made contact again for the first time, the first time since she had disappeared just after Chloe's first birthday, is still vivid for me.

Looking at Chloe then, especially tall in her new boots, I thought about all the anxiety that call of Maggie's had engendered, and the much-negotiated, much-monitored eventual reunion. It had all come to this, all that turmoil, mellowed to so much casual conversation on a railway platform.

"How is she?" I asked

"Oh, she's fine. She sent a book for you."

It would be a book about healing, about the cyclical nature of things and the danger of burying emotions, a book about the mind's effect on illness. I didn't need a book to learn about things like that.

I smiled and looped my arm through Chloe's, and at the announcement of our train, we walked together, trailing Phillip, luggage-laden again, down the platform to our carriage. Chloe's overnight bag was threatening to topple from its perch on top of our two larger, matching suitcases, and Phillip had to stretch his hand awkwardly to prevent the fall. He jerked his head to indicate where our seats were, and Chloe and I sat and compared magazines while he attended to the unloading. What a happy family we must have looked. A seamless happy family.

The weekend was like so many weekends before it. We fell quickly into the easy patterns of our history together, even in the shadows of those thunderclouds, even with my fresh hospital admission looming. Chloe lay about and looked lovely and leaned on things and picked at food and tossed her hair and talked. About her friends, about her job, about her boyfriend, Ed, about the decorating she was planning for her flat. Phillip and I, from old habit, caught conspiratorial eyes over her head, united as always by our adoration for her. Things like that don't change so readily.

I was feeling well and considered the fact that I had never really felt ill. I felt no more ill knowing that the tentacles of something sinister lurked in the deep recesses of my abdomen than I had before I had known it, and that other concern, that anxiety that had set the fear really clanging, was beginning to seem less real too. If Phillip was willing to give up his London time and stay at home with me, then perhaps after all I had exaggerated the thing in my own mind. I knew that I did not believe this, but I also knew that I needed to accept it to some extent, to convince myself of it, in order to avoid the damage that dwelling on the possibilities would do. I was just managing to haul myself up onto this high, level plain of reasonableness when Phillip made the announcement that sent me scrabbling for a foothold again.

Chloe was stretched on the sofa, half reading, half sleeping, absently stroking Hobo, who is rather a cross old cat these days, though he still succumbs to her charms.

"Weren't you going to see Emma?" I asked her.

She looked over at me and rolled her eyes and grinned. "Don't worry," she said, drawling a little for affect, "I won't miss my train."

I laughed, because that was exactly what I was worried about. Chloe always leaves things until the last minute and, as it was, she was planning on taking the late train after she'd been up to the village to catch up with Emma. Chloe and Emma were at school together, and Brownies, and swimming club, and ballet. It was that kind of friendship. The kind that dims and flares again all through life.

"Put your things in your bag at least, and put the bag by the door. That way I'll feel more secure," I said

"You needn't display so much unseemly desire to be rid of me."

She got up though, dislodging Hobo, who looked displeased, but soon managed to settle himself smoothly into the warm spot she had vacated with that absolute indolence that only cats can manage. Crossing to my chair, she bent and kissed me.

"People get fired," I told her, "even little hotshot magazine writer cookies like you. They get fired, they starve, they end up on the streets, they turn to crime. I worry."

"She worries," Phillip said, joining the game. We all knew our parts.

"Oh, I'll do fine on the streets," Chloe cooed, twisting herself into a cartoon hooker's swivel.

Her father hit her rump with a roll of Sunday newspaper.

"I'll take the train to London with you," he said. Then he offered to make tea with no change of tone.

I don't know why I had assumed that his permanence in the house would be immediate. He had never said so much, though it had been implied, I was sure, that he would stick with me now, until we knew that I was entirely well again. I still thought that way then, that I would be entirely well again. In fact, I had begun to think that the illness, like the other thing, was some sort of aberration, a brief, nasty interlude, soon to be swept away by a cleansing wave of normality. But I wanted Phillip with me in the meantime. Phillip's physical presence was part of the confirmation of this.

When he came back with the tea, pulling a footstool toward my chair to put mine on, I said, "I had in my mind that you would be here this week."

He sat, balancing his own cup at chest height.

"There are a few loose ends, sweet. I need to get everything tidied up at the office, make sure Carla can cope and Tom's up to speed on everything. That way I'll be able to manage things from here from now on."

I nodded because, on the face of it, this was perfectly sensible. There was no logical reason why the acid should have begun creeping in my stomach.

"Anyway," he went on, putting his cup on the floor at his side, leaning back, casual now, "you're seeing Sonia tomorrow. I'm sure she'd stay"—his tone softened then—"if you don't want to be on your own. It's only two nights, though," he added. "I'll be back on Tuesday."

I reassured him, I would be fine. Sonia would certainly stay if I asked her and perhaps I would, but there were things

I wanted to get done before next week, the hospital week, so a day or two to myself would be useful.

Chloe had gone off by then, to get her jacket and comb her hair I suppose, and Phillip and I slipped effortlessly into the kind of conversation—about packing, and train times, and what's for supper—that people have in marriages. I cannot remember a word of it, though only a few months separate me from that afternoon and now, and yet I do recall, with sunlit clarity, every detail of every moment that I spent with another man twenty-three years ago.

· · ·

It was Richard Luke who collected me that long-ago Sunday after Maria's party in a big navy Buick with ivory leather seats. He patted the dashboard affectionately. Good cars, he told me, Buicks. His father had sworn by them.

The car cruised along smoothly till the buildings began to thin out and huddle together. There was a rubbish dump at the edge of town, a gaudy tangle of trash, bordered at the back by a billboard advertising cigarettes. Children, boys mostly, played on the road nearby—improvised games with stones and cans. Richard slowed and gave the horn a mild slap with the flat of his hand. A woman, scavenging, looked up briefly and the children scattered then chased after the car, laughing and shouting, as we pulled off again. Richard glanced in the rearview mirror. He had two boys of his own, he said. He gave me a look that implied he knew an awful lot about boys.

Soon, the macadam ended and we were on the long straight of the dirt part of the road. Red brown earth, peppered with scrubby trees and cactus, stretched endless on either side.

I pointed. "One of my students asked me once 'How do you call this in English?'"

Richard turned his head. "You mean cactus?" he asked.

"Yes. That's what I told him, 'cactus.' But then he said, 'And what about this and this?'" I made little stabs with my index finger at the windows.

"More cactus," Richard said flatly.

"They distinguish between them, people who live here."

Richard's softly freckled face was uncomprehending.

"They don't just call them *all* cactus," I explained. "It's like Eskimos, you know, having dozens of words for snow."

"Aaah," he replied vaguely.

The car sent up a thin cloud of orange dust. Sealed inside, strangers, a light unease divided us.

Eventually, Richard bridged the chasm with chitchat about his children, Hudson and Howie. Howie was eight and Hudson was some number of months that meant nothing to me. Richard said that he'd been giving Howie tennis lessons this vacation and that the kid was getting along just great.

We saw the tennis court as soon as we passed through the high arched gate that broke the wall surrounding the house. Two teenage girls were standing near the net. One, taller with a rope of blonde hair, was flipping a ball idly up and down, up and down on her racquet. I was conscious of her watching us as we got out of the car.

Up close the great creamy sprawl of the house was too much to take in. I stuck close behind Richard, who ignored the vast, double-fronted door we had parked beneath, and headed instead for the sharp right angle of a corner to the left. Rounding it we were greeted by the perfect blue of an oblong swimming pool, and beyond that, over a wall that dipped with the contours of the cliff, the boundless azure of the glittering Pacific.

Mason was in the pool, swimming. Intent on lengths, he didn't react to our appearance. I followed Richard through some open glass doors where, in a big, airy room that looked onto the patio, Ned Newson grinned his slim grin.

"Hello, Frankie," he said.

"Hello," I smiled.

"Good. Now that Frankie's here it's a party," Mason said, suddenly behind me, wrapped in a towel. He bent and began to pull glasses out from a cupboard under a sideboard, the skin on his back still sheeny with damp. "Go sit out by the pool. Swim." He gestured with an empty tumbler toward the bright outdoors.

"I'll take you."

I looked down to see a small girl with light, tousled hair falling almost to her waist. She was all curves, like a peanut.

"This is my daughter Jenny," Mason said.

"And this is Jessica," said Jenny. There was another Severance child, thinner, but in other respects matching, standing in the doorway, worrying at the edges of her swimsuit. "We're twins."

The little girls tugged at my hands leading me back out to the pool. Then they swam while I sat on the mosaic edge, swinging my legs in the water.

"Frankie's a good name," Jenny said, kicking her feet near my knees.

"Thank you. Ned gave it to me."

"You're welcome," Ned said with a bow, appearing beside me.

Jenny arced off, swam to the other side of the pool, and looped back. She was a dolphin.

"We're nine," she said, "nearly ten. How old are you?"

"Twenty-two."

"Damn you," a woman's voice said from the doorway, though without vehemence. It was Bee Bee in owlish sunglasses and a tangerine ensemble that bared her midriff. "It's bad enough having Patsy down here parading her pert little rear." Despite the confidence of her appearance her movements were tentative. She stretched herself gingerly onto a white lounge chair. Once she was horizontal she gave the salt-rimmed glass she was holding a deft upward toss. "Cheers."

Mason handed me a drink. "To twenty-two."

"To tequila," Ned said.

"To temperatures in the high eighties," Richard added, with a small, stiff flick of a toast. His words, though, were drowned slightly by Howie's arrival at the pool. He joined Jenny in the water with a shrieking yahoo and a lot of splashing.

Patsy Luke came out onto the deck then, holding Hudson, hands around his chubby chest, at a forearm's length from her body. Both mother and child looked rather detached from the process. She set him on the ground next to Jessica, who was seated near the edge of the pool.

"Watch Huddy for a minute, honey," she said, "while I get a drink."

Jessica, water beaded on her narrow shoulders, seemed too slight a child for such a robust responsibility. She watched nervously as the baby creased his dumpling face and began to whine.

Howie yelled, "Put some soda on your finger."

Jessica dipped her littlest finger into her Coca-Cola and offered it timidly to Hudson, who clasped her hand and began to suck happily.

"That always shuts him up," Howie said. Despite his rambunctiousness he was a boy with a resigned look about him.

"Hi," a new female voice said.

I looked up. It was the taller girl, the blonde, from the tennis court. Her greeting had been directed at Richard. She was staring at him now, fixedly.

"That's Paige," said Jessica, "our sister. She's fourteen."

"And she *luurves* Richard," Jenny added.

I watched as Paige Severance, her eyes hard on Patsy's husband, settled herself in an upright chair, draped an elbow over its slatted back, and crossed her bare legs. If Richard was aware of the shock of sensuality revealed in the faint trace of blue at her wrists and the exposed milky cleft of her elbow, he made no response to it.

Paige was followed by Lesley Newson. She was younger, thirteen, Jenny informed me, and coltish with springy auburn hair. She was like her mother, I thought, glancing at Bee Bee. Their faces were similar, handsome rather than pretty, although Bee Bee's, even then slackened by prone slavishness to the sun, hinted at something that Lesley's didn't. Something almost hard.

If Bee Bee's face had a story to tell, though, I was too green to recognize it, so my attention was not diverted for long from the pleasant scene developing around me. I was rather dazzled by it all. The nonchalant polish of the people. The gentle flurry of staff. Everything glowing with poolshine.

"Mason, don't stare at your daughter's breasts."

I started at the sound of Sally's voice and flicked my eyes

up to the level of her fingernails at my side. They were perfect as seashells.

"Breasts!" Jenny hollered. "Bazooms!"

Paige, flushing, threw a towel at her. "Oh ha-ha."

The towel hit the pool. Jenny, ducking it, slipped under the water and rose next to Howie. She dunked him, hands neat on top of his gingery head. Howie, clumsily attempting to retaliate, hurled an inflatable sea horse, which splashed Hudson, who began to wail. Paige disappeared into the house.

Mason, apparently oblivious to his wife's remark and the melee it had sparked, lowered himself to sit next to me. His thighs, I noticed, already had a dusting of Mexican tan.

"Are you a swimmer, Frankie?" he asked.

"Not really."

He looked at me as if my answer required further explanation.

"My parents are Scottish."

He laughed. Across the pool, Patsy took a quick mouthful of her drink and put her glass down. She reached back and looped her smooth chocolate hair into a ponytail, before standing, diving, and swimming a clean length.

"Patsy's a swimmer," said Mason, watching her, "and a skier, and a sailor, and a polo player . . ." We watched Patsy's flip turn and her effortless progress back to the point where she'd started. "*Her* parents are rich."

Patsy climbed out of the pool and draped a patterned robe around her shoulders. It was the oriental kind with deep square pockets. She pulled a packet of cigarettes out, removed one with her long tapered fingers, and lit it with a silver lighter that I have since learned was recognizable to other people as having come from a famous New York jewelry store.

"Rich ain't a big enough word for what Patsy's parents are," Ned said as she exhaled, her Venus neck stretching her chin skyward.

"Show your mother your backstroke, Howie!" Richard yelled over our heads.

Howie squinted toward his father, his hair cowlicked from swimming.

"Your backstroke," shouted Richard, "like I taught you." He was making loping swimming movements and nodding his head enthusiastically.

Howie stared.

"Yeah, like this, kid." Ned, rotating his arms, Charlie Chaplinish, walked backward into the pool. He was fully dressed and still holding his glass.

"Never have yellow for an awning. Or a marquee," Sally said.

We were sitting at a long table under a bougainvillea-covered arbor. I looked out over the pool. There were yellow canvas sun umbrellas shielding two round tables on the far side of it. I thought they looked rather glamorous. Like something from an expensive hotel, or one of those beach clubs you see in films, old films full of immaculately made-up women.

"Pink," she said. "Pink or red. The light from them is far more flattering."

She had removed her hat, loosing a vanilla blonde sweep across her forehead. As she turned I saw that there were tiny, feathery lines at the corners of her eyes. She was, perhaps, fifteen years older than me. Her beauty, though, had lost none of its power. She signaled to a maid.

"Thank you, Christina," she said softly as her plate was cleared.

I looked at Christina. I had heard her speaking Spanish to the other staff, but I was sure she wasn't local.

"Christina is our own housekeeper," Sally said, following my gaze. "She came down ahead of us to open the house and organize extra help. I depend on her."

I nodded, feeling a little awkward. As if this were the sort of thing I ought to have realized for myself.

At four o'clock we were still sitting at the table, apart from the children who milled at the edges. Coffee things were brought. Howie made a darting grab at a dish of butter cookies and managed to net several. He pushed them, all at once, messily into his mouth, spraying crumbs and unleashing a wail of complaints from the girls.

At the other end of the table, his mother, Patsy, was oblivious. She was sharing some joke with Mason, her laughter mixing throatily with his. Sally, looking toward the sound, said crisply, "Christina, take that child and have some dry clothes put on him."

So Howie was led off, suddenly meek, goosebumpy in his nylon swimsuit.

"How long will you stay?" I asked a bit too loudly. Sally's flash of brusqueness had unnerved me.

It was Mason who answered. "Who knows," he said, smiling down the table and spreading his hands.

"We're refugees from the icy East Coast," Patsy added before turning to Bee Bee. "Were you at that party at the McFees's last week? Lizzie Calder kept her mink on all through dinner."

Bee Bee laughed. "I happen to know how Lizzie Calder came by that mink," she said, "but that's another story."

"We got out of school before spring break even started," Jessica announced, rerouting the conversation from the adult turn it had taken. "And we probably won't even go back before the beginning of next semester. We'll probably miss that too." She looked happy about this possibility, but suddenly a little taken aback by the boldness of her little speech. Everyone was looking at her.

"Yes, we must all show our gratitude to the demanding wife," Bee Bee said. "Here's to a much underappreciated species."

Jessica, as lost as I was, just stared at her. Mason must have noticed our confusion. "The owner's wife isn't keen on Mexico," he explained to me, Jessica having lost interest. "She'd like something similar to this"—he swept his arm, taking in the rambling spread of the house horseshoed around us—"a little closer to Palm Springs." There was general laughter. "They're friends. I said I'd take a look."

Mason was an architect. When he had told me that earlier, Ned had commented, "That's like saying Mr. Kellogg makes cornflakes."

"Actually," Mason went on, "the house is for sale. I think the idea was that I might decide I couldn't live without it. That's why I invited these idlers—they're backup potential purchasers."

"How do you like that?" Ned complained. "Dragged around by our wallets."

"Some of us can't be away for too long, though," Richard said seriously, unintentionally dampening the mood.

"For Christ's sake, Richard," Patsy snapped, "don't start raining on the parade yet." There was genuine irritation in her voice, but her husband's unresponsive shrug seemed to dull it.

"Whaddya gonna do?" she sighed, playing to the crowd. "I married a t-crosser."

Ned slung a loose arm along the back of Bee Bee's chair. "Well, they won't shake *us* off too easy, will they, kid?"

Bee Bee picked up her drink, tapped it against her coffee cup, and drained it. "Nope," she said. "Better people have tried."

"Call yourself a host?" Ned scolded Mason then. "My wife's glass is empty."

Smiling, Mason stood as Sally turned to me.

"I'll have a room made up," she said. "I don't think anyone is going to be driving you home."

In the morning, waking in the very quiet of that great, slumbering house, I felt strange. But it was early. The stripes of sunlight that had begun to creep through the slats of the shutters lacked force; it was still cool enough for two layers of bedding. I gave mine a tug, straightening the heavy cotton spread, and reached to switch the ceiling fan setting to low. Under the lullaby rhythm of its gentle *thuk-thuk*, I went back to sleep.

Richard and Mason were drinking coffee under the bougainvillea when I emerged. Mason stood and pulled a chair out for me. There was a round of the sorts of mildly awkward greetings and enquiries about sleep that always elicit the same responses, and then we sat for a moment in silence. My arrival had interrupted their conversation. Richard handed me the coffeepot and I poured some, though I didn't really want it, into a fat, patterned cup. Then, with an apologetic nod in my direction, he briefly spoke to Mason again about something businesslike before turning back and commenting courteously on the view.

"It's wonderful," I said.

It was.

We were interrupted by Jenny yelling from the patio doors, "Who's going to take us to the beach?"

Christina, passing, shushed the child mildly and told her not to disturb her father.

Jenny held still for an instant, and then shouted again, "Who is?"

Jessica and Howie joined her.

"Yeah," Howie called. "Who is?"

Richard, his back to the clamor, ignored it. "Where can I buy a U.S. paper, Frankie?"

I told him about the little store on the square in the middle of the town where they sold English-language paperbacks and postcards and candy.

"They sometimes have them. But they're usually out of date."

"Worth a try." He put his cup down. "Do you need a lift back?"

I paused, buttering the toast that Christina had brought, the prospect of the rest of the day unreeling before me suddenly, in limitless empty hours.

"Nooo," Jenny moaned theatrically. She was bouncing at the tableside now, like a cartoon, lurid in pink stretch swimming things.

"Nooo," Jessica echoed, although her actions and voice were milder versions of her sister's. "Come to the beach with us, Frankie. And Daddy."

Richard stood and hitched his waistband. "Howie, do you want to ride into town?" Howie sniffed and shifted his weight. Richard, ready to go, half raised his eyebrows—at me, at then at his son. Howie's nose wrinkled.

"It's okay," Mason said, his chin in Jessica's hair. "Frankie and I can keep an eye on him."

You could walk to the beach from the house, but the children wanted a ride in the jeep. It was one of three cars, Mason explained, supplied with the house. In addition to the Buick there was a big old Chevrolet that had been designated for staff use. Howie, jittery with excitement, sat on my knees and Lesley, who had just come downstairs, shared the back with the twins. The engine turned over on the second try.

"Byeee!" the girls called as we left, waving at the receding bank of glittering windows without looking back.

"Have you been to this beach before?" Jessica asked a few minutes later when we'd pulled up on the flat end of the dirt track and clambered down from the jeep.

"Yes, but I always came here by boat."

"Howie says there are sharks."

"I've never seen any," I said.

Howie looked downcast.

"But I saw a whale once," I added.

"Up close?"

"Quite close."

"Did it crash into your boat?"

"No."

He looked downcast again.

"But we rocked a lot." I grabbed his shoulders and rocked him to make up for the lack of a crash. Then we all stood still for a minute, looking out at the horizon, as if the whale might suddenly break the clean line of blue.

"I think Frankie has had a lot of adventures," Mason said.

The children turned and looked up at me. I had a lot of pale hair, a heart-shaped face, and I was five foot six inches tall. My dress was hopelessly creased from two days' wear. They squinted suspiciously. Then Lesley pulled her T-shirt over her head and broke, loose-kneed, for the sea. The other three followed her.

Mason and I sat on the sand and watched.

"They're like puppies," I said, and he laughed. He was an easy person to be alone with. He leaned back on his elbows, and we listened companionably for a while to the children's shouts, drifting back to us through the condensing warmth of the late morning.

"Where's the boyfriend now then?" he asked eventually. He must have remembered from the party.

"Spain," I said. I lifted my hands and made them fly. "Adios . . ."

He smiled. "Adios," he repeated, and closed his blue eyes.

When we got back to the house Paige was sunbathing by the pool, lying on her stomach in a red swimsuit. She pretended not to notice our arrival. Jenny, flapping a towel, sent a scatter of sand in her sister's direction and Paige, dramatizing her annoyance, brushed briskly at her oiled shoulders.

"We went to the beach," Jenny said. "That's why we're sandy." She gave the towel another flap.

Lesley, as if keen to dissociate herself from anything so childish, sat down next to Paige.

"Frankie saw a whale," Howie announced.

Paige looked at him and then at me.

"Not today," I explained, "another time, when I came to the beach by boat."

"I thought it was our *private* beach," she said, sitting up and wiping her dark glasses with the corner of her towel.

"Perhaps it is," I said. She glanced up and stared at me for a moment, almond eyed, then picked up her magazine. Lesley, stretching out beside her, reached for a plastic tub of coconut oil, unscrewed the lid, and began spreading the stuff, with intense concentration, on her scrawny arms.

"Good morning. Good morning," Ned sang when Mason and I went inside. They were all sitting around the room amid a scattering of coffee cups. Patsy, one leg bent under her against the calico of a summery chair, raised her million-dollar face and asked evenly, "Where did you two get to?"

"We took the children to the beach," I answered, aware as I did that I had spoken too quickly. She was looking at Mason.

"I know," she said, without breaking her gaze.

"They're nice in theory, children," Bee Bee cut in, "but their zest for life is depressing."

Taking the drink Ned handed her, Sally glanced down at the floor and said, "And they're tracking sand all through the house." But her expression, when she looked up again, registered no particular annoyance.

Christina nodded, apparently indicating that lunch was ready, and we all stood to follow Sally to the table.

"I met a guy in town who said he'd take us fishing," Richard said, pulling Sally's chair out for her. "You get all kinds of stuff down this coast, evidently. Marlin maybe. Wanna catch a marlin, Howie?"

"Or a whale," Howie suggested.

Richard tugged my chair out too, automatically, before taking his own and flapping a napkin into his lap while, at the other end of the table, Mason performed these same rituals with Patsy and Bee Bee.

"We're not going to catch any whales, Howie," Richard said.

"We might," Howie returned, petulant. He tore at a lump of bread.

"You don't go fishing for whales, Howie," Richard emphasized.

"Frankie did."

"I wasn't fishing for the whale, Howie," I said. I felt bad, siding against him. "I just saw it." I winked to soften the contradiction.

"Did you?" asked Ned.

"Yeah, and it rooocked the boat." Vindicated, Howie rocked wildly in his chair, watching his father for a reaction.

Richard looked thoughtful. "Really?" he asked. "Around here?"

"Right here, off the beach," Mason said, picking up the story as if it belonged to him. "Three of them in an outboard came across a mother and a calf." I had told him that part when the children were swimming.

They all turned then and looked at me, the way the children had at the beach.

"My," Sally crooned into the pause, "won't it be exciting having Frankie staying with us?"

TWO

PHILLIP OFTEN TAKES the train to London. It is difficult, he says, to park the car. Anyway he can read on the train, catch up on paperwork, that type of thing. After he and Chloe had left me that Sunday, had hugged me and promised to call, I imagined him, in some brief absence of Chloe's, some trek of hers to fetch coffee or cellophane-wrapped biscuits from the tiny coffee shop at the station, phoning his mistress from the booth outside, framed in a grid of damp glass.

I imagined this while I put a load of washing in the machine and treated Hobo to a small dish of leftover chicken, and ran the bath, and then I stood for a while staring into space imagining it all over again until the telephone rang. It was Sonia confirming our arrangements, asking how I was, how Italy had been. Talking to her was soothing, grounding somehow, and so after my bath I got into bed and was able to go to sleep almost immediately. I awoke at five a.m. and lay a long time, blankets bound around me, feeling cold, and afraid, and terribly alone.

For the first time in many years that story—my own story, though it had seemed for such a long time to belong to someone else—really came to me in its entirety. During the comfort years with Phillip and Chloe and Hobo, and a number of goldfish and a short-lived spaniel, during the years when I had become a good cook and a reasonable gardener and learned to drive and honed my drawing skills and played a lot of tennis at summer house parties, only splinters of it had pricked my consciousness, and I had had plenty to salve the punctures with.

The past cannot be controlled of course; it is too woven into us. But we try denial, don't we, as a defense? That night, despite the relentless march of the memory ghost, its muted tread seeming to build to an eerie clatter, I made a determined effort to convince myself that all my concerns were in the present and, what's more, external to me. I decided, in that fear-filled predawn, that the important thing was to know, to know absolutely about Phillip and Josee. I decided that having some sort of incontrovertible evidence to hand would generate a solution. I decided that, after my lunch with Sonia, I would go on to London, and I would spy on my husband.

The next day I met Sonia in Grantham as planned at a small restaurant with a flagstone floor and wooden slat blinds on the windows. It is the kind of restaurant that only Grantham, of the local towns, offers. The others, too far from the A roads and the motorways, have only pubs and fish-and-chip places and a hodgepodge of tea shops and hotel dining rooms. This restaurant is run by a Dutch couple, and I wish that they would put a rug on the floor, but the food is good.

Sonia did not say that I looked tired, though I knew I did, and I was glad that she let it pass unremarked, kissing me effusively instead and calling me darling. We sat and both ordered the same lunch, baked cod with some kind of top-ping, and twin glasses of French white wine, though we both knew without saying that Sonia's would be refilled before mine was half drunk.

"How's himself coping?" she asked as soon as the wine had been set before us. She meant coping with my illness of course and was referring to Phillip. She often calls him things like that, "himself," "his lordship." I was suddenly aware, in my new more sensitive state, that these labels were tinged with sarcasm.

It occurred to me that Sonia did not like Phillip very much, that she never had, though in the past I had put any negativity of hers down to a general distrust of men. Sonia has been married twice, and neither relationship ended happily. Now, though, I caught something more specific. It was a surprise. I had always thought of Phillip as a mild man, likeable. Had she seen something that I had missed, missed for years?

"It's hard for him too," I said, knowing as I did that any possibility of talking to Sonia about Josee had evaporated. Sonia would despise Phillip if she knew, and a scene would be inevitable. She would come, in her dramatic way, charging to my defense, a rally I did not deserve. Sonia and I know an awful lot about each other, and we have loved each other for a long time, but she is nevertheless ignorant of that key aspect of my past. That thing that makes me not who I am.

"Oh, I'm sure," she offered, not about to argue this point, and then she asked after Chloe, and I asked after her son, Ollie, and we talked a little about Catherine and her children, and we went on and had a pleasant lunch. And if I was a little volatile, talked a little faster or a little more or even a little less than I might have done some other time, well, there were circumstances enough to put that down to without the disclosure of new confidences.

There are very few people who, having attained more than forty years, can keep all normality, all mundane run-of-the-millness from intruding on a drama. At twenty, even thirty, you can do it. Women particularly subsume themselves in heartache, miss the bus in the midst of elation. But it changes. Commonplace things become the more powerful stuff of existence. The drive from Grantham to London took just over two hours, and, listening to the radio to distract myself from the dull hum of the motorway and my own bleak thoughts, I heard myself at one point commenting on the pompous pronouncement of some politician. Just as if I were on an ordinary drive on an ordinary day.

I had made a reservation at a hotel that morning before I left, and I went there directly and checked in and left my overnight bag. It was only five so I sat in my room for a while, watching television, distracted. At six I drove to Phillip's office, which is located in a beautiful thirties-era building on the north side of one of those lovely squares that makes London London. The trees were in early bud.

I parked on the far side of the square, having circled twice, and put a lot of money in the meter, and then I watched, through the passenger window, across the spring green of the central grassed area, until eventually he came out. He was with Tom. They spoke briefly on the wide steps at the front doorway, and other people coming out and passing nodded and said things to them. Then they parted and Phillip turned away and walked toward the tube station, which was on the corner nearest to where I was parked, and I got out of the car, and I followed him.

It was, of course, all faintly ridiculous. What if he had seen me? What if he had simply gone back to the flat and stayed there? He did neither of these things. I was able to track him unobserved quite easily thanks to the after-work crowd and his distraction. He seemed, even at the distance I was careful to maintain, weighted by his thoughts.

In the station he stood on the platform looking down at the tracks, and after a few minutes he boarded a train that would not take him toward the flat. I got on too, two carriages behind him. The difficulty then was to stay near to the exit despite the crush of people, people with normal, sensible plans to go home, or to the pictures, or to meet their friends, people whose lack of agitation I envied.

At the third stop, when I leaned toward the open doors, I saw Phillip get off and head for the exit escalator. I think perhaps I might have abandoned my grim mission at that point, given in to the warning voice in my head, or somewhere lower, my gut, if I had not realized that the stop that he had alighted at was the one nearest to Josee's office.

I pressed on, surrendering my thumbed ticket to the turnstile, knowing that if he was going where I thought he was going, he would take the pedestrian tunnel to the south side. There was a boy in the tunnel singing "Nessun Dorma" in a voice too meaty for his slight frame. On a different day

I might have stopped for a moment, and listened, and put a cheerful pound in the boater at his feet.

At the corner of Arundel Street my husband met his lover, but he did not kiss her. He simply touched her hand and looked into her eyes, holding her gaze for a moment, for a heartbeat. Then they turned together, synchronized, and walked three, four blocks until, perhaps by arrangement, they went into a small dark bar on a side street where they could be alone. London is like that: there are secret places everywhere.

My onward progress was interrupted then. If I went into the bar they would see me, and although I had, I suppose, entertained vague notions up until that point of confronting them, of making my presence known in some bold way, I suddenly did not want to. I felt tired, from the day, from the drive, from the lack of sleep the night before. I realized, too, that I must look dreadful. Strange, these little vanities; I could not face my husband's beautiful young mistress with uncombed hair and faded lipstick. I went into a coffee shop and ordered a cup of strong tea and sat at a plastic table on a plastic chair near the window and thought about the letter that had set me on this trail.

The letter had said: *Here is the response from Ellis & Co. Just F.Y.I., H.H., Josee.* Not much, was it? Not much to have taken me there, more than a hundred miles from home, not much to have concealed from my closest friends. But you see, it is not always the physical realities that matter most, not just the words, the letters, the ink on the page that carries the power. It is the great swathe of meaning behind them. I had seen in that flimsy script, beneath the yellow, desk-lamp light, force enough to send a shudder to the very foundations of my world.

When they came out of the side street it startled me. I had sat for an hour over the tea, ordering a second one and a small dry cake that I did not eat in order to justify my place. It was a kind of delicatessen. People had been coming in to buy salads and tuna fish in plastic containers to take back to their flats, and a man was asking for a carton of orange juice when I saw Phillip. I got up quickly, took some cash from my handbag, and tucked it against the plate with the uneaten cake on it. Then I held back for a moment; Phillip and Josee were right across from the coffee shop on the other side of the street.

They walked back to their meeting corner—I guessed that they had met there many times. And if in fact it was not so many, it would still seem as though it was to them. Love affairs are like that, things take on significance, time becomes protracted—events are multiplied.

I followed them, twenty paces or so behind, on the other side of the road. At their corner they stopped, and this time they did kiss. It was not the kiss of melodrama, offered as proof of infidelity, nor the kind of kiss that two tipsy people, who in fact care little for each other, might indulge in on the street after a party. Instead my husband put his hands on another woman's shoulders and pulled her toward him with a tenderness that was palpable. Then one hand strayed to the hairline at the nape of her neck and he touched his lips to her forehead and held them there, as if to a rose.

I cannot say that it was the most shocking thing that I have ever seen, but it was shocking enough. For a moment I felt that my legs might give way under me, that I might lose whatever dignity I still had and bend over the curb and retch. I clutched my handbag to my chest like a shield and stared as

Phillip and Josee parted. He turned and walked with a steady stride and a flat expression back toward the underground, after a half dozen steps twisting momentarily and looking back at the point where they had stood holding each other. I was too stunned to move. He might have seen me, but he didn't. Nor did she.

She had watched him, motionless, almost to the point when he had turned. She had missed that. In a film it would have been a poignant moment. The moment when you felt the burn in your throat in the dark. I watched it with no such distinct emotions.

Somewhere in my mental disarray some instinct took over and my feet began to move, one after the other—which in the end is all that is required, isn't it?—toward the end of the street. I was following Josee. She did not walk far. There was one of those car park, the kind that is a flat lot with a man in a booth at the front, around the corner. She went in there and unlocked the second car in the row closest to me, and as she did I saw that she was trembling. She got into the car and leaned her head on the steering wheel, and she began to sob. I could see her shoulders shaking. The man in the booth was reading his newspaper.

I don't know how long Josee sat in that car weeping, how long it was till she pulled herself up and forced herself to start the engine and drive home, but of course she would have eventually. At some point we do those things even when the circumstances seem to constrict us so much that all movement is impossible. We manage. But I was not there to see it. I went back to my own car and moved it to a parking garage with the same robot mechanisms that no doubt had got Josee home. Then I spent a restless night in the hotel.

At six a.m. I got up, ate no breakfast, and left. I wanted to be back before Phillip.

. . .

I had arrived in Mexico almost a year before I met the Severances with four hundred Australian dollars and a Welsh boyfriend. By the time I met them I was living alone and eating a lot of melon, which was what teaching English four or five hours a month bought, after rent and coffee. My visa had been extended, thanks to Arturo Rodriguez's influence and, particularly, his wife's need for an English teacher, but that was the extent of the organized aspects of my life. I had no reason to refuse Sally Severance's invitation, which had crystallized quickly into a formal one, and even less to question it.

"What about your teaching?" Mason was driving me into town to collect some things. It was midafternoon.

"I only have a few students now." I had two. Maria and a sweet teenager named Letty. "Since Adam left," I added. I wished I hadn't. His name felt strange in my mouth. Like cotton wool.

"Adam," Mason repeated, taking his eyes from the road for a second. "The boyfriend?"

"Yes." It seemed like a long time ago.

I lived in a two-story concrete strip of apartments near the town's only supermarket. They were painted the kind of color that looks as if it has been mixed from lots of other colors, an unwanted sort of ochre. Some children were playing out front with a half-deflated ball. They stopped when Mason parked the car.

"I won't be long."

"I'll give you a hand," he offered.

The children quit their game. The ball was tossed, nonchalantly, toward the smallest one, who caught it and held it firmly, arms against his chest. A neighbor of mine, jutting a baby on her hip, called "Hola" from her doorway. I told her I'd be away for a while.

"Sí," she said, diverting one of the baby's chubby hands from her chin and sliding her knowing eyes over Mason.

Fishing the key from my bag, I said, "You shouldn't really come in. Men wait outside here if your husband's not at home."

He grinned. "No husbands in there then?"

"No live ones."

He twisted his head over his shoulder toward the neighbor, who had edged herself around behind us. At his look she slipped swiftly back inside. He stepped through the door behind me.

My living arrangements comprised a single, tile-floored room and a bathroom. Mason sat in the only armchair and let his glance skirt the perimeter while I took a canvas travel bag out from under a chest of drawers and dropped it onto the bed. I began to pack things randomly. Books. Clothes.

"How did you get here, Frankie?" His voice was low, not particularly interrogatory.

"Adam taught a boy whose father owned the block."

"No, I mean how did you get *here*?" He tipped himself back in the chair and raised both hands, palms upwards.

I hesitated, considering the tale of my childhood, the lonely trail around the world in the wake of my father's career, army base to duller army base. The eventual quitting of it.

My mother's sad eyes when I gave up my first job as a nursery school teacher in Singapore. I bunched the soft fabric of the dress I was holding into the bag and zipped it decisively.

"Oh. You know. One adventure after another."

He smiled, stood, and took the bag from me. No more questions. I was glad. Lately, I had begun to find the shapelessness of my own existence disconcerting.

· · ·

Something had led me, of course, to that letter, to Phillip's desk in the first place. A hunch. A sense that something was wrong. Suspicion. She's a staple of men's angry humor, isn't she, the suspicious wife? And I am sure that they exist, those women whose insecurities turn every look, every conversation into something more, something with wickedness in it. But I am not one of them, nor, I think, are many other women. I am, however, like most wives, suspicious from time to time.

It did not occur to me during the first seven years of our marriage that Phillip would be unfaithful. That either of us would be. We seemed too sound for that sort of silliness, too stable. And I can say, too, that between years ten and eighteen I regained this sense of unassailability. But in our eighth year, the year that Chloe turned thirteen and her sweetness was coarsened slightly by the onset of adolescence, the year that I turned the playhouse in the garden into a studio for myself and took painting classes to replace some of her fading need of me, Anthea came to work for Phillip.

I met Anthea early in her employment because in those days I used to go to events at the office sometimes. It was a going-away thing I guess, or someone's birthday. Tom and Phillip are those modern sorts of employers who mark these occasions with drinks and expensive snacks from the local delicatessen or staff outings to nearby restaurants where the owners know them. Anyway, there was Anthea when I arrived, all plumply cheerful and as relaxed as if she had worked at Creel & Grace forever. She had been there for three weeks.

If I had forced myself to consider the possibility at that time that another woman could threaten my marriage, I would never have cast Anthea in the role. I thought her slightly stupid. It sounds arrogant, I know, but I did. On the days that Phillip worked at home she telephoned endlessly, checking details with him, lengthening these conversations with chat, like a teenager, though she was older than me, late thirties I guessed, about Phillip's age.

It was quite some time before I noticed that Phillip was not complaining about Anthea's calls, that he seemed instead almost to welcome them, his tone taking on a sort of fatherly, indulgent quality whenever he spoke to her. I did notice, though, when he went from talking about Anthea rather a lot to, too abruptly, not talking about her at all. I hunted then, for lipstick on the collar, those sorts of clues. Of course I found some; you always do, ridiculously attaching a moment of small triumph to each discovery—matchbooks from strange restaurants; tell-tale messages, kept and stuffed in pockets; some item, ambiguous, but with a female taint—a scarf. Things that set your nerves on fire and disconnect your brain from your actions.

Anthea had been around for about four months when I set upon Phillip with a clutch full of papery evidence and a belly full of suppressed anxiety. He naturally denied all wrongdoing.

It was his aggrieved expression, though, that set light to the ready tinder. He declared himself, too heartily, wronged, the victim of unfairness all around. Innocent as a baby.

Was he? Now I think not, of course, but I also believe that what he had with Anthea was a flirtation, whether consummated or not, a rather childish and potentially, pointlessly, corrosive flirtation fanned by attention-seeking on his part and overt flattery on hers. And I can admit now too, with the wisdom of distance and greater age, that my reaction may have been as futile and biting in terms of our relationship as whatever it was that took place between them.

We got over it, that fracture, but we were both a little scarred, and it took time. And, evidently, the healing was not absolute, because there was something, in the weeks before I went looking for whatever I was looking for and found Josee's letter, that reminded me sharply of that time. Phillip had stopped talking about Josee.

· · ·

The room that I had been allocated, during a subtle and almost wordless communication between Sally and Christina, was at the end of a long corridor on the second floor. The only other bedroom the corridor serviced was unoccupied. Christina, directing me, had pulled the door of the vacant space closed as she passed before asking, with a haughtiness I may have imagined, whether there was anything I needed. I had shaken her a distracted no. The bedroom into which she had ushered me, with its perfect balance of light and shadow, of open space and comfort, of simplicity and elegance, was to define my notion of luxury for the rest of my life.

I spent a pleasant dusk dozing, feline, on sheets that smelled of lavender. Then I got up to dress, knowing as I did that nothing I owned was adequate to my surroundings, or to the company I was suddenly keeping. I put on a simple, light blue shift, withered a little from many wearings. It was ankle length and made of some weightless stuff that clung when I walked. And then I went downstairs to my first night as an official guest at that golden house on the cactus shore.

It was like a lot of the nights that followed, but I remember it better. There was a pitcher of martinis. Patsy, all in white, stood in the corner holding one at her chest, her chin almost resting on the rim of her glass. She looked as if she had stepped off a billboard advertising something that a sultan would have to save up for.

Mason played barman. "Martini, ma'am?"

"Thank you," I said. I had never drunk a martini in my life.

After dinner, on the unnecessary excuse that my official arrival called for celebration, we drove into town, everybody laughing and carrying glasses, horns blaring and cars pulling over so that people could switch places for no particular reason at the roadside. Ned, in high good spirits, a cigar in one hand and a brandy in the other, steered the Buick the whole way with his knees.

We went to La Roseleda. It was an ordinary enough place, but they were thrilled with it, and in the stardust of their company, even the cakey orange smile of the familiar fat girl at the bar took on new glamour.

The owner, recognizing me, beamed at the clientele I had brought him and showed us, with novel pomp, to a table by the window. He took our drinks order himself and, a few minutes later, oversaw the careful work of a waiter unloading them from a tray.

Mason began to drum a soft fingertip rhythm on the table edge, and Patsy, next to him, put down her cigarette and jumped to her feet. "Come on," she said, taking his hand. Her hips swiveled figure eights as she wound him through the tables. At her back, Sally lifted her cigarette, which was still smoldering, between a manicured finger and thumb, and, expressionless, extinguished it, dropping the butt into a large black ashtray before brushing off her hand, as if some of the lipstick staining its tip might have adhered. It hadn't.

In front of the small raised area where the band played, Patsy turned and smiled, lifting her chin a little, and Mason, pulling her to him, smiled too. Watching them as they were drawn into the shadowy loop of the other dancers, I was surprised by a sudden tug of loneliness in the pit of my stomach.

"Frankie . . . Frankie?" Ned had to shout over the music. "Dance?" He jerked his head toward the dance floor and winked.

I was glad to dance with Ned. He was easy and smooth footed.

"Quite the little mover, aren't you?" He grinned.

I laughed. He twisted me away from him and spun me deftly back.

"You're a good kid," he announced suddenly, leaning back to look into my eyes. And then, settling his cheek again nearer to mine, he said, "Watch yourself," or at least I thought that was what he said; it was difficult to hear.

Back at the table, as I retook my seat, he stood behind me for a moment with both hands on my shoulders. It was a gesture that felt paternal.

The crowd had thickened with the night and the band was playing something loud when a man with a neat crease in his trousers approached our table and asked Mason's permission to dance with his wife.

"He says," I translated, "that she is a very lovely woman, and you are a husband very lucky and that, while he is dancing with her, he will leave with you his car keys . . . for security."

Mason glanced over at Sally and then turned to the man, who was staring intently at Patsy.

"He thinks Patsy is your wife."

"Shall we tell him?"

"No," I said. I was wary of the kind of embarrassment the contradiction would cause.

Mason put his shirtsleeved arm on Patsy's slender bare one and whispered into her hair. She listened, her brow slightly creased, with her head inclined. Then she laughed. When she stood up, the man took a set of keys from his pocket and laid them with some ceremony on the table.

"Tell him five minutes."

"Cinco minutos."

After the man had collected his keys and deposited Patsy, giggly, back at the table, tequilas arrived. With the compliments, explained the patron, gesturing toward the bar where the man raised his glass to the lucky husband.

"To lucky husbands everywhere," Ned said.

"To what?" Richard yelled, cocking his head.

"Lucky husbands."

"Oh, yeah," Richard grinned. "Here's to 'em."

Bee Bee raised her tequila. "And Patsy's pert little rear," she added.

Everybody laughed except Sally who, tequila untouched,

slid one corner of her silk shawl onto her shoulder, readying to leave. She spoke across the table to her husband. "You should dance with Frankie before we go. It's her party."

Mason, apologetic, asked me to dance. I was embarrassed. There was something vaguely adolescent about the situation, like being invited to parties by the prompted sons of my mother's friends, but I stood anyway and went with him to the dance floor. He put his hand on the small of my back and said, "I like your dress."

I was grateful for that; it made so many things easier. Then, drawn against him, I noticed the width of his shoulders and the smell, faint, at the base of his neck, of cloves.

On the way home we killed a dog. It was a stray, scrawny and ill-looking—the town was full of them—but Bee Bee, who had been driving, was upset, and drunk enough to turn maudlin. When the carcass had been hauled to the side of the road, Sally, laying her shimmery little handbag deftly on the dash, took steady control of the Buick while Ned and Richard and I sat sobering up to the heavy soundtrack of Bee Bee's sobs.

Patsy and Mason had gone ahead in the jeep, Patsy snatching the keys from Mason's hand under the soft light of a street lamp and running with them, her dress rising, sail-like, behind her. They had sped off, Mason laughing, clambering into the passenger seat after the car had already begun to move, like a television hero.

At the house they were sitting outside, opposite each other in the dark.

"I thought we'd lost you," Mason said, looking up at our arrival. He was leaning forward, lighting the cigarette between Patsy's lips with her silver lighter. When he edged back their knees disengaged.

"We hit a dog," Richard explained.

"Killed it," Bee Bee slurred, ragged now from drink and crying.

Sally, watching her friend with an expression that struck me as a bit pitiless, said in an even voice, "It was just a stray."

Bee Bee, her mascara-stained eyes wild-looking in the blue glow of the pool lights, stared, momentarily on the dangerous edge of anger, but Ned, nurselike, reached an arm out to her, and she acquiesced, letting him lead her slowly into the house.

"I need to get cleaned up," Richard said, holding his hands open like a child. He turned toward his wife, expectant. It was very late.

"It's very late," Sally confirmed. Then with the same cool expression she had leveled at Bee Bee, she turned to Patsy. "Let me relieve you of my husband, dear," she said.

Patsy drew hard on her cigarette, her eyes on Mason. He dropped his head and got to his feet.

"See you in the morning, Frankie," he said, passing me as he followed his wife inside.

Behind him Patsy turned toward the dark of the sea. She didn't answer when I said goodnight.

*　*　*

There are things, I can admit now, that I have kept from those days, or things that have stayed with me at least, despite my assurances to myself that I had closed the door firmly and securely on that chapter of my life. I have always remembered, for instance, that way they had of divesting themselves of all seriousness, all responsibility. It was a trait that I came to abhor in part, perhaps prematurely, perhaps making myself seem older, sterner at times than I am, but that is because I witnessed the outcome. Saw what lack of responsibility can leave in its wake. Nevertheless, along with the negative aspects, the carelessness, came the fun. It is such a small word, and corny, I guess. One associates it with garish advertisements for family days out. But it is the right word. I am not talking about joy, after all, or elation or anything on that grand sort of scale. I really mean fun. They understood it.

I tried later to emulate them in that—though I wouldn't have admitted it—particularly when Chloe was young. We had torchlit suppers in the playhouse with her friends; we had treasure hunts; we went on picnics and mystery bike rides, and more than once we turned ordinary, workaday rooms into fairy lands. Such a deliberate contrast, I realize now, to my own childhood. My parents seemed so untouched by my existence; there was never any trail, any messy clue of child in any of our neat houses. But I didn't learn it by myself, that frivolity; they taught me. The carefree Americans.

· · ·

With an eccentricity that I thought delightful at the time, Bee Bee disappeared at some point the day after we had killed the dog and came back with what she called a vacation puppy. It was a mongrel, with a triangular face and ears too big for its head. Bee Bee claimed that she had rescued the creature from a gruesome end at the hands of an unscrupulous chef, but Richard pointed out that she was confusing Mexico with

China. Anyway, the act had apparently afforded her some sort of catharsis. The run-over dog was never mentioned again.

The children were delighted. The puppy was fitted with a collar of red plastic beads, and somebody christened her Tallulah. Lesley fashioned a pasha's bed with the yellow silk cushions from the chairs in her parents' bedroom, and Tallulah was set upon it royally and fed with unsuitable tit-bits until she was sick. Christina's lips, as she set a bucket of ice for drinks on the sideboard, took on a scolding line. The children argued with her in chorus.

"She was still hungry," Jenny insisted.

"So we gave her some more dinner," Howie added.

Mason, sitting with his feet propped on a low table in the long, glass-doored room that faced the pool, just laughed.

"You can't just go on feeding and feeding an animal, Howie," Richard said.

"She was still hungry," Howie repeated lamely.

"I think she's cute." Patsy lifted Tallulah and kissed her head before dropping her back onto the floor, where Hudson made a swift grab for her tail.

Sally, watching, shelled a pistachio and let the husk fall into an oval dish near her husband's feet. "We'll all have ringworm within the week," she said.

Richard, at a slight disconnect from the hilarity as always, said, "I've set the fishing trip up for tomorrow."

Howie quit the writhing and shrieking that the mention of ringworm had triggered in him and looked at his father.

"Just us guys," Richard said, ruffling the boy's hair.

"What if there's a big storm?" Howie asked.

"I don't think there'll be a big storm, Howie," Richard replied, tender suddenly. "But if there is, we won't go."

"Because we might crash," said Howie, relaxing.

"Because we might sink," Richard answered patiently. "We won't sink, though. We'll just catch lots of fish, and maybe swim. It'll be great."

Richard leaned then and lifted Hudson, who was at his feet clutching a handful of trouser leg. Holding the child under the arms, he gave his round, dangling form a little shake, making him grin and gurgle, before settling him down again and sending him, with a pat on his yellow-rompered bottom, crawling enthusiastically in the opposite direction.

"Early start, though," he announced to the men.

Ned groaned.

"You Paul Bunyan types need to remember that my husband is a fine Chicago-raised fellow whose constitution runs best on equal measures of dry vermouth and nicotine," Bee Bee said.

"Someone," Ned insisted, cupping a handful of nuts to his mouth, "has got to fly the flag for bad habits and idleness." He crossed his long, lounge-lizard legs. They were clad that night in pink velvet trousers.

· · ·

Ned used to toast to high times. And that is what they were, for me anyway, high enough to threaten chasms, just as these rugged days do. It is the easy times that level. The easy times that lull us complacent, and cocksure too. Even I, with so little reason, believed for many years that life had become some sort of ordered pathway, that there were neat and fathomable rules to direct me. If . . . then. But dilemmas do not always turn up in the neat packages we imagine when none lurk. Predicaments have frayed ends and rough edges, and you can't always just seal them off cleanly and be done.

After watching Phillip and Josee part, I knew that I had witnessed a great love scene, the kind that closes an act. That my husband had ended his affair, but that it had been an affair of the heart, a passion. I had a husband who had left someone he loved, deserted her, for me. I could not fit all the pieces together. For the first time I felt that I was a sick woman, and it was a sick woman who Phillip came home to at exactly the time that he said he would.

My illness from that point took the same course as the illnesses of so many others; one minute steady, optimism surfacing, and the next laborious, effort at every turn. There are no real patterns, no absolutes, though we look for them, we sufferers, especially at first, heartened a little by the happy-ending tales that well-wishers are so keen to pass on. But after a while we know that, despite the similarities, despite the shared pain and the same prescriptions and the similar symptoms, we are on a lone journey, with its own peculiar variations and pitfalls, and outcome.

My journey at least has been undertaken in comfort. We live a life that is privileged, if lacking in glamour, so when I got back from that second, more grueling hospital stay, I did not have a lot to be concerned about in practical terms. Joan, the woman who has cleaned and babysat and cat-sat and watered plants for us for many years, had come to an arrangement with Phillip in my absence to work every day, rather than the two mornings that had been her previous quota. Since my return she has often taken it upon herself to prepare lunch, and she irons more now too, ferrying Phillip's shirts upstairs in soft, warm piles.

It has occurred to me that if the situation had been reversed, if Phillip had been the one afflicted, people would not have arrived with casseroles the way that they have, would not have been at such pains to relieve us of the burden of domestic things. They would have thought that I could manage the washing by myself. But that's how it is, isn't it, the conspiracy of men's helplessness? We are all complicit in it. And anyway, I don't want to seem ungrateful. I was glad, particularly, of Joan's help. She is a kind woman, and quiet, which mattered very much to me then. So many things were intruding on my peace.

Our house is big enough that a downstairs room could be dedicated as a dayroom for me. Phillip chose which one, and organized it, for which he was rather proud of himself, while I was away. I agreed with his choice. There are good windows in that room and a wide ledge beneath them. There is a fire too, and Phillip lit it the day of my return, to ward off the chill of the early spring afternoon. The air smelled faintly of lemons, and there were daffodils winking in a jug on the mantel. A wide sofa that usually lives elsewhere had been moved in to serve as a resting place, and next to it a piecrust table, polished to gold, had been stacked with magazines.

I did not need that household sanctuary then the way that I do now, but I nevertheless took to sleeping there in the afternoons. The days had begun to draw out and I would wake around five without the unsettled feeling that waking in early evening brings. Phillip, as promised, was at home all the time, and we fell into new routines, brought forward our customary six o'clock drink to five thirty and took to having it on the terrace, sitting in the cast-iron chairs, extra sweaters over our daytime clothes.

Chloe came most weekends, often with Ed, who is good-looking and polite, and funny too when he relaxes. In some ways it was a strangely happy time, one of those limpid spells in life that feel like they will last forever.

. . .

On the day that the men went fishing and left the women alone, I went to Maria's house to give her an English lesson before anybody else was awake. I called her first from the little vestibule near the hardly used front door. A creamy telephone sat in there on a purpose-built shelf. There was a virgin white notepad next to it and a freshly sharpened pencil. Then I waited on the front step for Arturo's driver to collect me, watching cotton clouds scud across the blue helmet of the sky. They darkened patches of the sea from turquoise to navy.

Maria was even less interested than usual in her lesson.

"Es muy grande, sí?"

"In English, Maria." She paid me whether I taught her anything or not, but I felt that I ought to at least try. It was such a happy arrangement.

"Biig, la casa?" She opened her arms, offering her palms to the ceiling of the shady room at the back of her house where we always spent these fruitless hours.

"The house is very big, yes," I answered her.

"E beautiful?"

"Very beautiful."

"Piscina?"

"There is a swimming pool."

She sucked the air in between her teeth.

"It's a very big house, with white walls and shining floors and many lovely paintings and you can see the sea and the sky and almost all of Mexico lindo from every room," I said. I was very fond of her.

She grinned. She wanted to know how many servants.

"The Severances' housekeeper Christina, who traveled with them. Puerto Rican." She was unimpressed by this. "And maybe six others, local, who came to help with the cleaning and the pool and the garden." This she liked.

"Café?" she asked, patting my shoulder affectionately. "Coffee?"

"Thank you."

She went to call the maid.

When I got back, the house was still quiet, so I walked the cliff path to the beach. I sat under the ridge where the earth turned the bleached color of bone and let a handful of sand run through my fingers. Then I lay back and closed my eyes. As the sun stained the underside of my eyelids, uncertainty swamped me. That had happened often lately.

What was I going to do?

Adam had asked me, over and over, in those emotional days before he had left, but it had only been on the walk back, alone, from the goodbye at the bus station that I'd felt the first real prick of concern. What was I going to do? My mother's letters, little stone weights in my life, were full of niggling inquiry.

I didn't know.

I sighed. The sultriness of the air, so early in the day, was a reminder of the exhausting heat that the touristless summer would bring. I'll make a plan, I thought, soon, and gave my head a shake to free myself from the necessity of it. Then I took my clothes off and swam so as to walk back cooler.

The water was lagoonish, shallow for a way, with firm ripples of hard sand underfoot. I waded, feeling the chill edge creep cleanly up my legs, and when I was waist-deep I let my feet rise and my head drop backward. I floated, spreading my arms like wings.

Suspended there staring at nothing, I thought, not for the first time, how simple life was for women like Bee Bee and Patsy and Sally, their days so full of children and husbands and amusing diversion. Their lives rolled out easily and evenly ahead of them. They have everything, I thought, everything. Especially Sally.

Men came each morning, early, to water the garden and clip dead heads from the flowers in the marble planters around the pool. I was almost back at the gate that divided this lush oasis from the ragged hillside when I heard a scream. Even at that distance from the house the alarm in the child's voice was apparent. I ran.

"What's happened?"

The twins rushed at me, urchinish in cotton nightdresses. "Tallulah's lost."

I leaned over, hands on my thighs, my face level with theirs, and let my breath steady. "Really lost, or just hiding under somebody's bed?"

"Really lost."

Fifteen minutes of anxious hysteria followed. Lesley and even Paige were roused from their beds to join the search, though their contribution was aimless. Lesley pushed the hair from her face with the flat of her palm and sang "*Talluuulah*" at intervals, while Paige ambled along the fence line with the T-shirt she'd slept in riding up against the lace edge of her underwear.

Tallulah was asleep, of course, in a basket of fresh laundry in the basement. This discovery was met with a fresh round of hysterics and a "*Ssh*" from Christina. The mothers were still sleeping, partnerless, in their ivory rooms. The men would be bobbing way out on the wilderness ocean by now. I wondered if Howie would get sick.

I put a finger to my lips. "You'll wake your mother," I said to the little girls, who cheerfully ignored me.

Christina, busy with breakfast things and overseeing a maid who was feeding Hudson mashed fruit, made no response either to my weak attempt to support her authority, and Paige eyed me coolly.

"We won't wake our mother," she said with exaggerated patience.

Jenny lifted the lid from a blue and white bowl, removed a lump of sugar, and held it pursed between her thumb and forefinger. She licked at it once and said, "Mommy takes a pill, and it makes her go to sleep, and she never, ever wakes up until Christina takes her tray."

I was surprised, after we had eaten, when Paige followed me to my room and sat, uninvited, on the corner of my bed. It had been tidied already by an unseen maid.

"Can I borrow your blue shirt?" she asked.

I looked at her. "Sure."

It was a small thing, but it seemed to be enough. She smiled. Suddenly warm. A softly pretty version of her mother's thoroughbred beauty.

"Thanks."

I guessed that meant we were friends now.

Paige wore the blue shirt to lunch. We went to a beach restaurant on the other side of town. Patsy, Bee Bee, and Sally, their female offspring, and me. Outside we could see pelicans diving, framed by the sloping line of the roof. I watched them, aware briefly of a mild shiver of not belonging. But then Bee Bee grinned at me, pulling me into the crowd, and said, "Hot, ain't it?"

Patsy finished her drink and put her hand up for the waiter. Earlier she and Bee Bee had slid behind the painted breeze-block bar and shown him how to make daiquiris the way they liked them.

"Keep up, Frankie," she said, noticing mine, half full.

"Frankie's not much of a drinker," Sally said.

Bee Bee hoisted her glass. "Drinking is key, Frankie. Drinking helps you to forget."

Sally laughed lightly. She and Bee Bee had known each other since childhood, Mason had told me. I could see it. The long association. "Maybe Frankie hasn't got anything she wants to forget," she said, looking at me.

I smiled at her. She had been very flattering to me the night before in that offhand way she had that I never knew how to take, commenting to Mason that my looks were an ideal mix of Celt and hothouse.

"Everybody wants to forget something," Patsy declared. She had a gold chain belt around her hips. It jangled as she shifted in her chair.

Sally, with an icy kind of evenness, leaned forward over the table.

"Well, sure, honey, a little forgetfulness can come in real handy sometimes."

Patsy's voice had a hint of the South in it. Sally had mimicked it exactly.

I did not know what had happened, but I knew that something had by the way my breath held tight in my chest while I waited for what would happen next. Patsy stared at Sally, and Sally held her gaze, and then Patsy laughed, a little falsely I thought, but Sally smiled, and, at that, Bee Bee smiled too. And I realized that whatever was happening was happening way over my head, so I volunteered to go and check on the children, who had wandered, bored, out onto the beach.

I rode home with Patsy in the jeep. About a quarter of a mile out of town she said, "That high-and-mighty act Sally puts on is going to cost her eventually."

She had sobered a little, but I put her fractiousness, nevertheless, down to too long a lunch. That and the inevitable sparking of temperaments. Sally, it seemed to me, was queen to Patsy's princess.

"I'll tell you one thing for sure," she continued. "That marriage of hers isn't the fortress she likes to think it is."

Suddenly she turned and winked like a little girl with a secret.

I smiled back, caught, uncomprehending, in whatever amusement had diverted her.

The men got back not long after us. I was pleased to see them, sunburned and bedraggled in their open-necked shirts. The room filled up again with deep, men's laughter and squealing, teased children. The edgy flicker that had flared over lunch faded and seemed completely forgotten.

THREE

T HAD BEEN twenty-one months and almost as many days since Adam had smiled at me across the tanned thighs of another girl at an overheated party in Los Angeles. He had been heading east and I west. We were both voyagers, drifters really, like so many people were then, seeing the world. I followed Adam's smile almost directly to bed and from there to San Francisco and from there to New Orleans. All together, with him and before, I had been traveling for more than three years and thought myself, in the wake of this slim history, rather sophisticated. But then the Severances had come along, with their gay friends and their grandly casual outlook on life, and I had begun to realize there was a great deal of the world that I did not know at all.

"Dear girl," Patsy said, "they're *honeymooners.*"

I felt horribly naive. We were picnicking, all of us, on the beach and I had commented, watching Bee Bee and Ned at the water's edge, on their apparent affection for each other. Now, in the distance, we saw Ned trip a playful hand over the curve at the base of Bee Bee's spine.

"That marriage is barely broken in, honey," Patsy went on. "It's still chock-full of high-school freshness."

The laughter was general.

Mason, rescuing me, explained, "Ned is Bee Bee's third husband."

"She got Lesley from the first one and a darling little fortune from the second one," Patsy finished.

Richard, his fair eyes straining against the sun, looked at Mason. "How'd that second guy make his money?"

Mason shrugged. "Steel . . . stocks . . . dime stores. Fingers in a lot of pies, I gather."

"And a lot of cocktail waitresses," Sally added blandly.

I stared. Her appearance was so immaculate that any hint of crudeness from her was mildly shocking.

She picked up a magazine. "The man was a philandering lowlife. Bee Bee earned every cent she wrung out of the bastard." She plucked at a glossy page, pinching the corner grimly. "Where men are concerned, Frankie, always go straight for getting even. Getting mad isn't worth the frown lines."

I was freed, luckily, from having to produce the kind of response for which I lacked the wit by Richard's low, admiring whistle. "She sure got herself a sweet deal."

Sally ignored him. Her eyes, lifting from the magazine, took on the flinty look I had seen there before. "Divorce is *bloody* for women," she said. Then, just as suddenly softening

again, brushing off the thin fizz of attention the strenuous-
ness of her remark had generated, she went on lightly,
"Well . . . everybody blames the woman, don't they? The
man just dusts himself off and moves in with the new version,
generally shinier, while the old has-been wifey is left to stew
over her failings and save up her alimony for plastic surgery.
And the social life, forget it. The husband and the floozy get
all the invites, and the divorcée gets to opt for a quick, trade-
down remarriage or a series of endless, inebriate lunches with
other divorcées." Patsy tittered at this, and Sally smiled at
her, finesse fully recovered. "I swear half the restaurants in
Manhattan make a living out of those dames, bitching over
their noon martinis. They call all the waiters by name."

The others recognized this and laughed.

"Still . . ." Sally said wickedly, amusing herself now, "I
guess it's nice that they have each other to turn to when the
pool boy throws them over at the end of the summer."

Later, as we lay there in the roaring afternoon heat, Howie
begged people to swim with him.

"Not now, hon," Patsy said, lazily shrugging off his tug.
Her turquoise bikini, held together by gold rings at the corners, exposed the sharp line of her pelvis.

Richard stood. "Come on, son. I'll swim with you." He
leaned over Patsy, casting a shadow. She half opened her eyes.

"You're in my sun," she said flatly, closing them again.

Richard bent swiftly and scooped his wife up as if she
were straw. As he carried her to the sea, we could see her legs
flailing and her fists pounding ineffectually at his neck. The
children exploded, squealing and splashing, when he dropped
her into the water. Patsy emerged instantly, adjusted the strap

of her bikini top, and waded shoreward. Richard, behind her, submerged his head for a moment before rising and settling his dense gaze on the retreating lower center of her back.

"He's such an *adolescent*," she said, reaching us back on the sand. She flattened her towel with irritated, fluttery hands.

"Oh lighten up, Patsy," Mason said. There was a tiny scowl in the sleepy, afternoon drawl of his voice.

Patsy, stretching, paused at it and twisted her face to him. He did not meet her look.

Jenny and Jessica, breathing hard, rushed up to the edge of the cluster of adults on the sand. "Come and swim," Jenny said.

Jessica was clutching Tallulah, who was shivering miserably. "Tallulah loves it. You put her in the water, and she swims, but then, when you lift her up, she keeps swimming."

Jenny, giggling, imitated a dog's frantic paddle. "Come and see," she urged.

"All right," Mason agreed. "Frankie?"

I looked at him.

"Coming?" He lifted his arm slightly, beckoning, and the silver of his heavy watch flashed.

I looked around. Patsy was on her stomach, the strap of her bikini top undone. Lesley and Paige, their heads and towels together, were huddled at a safe distance from the adults down the beach. Everyone else was swimming or sleeping. Sally smiled over her dark glasses and signaled with a tiny, queenly movement of her hand that we ought to just go.

"I'm happy here," she said.

"What's around the bend?" Mason asked over the children's heads. We were standing thigh-deep in the water.

He looked back toward the rocks at the end of the crescent of the bay.

"More rocks. One big one that looks like a wineglass. Narrow at the bottom and wide at the top."

"Show me."

"All right."

We left the girls swimming and walked up onto the sand toward the rocky curve.

"See. Like a wineglass." I made my hands into a V.

"Yes," he said, "it is." And then: "How was yesterday?"

"Fine."

He looked at me. "Women never mean fine when they say fine. How was it?"

"A lot of drinking."

"Yes, and?"

"I don't know . . ."

He smiled. "Don't you?"

We had wandered beyond the wineglass rock and stopped on the far side of it, in its shadow.

"Sally and Patsy got a bit edgy with each other."

"Patsy shouldn't drink," he said mildly.

"No." I toed the sand, wishing for something cleverer to say.

He put one hand at the back of my head and kissed me.

"Don't mind about them," he said, "Patsy and Sally and Bee Bee."

My brain couldn't catch up. "I don't."

"Yes you do." He laughed and took my hand.

He held it, walking ahead of me across the rocks, until I disengaged my fingers when I could make out the shapes of others, vague through the veils of haze.

That night we ate formally, as we did sometimes, in the vaulted dining room. Sally presided over those occasions with a majestic mix of grace and authority, but that wasn't the sort of thing I realized at the time; I was too caught up in the constant, joyful undercurrent of anarchy. So much charm and beauty, so much heady entertainment, all in one room. I was giddy with it, that night in particular, though Mason's seat, assigned by place card, was at the opposite end of the table from mine.

Between us the children were in revolt.

"Not fish again." Jenny's plate had just been laid in front of her. Soft fingers of lemon sauce spread across the white of the porcelain.

"Good fish," Christina said sternly, "from your Daddy."

"Probably I caught it," Howie announced.

"No," Ned insisted. "I recognize that one. He's mine."

"It's disgusting," Lesley groaned, pushing a fork in a listless half circle around her plate.

"What's wrong with it?" Richard asked.

"We don't like it," said Lesley.

"I do," Paige said. "I think it's delicious." It was painful, her crush on Richard, and all the harder to watch now that I was beginning to like her.

Howie forked a chunk of fish and dipped it in his sauce, then licked at it before spitting theatrically.

Richard's disgust registered clearly on his face. "What *do* you like?"

"Spaghetti."

"That's all they ever eat. Spaghetti and hot dogs and candy."

"They're barbarians," Sally commented blithely. "It's best

not to attempt to civilize them." She lifted her wineglass and sipped. "That way they grow up better prepared for the perils of adult life. Like guerrilla warfare and marriage."

The twins, their hair, almost white now, tumbling uncombed over their shoulders, gazed at their mother.

"We like hamburgers," Jessica offered.

She seemed confused when everybody laughed.

I stayed up late that night, drinking brandy and flirting, feeling distanced from my earlier gaffe over Bee Bee and Ned by an effervescent new mood and a sense that something had changed, that I was a small step closer to becoming one of them, a member of their ill-defined, faintly hedonistic club. When, eventually, I said goodnight and went to bed, my skin still damp from moonlit swimming, it was to dream, on the frothy foundation of one tiny, unrepeated kiss, girlishly of Mason.

· · ·

There are stories, aren't there, plays and things, in which the central plotline involves one person driving another mad through all sorts of contrivances that leave the victim doubting the evidence of his or her own eyes, ears, memories? In life, of course, it's simpler. One person only needs to lie to another patchily but regularly for a reasonable length of time for the lunatic edge to set in.

In the three months since Phillip had come home to me, and stayed, he had been a model husband. Concerned and caring, he took on all kinds of new tasks and accomplished them with bachelor aplomb. He complained, comically, about the price of fruit juice, the difference between the good kind and the processed kind, the kind we did not like. Pressing home to me, through this exchange, the marvelousness of his realization that we needed fruit juice, and that he could not just leave Joan to reach for the first and cheapest one that caught her eye. I had to praise him.

Then, when praise wasn't quite enough, he caught a cold, or a sore throat at least, and though lousy with it, ventured out on a chilly day to spread some gravel on a pothole in the driveway. I had commented on the pothole the day before, on our way to Dr. Griffith's office. Phillip blamed the visit to Dr. Griffith's office, the crowded waiting room in particular, for the sore throat.

As a result of the damp gravel spreading, the sore throat naturally flared and I was aware—and not as cross about it as you might suppose—that Phillip wanted nursing. That he wanted me to fuss over him; that he wanted soup. And, when I obliged, he lapped my attention up like a greedy puppy.

At other times, away from my gratitude, or concerned inquiries, he was quieter than he might have been, more distant. But one could put that down, if not in possession of the facts, to writing pressures, to the difficulties of running a company from a distance, to the days when I really did need him and some expression, some new paleness perhaps, alerted him to that fact and frightened him as much as it did me.

Actually all of these things did strain him and eventually began to take their toll. He was tired. I heard his mother, Helen, a frequent and welcome visitor, say to him in the kitchen one evening: "You must take care of yourself, dear. You're no use to Frances if you're ill too."

She is a decent woman, Helen, and would not have wanted

me to hear this remark. In my presence all her concerns are directed at me. I feel for her. It has not been so long, three years, since she lost her husband. And now she is worried again, for us, for me, and Chloe, and Phillip. She sees in Phillip, of course, only the dutiful son, the devoted husband. I wish that that was all I saw, that no vision of him as someone else's lover ever wandered unbidden across my eyelids when I close them to sleep.

One warm evening a short while after that visit of Helen's, I joined Phillip in a whiskey and soda. I rarely drink whiskey, but that night I wanted one, a premonition, perhaps, of what was to come. Whiskey is such bracing liquor. Phillip, sipping his and gazing sternly at the skyline, said that he needed to go to London. He had tried to avoid it, but there was nothing for it; some campaign, some new client demanded his presence. He would probably need to spend about a week away, so he had asked Helen, and she had said she would stay with me. Chloe had even offered to take a week off work and come down too if I liked. Or maybe I'd prefer it if Catherine came.

I would prefer Catherine, I thought, and then I told him so, rather slowly, feeling as though I was watching us having this conversation from a distance, wondering when he had discussed his plans with all these people. When he had stopped discussing his plans with me. I realized with a small shock that this lack of communication predated my illness, predated even his affair with Josee. We had been sliding for a year or two, maybe even three, toward this vaguely detached state.

"Right then," Phillip said, and he brushed my hand,

which was resting on the tabletop, before getting up to fix us another drink. I didn't want one.

Why was I so sure that after three months of apparent and admirable devotion, after three months of, if not forgetting, at least distancing himself from his lover, my husband would take this opportunity to see her again, had perhaps already arranged to do so? I stared at his empty chair. H.H., I thought. That's why.

H.H. was a device that Phillip had concocted when Chloe was not yet in her teens. She went through a phase, as most children do, of exhibiting acute and noisily disapproving embarrassment at any sign of affection between us. Once, when Emma was visiting, she gave a display of particular horror when Phillip attempted to kiss me over a bowl of coleslaw.

"H.H. instead then," Phillip had said to me.

H.H. meant nothing. It happened that these were the initials on a serving spoon that I had bought at a flea market and that Phillip was holding at the time, but Chloe did not know this and incredibly has never figured it out. Throughout her childhood, she would beg in that wheedling way offspring adopt with parents to be let in on the secret, because for Phillip and me it became a constant code. It was our way of expressing love in public, secret to us, immensely private. Until Josee.

H.H., she had written. *H.H., Josee.*

How could anything that had breached the privacy of our marriage so profoundly simply evaporate?

. . .

There were to be more guests in those gilded halls, I had discovered in the course of casual dinner conversation the night before. The idea, through the passing of a glorious morning, began to make me faintly edgy, as if my own fragile standing were threatened somehow. By the afternoon, with the arrival imminent and then announced by the hiccup and sudden cut of a throttley car engine, a soft murmur of nerves had set up in my stomach.

The girl in the convertible did not open the door to get out; she just stood on the buff leather of the bucket seat and slipped one golden leg and then another over the side of the shiny red chassis. When she landed in her bare feet on the gravel, she gave an easy little hop, slipped the seal-sleek curtain of her hair back behind her ears, and stared at the house for a moment the way I had once tried not to. Then she looked back down the sweep of the driveway, toward the tennis court, across the fresh emerald of the perfectly clipped lawns, before turning back to face us with a small, sincere sigh.

"Great place," she said.

I felt my nerves dim and fade, and a different, female part of me spark. Here was another extraordinarily pretty woman, wearing a string bikini top.

Mason smiled.

The car's driver exited the vehicle more conventionally than his companion. "This is Skipper," he said in her direction. He stretched slightly, and stood easing his back. The movement drew attention to the difference in their ages.

"Good to see you, Carl."

Ned and Mason advanced at once to shake Carl's hand.

Patsy and Bee Bee had not joined the welcome committee on

the gravel driveway, though it had been Bee Bee who had told me the night before that Carl and Skipper were coming. She had known Carl a long time, but was no fan of Skipper's. Evidently Carl had a wife somewhere who was Bee Bee's friend.

"He ditched her for the babysitter," she had explained. "They'll do that, you know."

Now, by the pool, a small clutter of necessities dividing them, the two women were spread, shins and arms and cleavages gleaming with suntan oil, impervious to the recent arrival, though it was heralded again by Howie, fantasy-driving Carl's car around an imaginary bend. He skirted the pool and skidded to a noisy halt near his mother.

"That man's got a sports car, Mom."

Patsy opened her eyes then and stood to be introduced. She and Richard had never met Skipper and Carl either. I was pleased.

Bee Bee sat up, limply, to receive Carl's kiss and waved halfhearted fingers past him at Skipper.

"Hi," Skipper said, beaming.

Carl had revealed a stump of ponytail when he bent forward over Bee Bee.

"You've been in California way too long, fella," Ned said.

When they left to say hello to Sally, who was in the house, Bee Bee inclined her head toward Skipper's skimpily denimed derriere and pushed her glasses back up her nose with an exaggerated gesture. "Poor old Carl," she crooned. "He hasn't got the first clue how much that pin-skinny piece of ass is gonna cost him."

Thirty-two hours had passed since Mason had kissed me, and there had been no further sign that he had. He remained his assured, charming self. Particularly, it pained me to note, with women. All women.

It was the evening of Carl and Skipper's first day. She had come to dinner wearing the same clothes she'd arrived in with the addition of a thin top, its narrow shoulder straps criss-crossing the halter tie of the bikini. We had eaten outside. It had gotten cooler during dinner and a breeze had come up. Mason lifted a shirt, one of his, from the back of a chair and handed it to Skipper. He left it there this morning, I thought, when he came out to swim.

"Thanks," she said, pulling it on and rolling up the cuffs. She raised an arm to her face. "It smells of the sun."

Leaving the shirt unbuttoned, jutting her hip and the soft curve of her belly forward, Skipper reached with one hand into the front pocket of her shorts. When she sat up again, leaning forward, elbows on her knees, she held up a joint, horizontal in her fingertips. "Do you mind?" she asked Mason.

He shrugged and lifted his hands.

"Carl?" she called. "Match?" She caught the box he tossed her easily with her left hand, lit up, and inhaled, holding her chest expanded for a second before breathing out again.

Carl moved to stand behind her and gave the nape of her neck a gentle stroke. She smiled, passing the joint over her shoulder to him. When he handed it back she half stood and sent it not sideways in Mason's direction, but across to Richard.

Richard hesitated, his grip slightly pinched. Then he looked at Patsy. When he had caught her eye he held it, put the joint to his lips and inhaled as deeply as Skipper had. He grinned as he exhaled the smoke. The broad stretch of his lips made him look, for just a moment, almost rakish.

"Nothing like a little Mary Jane," Carl said.

Later Patsy dragged the hi-fi speakers out by the pool, hurrying back inside with a little jiggy movement of her hips and emerging again on a wave of music with her wrists held together in the air above her head and her breasts swaying. She swung herself, describing smooth circles with her pelvis, past the clutch of Carl and Mason and Richard, who quit their talk and laughed as she plucked an orange from the bowl on the long table and tucked it under her chin. Limboing lightly she beckoned, her arms waving like an Arabian dancer, for someone to take it from her. It was a game; people played it at parties.

Ned, mirroring Patsy's movements, attempted to relieve her of the orange without the use of his hands. It rolled down the tender swell of her upper body with his head in steady pursuit. Eventually he caught it and, birdlike, twitched it from the open plain of bare skin near her belly button. I watched as Bee Bee took it from him and Richard from her as Ned, prone on the patio tiles, made a play of looking up Bee Bee's skirt.

Skipper stood when Richard turned from Bee Bee, triumphant with the orange locked under his jaw, and slipped Mason's shirt from her shoulders. She held her arms fractionally behind her, shimmied, and smiled as she approached him. His eyes smiled back, flirting. Everybody was.

"She's got even bigger bazooms than Paige," Jenny said, staring sleepily at Skipper.

The twins were nestled on an embroidered cushion that they had taken from a small sofa in one of the downstairs rooms, vaguely hypnotized by the noise and the antics of the adults, a shared bath towel encircling their shoulders. I had detached myself momentarily from the rest of the party to sit near them. Children's company has always been a sort of refuge for me and I was feeling separated somehow from the revelry. The dynamics had changed.

Paige cuffed her sister lightly. "Better not let Christina catch you with that cushion." But she didn't take her eyes off Skipper, who was squatting, knees splayed, feet together, heels raised, with her hands on her hips. The orange was rolling first left, then right along Richard's waistband, half held between Skipper's chin and the long stretch of her throat.

"It's too loud," Jessica complained.

"Let's go for a swim," Howie suggested. He had been amusing himself for the past fifteen minutes tickling alternate girls' ears with a straw, until Lesley had grabbed the thing eventually and destroyed it. "*With Tallulah.*" He leapt to his feet and grabbed Tallulah, squeezing her enthusiastically. She yelped.

It was the yelp that got Sally's attention. She turned toward us with a little swish of paisley voile and said, "You children should be in bed."

Howie whined.

"Now," she insisted.

I offered to take them.

On the way back from the childrens' rooms I met Mason standing in the long hallway, the warm light from a wall sconce bleaching his hair. He stopped me in front of him and lifted his hands to my face. I was just a little tipsy. I gazed serenely for a moment at the skin revealed in the uneven, open V above his shirt buttons.

"Are you all right?" he asked.

"Yes," I said, raising my eyes.

He kissed me. More seriously this time.

"Good." He turned me, holding my shoulders, back toward the party noise.

I rejoined the others with a new jitteriness in the pit of my stomach and, brightly light-headed, grabbed the orange from Carl. Mason, reappearing, ducked his head and took it from me. He spun then, arms spread, grinning.

"Well?" His voice was impeded by the obstacle at his throat. He leaned backward, gaily imploring someone to take it.

Sally was the only one who hadn't played. "You'd think we were in high school," she said.

Mason dropped the orange into his palm, then onto an occasional table in the big room where we often had drinks. It rolled a little, looking lonely, and came to a rest against the ceramic base of a Chinese lamp. Then, claiming concern for the children, he turned the music down. In the sudden quiet, the party slowed, but nobody went in. We all sat instead, in the moonlit dark, scattered amongst the ashtrays and half-empty glasses. Sally had sent the maids to bed.

"My father used to say that California girls had good teeth and no last names," Richard announced, too loudly, lagging behind the general mood.

Carl ran a drowsy hand under the strap of Skipper's top. She was sitting on the ground at his feet. "Who needs a last name?" he said.

"I think," Skipper offered slowly, turning her face up toward Richard, "that convention can become a sort of a prison."

"A prison," Richard repeated, nodding his head deliberately, creating a bond between them with the matching seriousness of his tone.

"*Oh spare us*," Patsy said, flouncing back in her chair. Her mood, at some unseen point, had dimmed from its initial spiritedness. I had heard her arguing earlier with Richard, their voices harsh whispers. He had shrugged after a minute or so and walked away, leaving her flipping edgily at the catch of her cigarette lighter.

"But Patsy," Sally, an elegant curve in the patio doorframe, said now, "I thought you were all for throwing off the shackles of society."

Patsy, twisting toward Sally, hesitated.

Bee Bee didn't. "To hell with all this throwing-off-the-shackles crap," she declared, puffing herself up as if she had said something regal. "It's all just a lousy excuse for men to think with their balls."

Skipper's was the warmest laugh, a chime over the gentle rhythm of the night noises.

· · ·

Guilt is such a feeble emotion. It surrenders so easily. Some might say, fans of pop psychology like Maggie, that this illness, this ogre that inhabits me, that cannot be removed, and is proving, too, resistant to the onslaught of chemical and mechanical weapons, was caused by guilt, or some such negative emotion looking for exit. And although it is hard now to escape those sorts of thoughts—thoughts of self-infliction—if pressed I would argue that such a theory was wrong, because life is full of random unfairness. Didn't I say so often enough to Chloe? Some things just happen, good or bad. But that is not the only reason that I would say that guilt cannot be the root of my disease; I would say it because I think I really forgave myself. And that is something that I cannot forgive now.

It was probably in great part due to Chloe, the self-bestowed pardon—because I did so much for her. Everybody said so; even Maggie, hesitant and chain-smoking, but heartfelt, said to me once, "You're doing a great job with her." And it's terribly easy to bask in, and absorb, what everybody says, isn't it?

My initial meeting with Chloe coincided with the first time that I spoke to Phillip, though I had often seen him pass my desk, parked near a drafty doorway in the advertising agency where I was working as a temporary something, I forget the title. Secretary would be too grand; office help is more accurate. Mostly I filed things and answered telephones and bought sandwiches for more important people, and sticky paper cups of coffee. Phillip was a copywriter. Phillip Grace. I had put his mail in the slot with his name on it once or twice.

Chloe was a dark, elfin thing, exquisite to look at even then, at four, almost five years old, and she was busy methodically emptying the drawers of one of the desks near mine. She did not look up when Phillip called her name in a clear signal for her to stop. I disliked the woman whose desk she was divesting of its contents, so I watched her unchecked progress with some amusement until Phillip, crossing to her and lifting her away from her task, said, "Leave it, Chloe," in a voice so edged with strain that his words were more entreaty than command.

Chloe reacted in a way one might associate with a much younger child, a child of two perhaps, a child at that age when frustration marks every communication. She stiffened, rigid against her father, so that it was difficult for him to keep holding her, and she wailed. Phillip, struggling with her small body and obviously distressed at the sound, looked thoroughly beaten. I put my arms out instinctively to that little girl whose tears, copious already on her plum cheeks, spoke to so many parts of me.

It's a cliché, I know, a man falling for a woman because of the relationship she has with his daughter, but that is what happened between Phillip and me. We were united over that small, unhappy head, perhaps instantly. Phillip had a meeting to go to, so I took Chloe, who came to me unthinkingly, quitting her tears, maybe from surprise at a stranger's face, maybe from some animal understanding of what would develop between us, and I offered to watch her for half an hour. I managed to distract her quite quickly with a box of paper clips.

The next day Phillip bought me a ham salad in the coffee shop downstairs, and the story of Chloe's difficult infancy, her mother's disappearance, the valiant efforts of his parents and various friends to help, came tumbling out.

"She really took to you, though," he said eventually.

"I took to her," I replied.

Ten months later we were married.

Recently Helen, sitting with me one afternoon while Phillip worked upstairs, interrupted some rambling narrative about a book she had just finished and said to me, "Did you never want children of your own, Frances?"

The directness was not typical of her. I was surprised and must have looked it, but she did not pull back, just gazed at me with those gray green eyes, the same ones Phillip has, and an expression of sincere interest.

"Once, maybe. But Chloe was like a child of my own. At least I don't think I would have loved a child of my own any more than I loved her."

Helen nodded and smiled a smile full of gratitude and acceptance and kindness, a smile that she had smiled at me many times before.

The real question, though, is whether a good deed cancels a bad one, whether evil is undone by penance. Some people believe that, don't they? My friend Catherine is deeply forgiving; I think she would believe it. Do I? Do I think these kinds of processes, addition and subtraction, will figure in the final reckoning?

I devoted myself to Chloe, devoured her. Spent all my energy on activities that calmed her and food that pleased her and making for her a whole safe little bubble of life that allowed her to be a bright, adorable child. Helen and Andrew had a granddaughter to spoil, and Phillip had a little girl to delight in. And I had my own private Jericho. Because mothering can provide a vast wall of protection from the outside world if that is what you are looking for.

Children's needs are so constant and so urgent that I daresay my attentions to my husband came second at times, but I was doing something right, wasn't I? Something important and decent and worthy. Phillip had a home and a lovely child; he seemed happy. Both of us wore Chloe's progress like a badge, like a confirmation of the meant-to-be aspect of our union. So when did that stop being enough for him? And if it was only fairly recently, is he still a good husband by virtue of his previous behavior? Does his erstwhile virtue cancel the lies I know he presents me with now?

What would Catherine think, with her compassionate soul, if I told her of the indecent haste with which Phillip had left the table, that night of the whiskeys and sodas, in order to fetch the telephone for me so that I could call her and ask her to leave her own husband and children and spend a week with me while he escaped to London? Would she think that twenty years of fidelity, if indeed it had even been that, canceled the debt of the past year? The debt I was sure he was about to redouble.

* * *

We were just two, Mason and I, at a poolside breakfast. Even the children slept late that day. I had woken early, and lain listening for the sound of him swimming as he did every morning. He had a routine. I got up when I heard the water disturbed and watched him from my window till he pulled himself out of the water, leaning heavily for a moment on his forearms on the ledge at the deep end of the pool. He wrapped a towel around his waist before going inside.

Over round pieces of hard bread, I told him I was supposed to teach that day.

"I'll drive you into town," he said.

I nodded and smiled. I felt weightless.

In the car, driving, he extended his arm without looking at me and rested his hand near my knee. I looked at it and then away, staring instead, intently, at the featureless view from the passenger window. We were on the long straight part of the road.

Suddenly he braked. I turned to him, surprised.

"Darling," he said, "you are an adorable girl, and I adore you. Don't spoil that by trying to understand everything."

I knew that he meant about Sally. I knew it because, feeling his hand through the fine cotton of my skirt, I had been thinking about Sally. I met his glance, a little dopey in the clutch of the endearment. Darling.

"Don't try to understand everything," he repeated. He leaned over then and kissed me very quickly and very hard, as if it mattered, before putting the car back into gear and continuing on. "It's all much simpler than you think," he said, lifting my arm and touching his lips to the hollow of my palm.

Letty had been my student for almost nine months, but that day was the first day that I noticed how starkly her immaculate neatness conveyed her poverty. Dressed, as always, in her navy pleated school skirt and white blouse, she lay her precise hands on her notepad and looked up at me from her seat at her mother's kitchen table, waiting for the lesson to begin. She was a sweet-faced, studious girl, whose family scrimped for the pittance I charged them. They wanted a future for her, a future that would probably take her north of the border and far away, to a country where she would in turn scrimp for her own children's education. Her English was miraculous.

"What are the interests of the American girls?" she asked.

"'Hobbies' is another way of saying 'interests,' Letty."

"Hobbies," she repeated, trying the word for feel, sealing it in her head. "What are the hobbies of the American girls?"

I thought for a moment, trying to fit a hobby on Paige or Lesley. It was difficult, matching them to such an organized concept. They were lazy, those girls, appealing, but lazy. It was all the maids, and the money, cleaning up after them.

"They like to play tennis," I said.

Letty nodded, but her forehead pinched momentarily. She had hoped, I think, for more common ground. "Perhaps," she suggested brightly, "they have a collection."

Letty had a collection of plaster figurines, dressed in the national costumes of different countries. Nine countries were represented so far.

"Perhaps," I answered. Then, "I had a collection when I was your age."

Letty was fourteen, like Paige.

"Of what your collection?" she asked, pleased.

"What did you collect?" I corrected. "Shells."

"Shells? Las conchas?"

"Yes. My mother used to say that they made my bedroom smell like fish."

She hesitated, processing, and then she laughed.

Later, before I left, she wrote *Hobby* and *What Did You Collect?* in her notepad, between faint lines the color of swimming pool water.

I stopped on the corner of Letty's street to comb my hair. I was glad that I had; he was standing already where we had arranged to meet.

"Hello," he said, smiling.

"Hello."

We bought gum for the children and papers for Richard. Waiting to pay, just for a second he took my hips in his hands with a deft possessiveness that blurred my ability to think. We crossed the square after that, him leading me by the hand, just as if we were any other couple. Any simple sort of couple, in love. We went to buy, just for the sake of it, avocados at the market, then we sat at a café for a while drinking coffee, looking silently out at the square with our chairs on the same side of the table and our thighs almost touching.

Driving back, he said, "Is it left here?"

I knew that he was asking for directions to my apartment.

He crossed the courtyard behind me, closed the apartment door purposefully at my back, and pulled me to him. I was neither completely naive nor terribly experienced those days, and I felt for a moment the way that they say swimmers can feel like when they're drowning. As if a conscious instruction to resist were battling a more seductive sensation. For a few thrashing seconds, in a pointless negation of my part in the rituals that had brought us there, I stiffened to him, but he persisted determinedly, with no new lover's tentativeness, and any will I might have had to stay afloat weakened. And was gone.

Later, on the blue cotton bedspread, when he began to snake his hands with intention over my breasts and thighs for the second time, I asked him to take off his watch.

"Why?" he said, his weight across me.

"It reminds me that we have to remember the time."

"Where's your watch?"

I felt a small thump of shock when Jenny asked, but Mason just said, "I dunno. Around."

85

"We bought him that watch, didn't we, Jessica? For his birthday."

Jessica nodded.

"We did, didn't we, Dad?" Jenny coaxed.

"Sure." Mason winked and lifted his daughter to swing her out over the pool. She squealed and clung to his neck. When he put her down, her swimsuit had ridden up over the peachy curve of her bottom.

Mason sat, and the twins settled either side of him, Jessica stroking the bleached hair on his arms. From the shade of the bougainvillea Paige, too grown up for her father's knee, watched.

Sally lifted the avocados from the chair next to her husband and said, "Wasn't it clever of them, Patsy, to think of avocados? I'll have Christina make a vinaigrette." She turned carrying the bag in front of her, one hand poised delicately underneath, as if it contained something unpleasant that might scatter at any minute across the terrace, and Patsy, without reply, turned a masked gaze to me for a second.

"Avocados are a perfect food," Skipper declared. She had the full bikini on today, stars and stripes, looped at the sides with stringy bows. "Like some nuts. You could probably live on them."

"Believe me, honey," Ned said, hoisting his glass, "you can't live on anything that you don't get a little buzz from."

"You don't need chemicals, though, to get a buzz, do you?"

"She means," Bee Bee suggested, "that you can always puff on a little weed when you need an escape from your careworn Californian existence."

"Well that," Skipper replied smoothly, "and, you know, natural highs, like love."

"Amen to that." Carl's ponytail bobbed when he bounced his head.

"I think Skipper's got a point about this eating thing," Richard said.

Patsy turned slightly, shifting her attention to her husband.

"It's like what I was saying about the kids," he went on earnestly. "They never eat anything with any nutrition in it. When I was a kid, we ate proper food."

"Good wholesome vittles. All served up on silver platters by three Irish maids." Bee Bee was hitting her morning high.

Carl, missing the wit, and the acid in it, stood and patted his stomach. "Your body is a temple."

Bee Bee sitting forward sharply, snapped, "For Christ's sake, Carl. You used to be a normal person."

"I'm still a normal person," Carl said, flustered. "I'm just a normal person who's expanded his horizons a bit, that's all." It was feeble. He sat heavily. There was a beat, the air left his lungs, and his shoulders dipped at the deflation.

In the silence Patsy began to pull her lounger ineptly into the sunshine. The legs scraped. She bent forward over the head end, accentuating the shadowy canyon of her cleavage, and her sunglasses slipped down her nose. She took them off.

"Give me a hand, would you?" she said, smiling at Mason.

"Of course." He leaped up and took the foot end, and she maneuvered the other. Once in position, she adjusted the backrest with his help and settled, one leg bent mannequin gorgeous.

"Thanks." She put her sunglasses back on, raising her eyebrows over the broad arches of the lenses.

Mason replied with a smile. Watching him, I felt my stomach contract. I was in love.

F O U R

TOM KISSED ME once, in the kitchen in the middle of a party. How pedestrian that sounds now. How suburban. But it was something then, because I wanted it to be. I kissed him back. Tom was single at the time—he had divorced his first wife and had not yet met Alice, who is his second—but I was not. But, just for a moment, at that night-lit draining board, Ella Fitzgerald and Sonia's laughter in the background, I wanted to be, wanted to give in to the feel of unfamiliar lips on mine, unfamiliar hands at my waist.

It had not been long since Phillip had hurt me, betrayed me, I half believed, with Anthea, and compounded that betrayal by clinging pointedly to his injured attitude. Rethinking the whole business, after the row had dwindled to a bicker and then to a silence that had refilled again, drip by drip, with life's undramatic business, I realized that his protests had focused predominantly on detail. He had been like a child accused of stealing biscuits when in fact he has stolen cake. Phillip had clung to the flotsam of my mistakes, the pinpoints I had got wrong, in stating his case, and left the dark undertow that had buoyed them intact.

Anyway, the whole thing had left me feeling adrift, insecure, which is a dangerous way for a married person to feel. But then—as Phillip perhaps had—I reflected later, after drink and sentimentality had turned Tom's departure sloppy, and Phillip and I had crept in together to check on Chloe, angelic in sleep, that the price of clinging to the wrong rock in order to escape such a feeling would be high. I remembered that I knew exactly how high the price could be.

That little kiss, though, turned out not to be so fluffy, because Tom and I have been better friends for it. For having got it out of the way, I suppose. It was Tom who showed my drawings to Stella Crewkherne, who then asked me to illustrate some of her books. They were children's books, and I made a bit of money of my own from them. The little red-haired people I painted for her, all cute outfits and exaggerated roundness, paid for the oil by one of the modern Americans that hangs in what is now my dayroom.

It turns out to be worth a great deal these days, that picture, but that's not what I think of when I look at it, musing often for hours, as I must now that physical capacity is so much taken from me. I think about that kiss in the kitchen with Tom, and others. Others that preceded it.

· · ·

The proximity of my lover's wife should have deflated the moony bubble of my desire for him. I am aware of that, was aware of it even then, but it did not. There were things that contributed to this, things that are somewhat hard to convey. The times, for instance. It seems feeble now, but there was then, and especially in that detaching, sensual heat, an atmosphere of general disregard, for practicality, for convention. And I was as convinced as the rest of the youthful world of the unquestionable rights of love, of passion, and of impulse. It seemed to me, anyhow, that Mason and Sally's relationship was on a rather mechanical, flat foundation, no deeper than habit. So once he was in my life in the way that he was I gave no time at all to searching for reasons to resist him.

He shifted the smooth curve of his shoulders toward me in the afternoon sun and asked, "Frankie, do you think we could get a couple of boats, maybe, and all go off somewhere for a day?"

I felt a flush rise in me at the mere sound of my name in his voice. He had kissed me only once, swift soft lips on the back of my neck, since we had arrived back from our tryst. We had eaten lunch with the others just as if there were no more sweetness between us than mere cordiality demanded.

"It's not usually hard to find boats," I said.

Richard broke in to this gauzy communication enthusiastically, "We could probably find those fishing guys again."

"I am *not* fishing." Patsy held up the flat of her palm for emphasis.

"We don't have to fish. We could go to one of those coves we saw . . . or something."

"It's a wonderful idea," Sally interrupted, her subtle authority sealing the plan instantly. She brought both her hands together, fingers meeting near her mouth. Her rings sparkled. "Frankie, would you mind being a sweetheart and going back into town to find out about the boats? These sorts of negotiations tend to go better if you speak the language. I'd come with you, but I've got a date to whip Patsy at tennis."

I thought Patsy looked mildly surprised at this, but I didn't think about it for long. Mason and I would have two more hours alone together before drinks.

At six Ned emerged from the kitchen with a pitcher of martinis and a triumphant expression. I was the only person in the room.

"Where'd everybody go?" he asked.

"Showers, mostly."

"I reckon hygiene's an overrated notion," he said, putting the pitcher down.

I laughed.

He sat next to me on a boxy chair with a flower-patterned cushion, tiny birds poking pretty heads from hand-painted foliage. For a long moment we didn't speak, watching, instead, the children playing with Tallulah out by the pool.

"You enjoying yourself, Frankie?" he asked, without turning to face me.

"Yes," I said, "very much." I was aware, though, of a deeper level of interrogation that the lightness of the question implied. I didn't like it.

"They can be a bit overwhelming," he went on, running a finger idly along the armrest of his chair.

I didn't reply.

He stood then and, opening one of the sideboard cupboards, took out a small dish and filled it from a jar of olives.

When he had finished, he turned to me. "I married into it, so I know what this kind of life looks like to an outsider. But you gotta remember, Frankie, they don't." Behind him condensation was forming on the martini pitcher. "This is it for them. How they've always lived. How they always will live. They sorta write their own rules," he finished, sighing a little.

I nodded uneasily.

"It's the kind of life that can make people . . . casual," he said, choosing the word, "about all kinds of things."

I looked down and saw, not my hands, but the abyss that was opening up before me. I was headed for it. I knew. Willingly deaf to the increasingly distant voices of my own intelligence, conscience, and upbringing, I set myself, determinedly, against Ned's tethering tone. What could he know, anyway, about me, or Mason?

I stood up.

"Yes," I said, ending the conversation. "Actually, I think I'll change now too, before drinks." And then, so as to soften my abrupt exit, I went over and kissed his cheek.

He clasped my arms for a moment and looked into my eyes as if about to say something more. Perhaps he saw from their bright deflection that I didn't want to hear it.

"Better put this in the icebox," he said, dropping his hands and turning to take the martini pitcher back to the kitchen.

It wasn't hard to put what Ned had said out of my mind. Standing in a corner later, momentarily alone with the now familiar-feeling shape of a martini glass in my fingers, I thought about my own futurelessness. In the face of it, a love affair with Mason didn't seem casual at all. It seemed concrete, solid, something to hang on to.

This conviction was soon rewarded. Mason joined me,

turned his wandering eyes from the scarlet ridges of an enormous painting on the opposite wall, and whispered, "Hello, sweetheart," in a voice that was as laden as I could possibly wish for, with promise.

. . .

I was sleeping when Catherine arrived and awoke to hear her voice in the next room, and Phillip's. I thought that they were probably talking about me; people do that a lot now, and I marvel at it because I cannot guess what it is that they think they know. What does the surface of me give away? I cannot imagine. The hidden parts are so deeply hidden.

"Hello."

Catherine, sensing my waking, had come in. She kissed me. Phillip, following, kissed me too. And then he said that perhaps he ought to be going, but, so as not to depart too abruptly and also to show manly usefulness, he spent a few seconds doctoring the fire, poking at it ineffectually. Catherine and I, recognizing this small maleness, this need to prod at something, looked at each other with no expression and absolute knowing, and I was filled with a rush of gratitude for her presence. And a desire too to be alone with her, for Phillip to be gone, no matter where it was that he was going.

"Thank Chloe for the bath oil," I said, relieving him of further duty. It was a cue he seemed pleased to grasp.

"I will," he said decisively, propping the poker back against its brass stand, and I knew that he would forget.

Chloe had sent the bath oil by messenger. It had arrived that morning encased in an elegant black box lined with lavender tissue paper. I had put the box on the sideboard, next to a photograph that had been taken in Singapore when we went to visit my parents. I wanted to show it to Catherine.

"I'll see her tomorrow," Phillip said.

Of course I knew this already. Chloe had invited Phillip to supper at her flat. Ed would be there too no doubt, and Chloe planned to cook. It is a new trick with her, cooking. She plays at it rather, adds ready-made sauces to pasta, that sort of thing. But we indulge her in it, as we do in everything.

Catherine, who is a real cook, began unloading the stocks she'd brought with her, holding packages and jars up for my approval: ginger biscuits, cheese biscuits, olives, plum jam, all stacked together in a basket we had bought together in Barnham market when Chloe was about nine, before Catherine's youngest, Ness, was born. Phillip went upstairs to get his things. While he was there, the telephone rang. Inside me something caught.

It was only Dan, though, Catherine's husband, with some spousely inquiry, some need which Catherine easily dispatched. They didn't talk for long, and by the time she had hung up and passed Dan's greetings on to me, Phillip had reappeared, garment bag in hand. He said goodbye again, and in the still evening we heard his car skim the gravel, signaling his absolute departure.

The September day had been warm, but it had given way to a surprisingly cold evening, and so Catherine got up and stoked the fire to a roar. Then she went into the kitchen to fetch herself and me a glass of wine. It was all so companionable. I was delighted with the dull domesticity of it and wondered if, despite my concerns about Phillip, there weren't just bigger things, more important things to be concerned with now. A lot in life had begun to seem small.

* * *

The boats for the day-trip had been secured easily enough by a run into town and a few American dollars, and the next morning we were aroused early by maids and children and greeted by the smell of pancakes.

Skipper, in a loose puff-sleeved top that slipped constantly from one narrow shoulder, licked maple syrup from her fingers.

"It's a completely natural substance," she said.

"Like opium," Bee Bee offered, still gravel-voiced from sleep.

Christina came to the head of the table and leaned toward Mason's ear. "Madam says go without her."

"Without her?"

"Yes, sir. She will sleep some more."

I finished my coffee, listening, of course, with keen attention, but wanting to appear distanced from this exchange.

Bee Bee, at Mason's side, stood. "Hey. If *I* can get up, Lady Severance can get up too." Then, catching Christina's glance, she sat down again.

"She says you should go without her," Christina repeated to Mason.

"She told you this just now?"

Christina, her hands clasped neatly in front of the white half apron she wore over her black uniform, bent from the waist to lean in closer to him. Lowering her voice, she said, "No sir, last night."

"*Last night?*"

"Yes, sir. She asked me not to wake her this morning, just to tell you that you should go without her." She stood upright, duty done.

Mason tapped his glass with a butter knife and announced, "Madam sends her regrets."

Howie quit his pancake for a second and glanced quizzically at Jenny, who had listened, from her seat near her father's, to the entire exchange with Christina.

"Our mother," she explained, with a small sigh and deliberate patience, "is going to stay home instead of coming on the boat with us."

"Oh." Howie picked up the maple syrup with two hands and poured some clumsily onto his plate. "Good. She can watch Hudson."

Bee Bee tipped her head back and hooted.

Bee Bee demanded a sedan chair for the wade through the water to the boats, which were moored, canopies fluttering, in the bay. She had to make do with a hoisting hand each from Ned and Richard. She clutched her backside protectively as it was released. "Hold the smart remarks," she said, lifting a warning finger to Ned.

Ned blew her a kiss and then saluted before wading back to shore to help with picnic things.

"Keep up the b.s., sailor," she called after him. "It's part of your charm."

Skipper rose effortlessly from the sea next to Bee Bee and, standing sure-footed in the boat, turned and put her arms out. Children and baskets of food and beach things were passed to her. Mason and Patsy and Richard and I got in one of the other boats with Howie.

"Give me Tallulah," he shouted.

But Lesley, who was holding the dog, pretended not to hear. Tallulah, head poking from Lesley's clutch as Ned ferried them both through the glassy water, looked as she always did: petrified.

"It's okay, Tallulah," Jenny called from her perch next to Bee Bee. "It's just a boat ride." Then she squealed as the outboards started to cough and grabbed excitedly at Jessica.

"Keep still," I called, but they didn't hear me. Their hair was already beginning to whip back from their faces.

When we rounded the bay and passed the wineglass rock, Mason leaned toward me, put an arm across my shoulders, and pointed to it. I nodded, as if acknowledging a minor pleasantry, and we exchanged a smile. When he took his arm away, I turned and lowered my hand into the froth of soft, salt spray.

We were to be in the boats for twenty-five minutes or so, but it was only fifteen before we saw the dolphins.

"Shaark," yelled Howie, leaping up and pointing, his arm extended. "A shark."

Richard, holding the child's waist, tugged him back into his seat.

"Delphina," said the boatman.

"Dolphin, Howie," I said, unnecessarily. They were clearly visible now, half a dozen of them, arcing in rhythm on the seaward side of us. Everyone had seen them. Carl, in the boat ahead, held the twins, one tucked in either arm, over the side near the bow for a better view. The dolphins peeled off and swam out to sea only as we turned and, with a gentling of motors, put-putted into the cove.

"Is four o'clock all right?" I asked Mason, translating the boatman's question, arranging pickup.

Mason looked around. Behind him the sun had turned the U of the cove silver. "Sure," he said, raising his palms and smiling.

"Get Mommy a drink." Patsy leaned on her elbows and tipped up her hips, sacrificing herself to the heat. "And a beer for Aunty Bee Bee," she called. But Howie paid no attention. It was Paige, less teenagery than usual in a pretty spotted sundress, who handed out bottles, beaded still from the chill of the cooler.

"Richard?" she asked.

"Uh-huh."

"Would you like a drink?"

"No thanks," he said, waving her off, folding the sports section of yesterday's newspaper, and creasing it with a snap.

Paige, discharged, sat with a little crestfallen thud.

"To Mexico." Bee Bee raised her beer to the Pacific's blue horizon.

"To Mexico," we repeated.

"Mexico lindo," I said.

"What does that mean?" Skipper turned her soft face toward me.

"Beautiful Mexico."

"Yes." She cradled her bottle to her cleavage. "It is."

The bay stretched maybe a mile end to end, curved against a hillside that rose shallowly at first, the white of the sand turning gradually to yellow brown dust, then sharply to a cliff. At either end the dirt gave way to good-sized rocks. Azure-tinged sea lay trapped in the shallows at the bases of them.

"Let's take Tallulah to those rocks," Jessica suggested.

I said I'd go with them. I was in a mood to please. Paige slid her eyes over her knees, first toward Richard, the newspaper resting on his thighs, his face halved by the shadow of his hat brim, then to Lesley. They agreed by some clandestine adolescent signal to join us. Lesley stood up.

Mason, watching, got up too. "I can come, can't I?"

Paige, to whom the question had been addressed, shrugged. "I guess," she said with a smile.

The rock pools were deep enough for the twins and Howie to splash around in. The water was already sun warmed. Paige and Lesley took off their sundresses and waded.

"It's cold in this bit," Howie said. He was lying on his stomach, his chin jutting from the water and his hands spread like starfish.

"You're in the shadow of the rock there," I called.

I sat down, rubbing grainy flecks of sand from my palms, then lay on my back. Mason lay beside me. I turned my head toward him; his face, a few inches from mine, was double exposed. I had to squint. He smiled too before we both closed our eyes. Lying there, in his handsome nearness, I thought about Sally's absence. I had been deeply comforted by Mason's clear ignorance of her intention not to join us. Mentally, I began a checklist, evidence of their estrangement. Worlds away I could hear the muted, singing voices of the children.

I felt Mason sit up and heard him shout, "Don't drown the poor thing."

I opened my eyes. Howie had Tallulah aloft in his hands on the top of the rock. He was about, despite the shrieks from the girls beneath, to drop her.

"She can swim," he called, defiant, but he retracted his arms to his chest nevertheless and looked toward Mason.

"Yes, but she can't high dive," Mason said, getting up. He walked over, stepped into the water, and reached up to take Tallulah from Howie. Rescued, she was fallen upon by a rush of cooing girls. Mason lifted Howie down.

"A dog isn't a toy," Lesley said to him, her face pursed with deep disapproval.

Howie, near tears, hung his head and kicked some sand into the water, clouding it.

"It's okay, kid," Mason said, squeezing his shoulder. "You just need to take it a little easier is all."

Paige, cradling Tallulah, looked over at her father. "High dive," she said, and started to laugh. She pushed Tallulah's front paws together in a mock-diving pose. "Like Ethel Merman."

I was surprised that she knew who Ethel Merman was.

Mason laughed too. "We could get her a fancy bathing hat," he said, reaching over to pat Tallulah's head. "It'd have to have ear holes, though." He tugged gently at one of the dog's disproportionately large ears, and then he pinched the lobe of one of Paige's. She giggled.

"Come on," she said. "She probably wants a drink." She turned to walk ahead of us along the beach, the tops of her thighs blossoming into pale half-moons from the back of last year's swimsuit.

"Daddy had to rescue Tallulah," Jenny declared, small-girl superior, when we reached the others. "Howie tried to drown her."

"Did not." Howie sat, stiffly distanced from everyone, particularly the little dog who had been settled to recover under a soft oval of sun umbrella shade. He rubbed sulkily at his shins.

Skipper shook her head and let several drops of seawater fall onto Richard's newspaper. She had been swimming. "Hey," she said, smiling, "there's a big world out here."

Richard smiled back at her.

"It's a beautiful one too. Mexico lindo," she said, sitting

beside him. She twisted the sea from her hair. Thin rivulets trickled down her back.

"The water's good, then?"

"Magic," she answered.

The water was good, and safe for swimming, with no rips. The color changed subtly from opaque green at its frothed edge to clear blue as you went farther out. Bee Bee floated with her knees breaking the surface and her thin hands rotating just beneath it.

"Not bad," she said, "as exercise goes."

I flipped onto my back beside her and let the air out of my lungs and laughed. It was one of those days when nothing that isn't immediately visible seems real.

In the gorgeous waterborne ebb and flow of bodies Mason and I were alone for just a few moments.

"I miss you," he said.

"I miss you too," I replied, knowing that we were talking about the kind of missing that besets new lovers when they are unable to touch. The kind of missing that teases hours into millenniums. His deft hand reached for me below the water, and I closed my eyes against its directness.

"You look very beautiful with your hair wet," he said.

After a lunch of cold chicken and chocolate cake, I slept on the sand. Lying for a while first, watching the lazy rise and fall of Patsy's concave stomach, I marveled, in my hot, half-dreaming state, that it bore no memory of her pregnancies. Everything about Patsy seemed untouched, unimpeded by anything. I liked that. I liked the way she didn't care who saw her sulk or snap at her husband. I liked her impulsiveness and her inconsistency. These seemed to me brave sorts of traits.

Not like the ones I had been raised to: politeness and concern for other people's regard.

Of all them, I decided, closing my eyes, the sound of my lover's voice in the background somewhere, of all of those women, I liked Patsy the best. I fell asleep then, adrift on affection and sunshine and happiness.

"Here they come. Here they come." Howie, shouting, did a little whooping dance. The boats had arrived in convoy around the headland.

I sat up. At the waterline, Skipper and the twins were setting a row of shells along the base of an enormous sand castle.

"What will happen to it?" Jessica asked as a thin wave-edge stretched toward her toes.

"The silver sand king and queen will rule over it forever," Skipper answered.

In the boat, as the engines started, Jessica lay her head in my lap. I looked down at her small, sleepy face and brushed a string of hair from her cheek. When I looked up, Mason, across from me, smiled. It had been a perfect day.

"Well," Sally said when we reached the house, a rabble, sand-laden and disheveled in contrast to her fresh, cocktail-hour neatness, "how was the expedition?"

"Lovely," I said. My voice sounded false.

"Mason," she went on, acknowledging me with a vague smile, "there was a message for you."

Mason nodded and followed her inside. Heading to my room to change, I paused near the door that led to the front entrance where the telephone alcove was. Sally had evidently written the message on the notepad there. I watched as she held it up and Mason, framed in the doorway, leaned toward her. He read without taking the paper from her hand, exposing the nape of his neck above the soft collar of his blue shirt. Sally spoke then in a low voice while he, in three-quarter profile, rubbed the bridge of his nose with his thumb and index finger and nodded. They looked, standing there, very much like husband and wife. I turned, a jumble of beach things in my arms, and walked quickly away.

After dinner Sally asked, "Did Mason mention inviting Arturo and Maria for drinks?"

I felt, as always, flawed under her gaze. She was wearing a sleeveless linen dress, her hair flipped just at her shoulders. She tipped her head slightly toward me. The movement made her earrings quiver.

"Yes," I answered. He had. Ned was performing a magic trick for the children that had so far resulted in irreparable damage to two glasses and Richard's shirt cuff, but even above the riot, I was aware of the small, brittle clicking sound my coffee cup made as I placed it back on its saucer.

"Do you think they'd like to come?" she pressed.

"I think they'd be very pleased. I can ask Maria tomorrow if you like. I'm giving her a lesson in the morning."

"Perfect," she said, and then, "I'll ask Mason to drive you. He's an early riser too."

Mason's watch was still sitting next to half a glass of water on the chest of drawers near the bed I had once shared with Adam. The water had bubbles of stale air in it.

"Did anyone else notice?" I asked. I meant apart from Jenny, but I didn't want to mention his children here.

"No," he said, understanding.

We both looked at his wrist where the white mark had begun to tan over. I was pleased that Sally was so unobservant of him that the disappearance of his watch had gone unremarked. I turned to face him, and he put his arms around me and kissed me. We stood like that, kissing, for a long time. I had worn a loose blouse with a drawstring neckline and he undid the drawstring and drew the blouse down over my shoulders to kiss each of my breasts. Lifting his head, he smiled before taking my hand and pulling me down onto the bed. The covers still bore the creases of our last visit. Afterward we lay silent a while. I folded myself against him, gazing across the sweet, undulating ocean of his chest at the room in which I had spent many months and thought, suddenly, that it was too dark. Or, rather, that there were too many dark colors. It was not the sort of thing that I had ever paid any attention to before.

"Darling girl," he said eventually. Then he sat up.

My skin, peeled from his, felt chilly.

Showering, dressing, he was cheerful, businesslike. Ready again for the outside world. He slipped his watch back on, clipping it with a deft, habitual motion. I reached for him and kissed him intensely, to get him back. Back to how he had been that morning, in the car, kissing my fingertips with tender seriousness when we arrived at Maria and Arturo's wrought iron gate. His smile had sent me off, across the courtyard, past the spitting fountain, and up the steps, with a tingle of euphoria that had lasted all through Maria's lesson. Now, he reacted to my fervor with a little laugh.

"Darling girl," he repeated, and, mistaking the tenseness in my smile for playfulness, he gave me a gentle, shooing pat.

A sudden, shocking sense of panic rose up from my gut.

. . .

Catherine is a midwife and a redhead and an undemanding presence. She presents none of those stereotypical qualities that her coloring and heritage are supposed to endow and is the gentlest person I know. Her fingertips, which I have now experienced, delicate against my pulse, are violinist-sensitive to the secrets beneath the skin. She was the ideal person to act as nurse, caretaker, that week while Phillip was in London. That week that marked the full stop at the end of the three-month hiatus. The three months when we had forgotten at times that we were no longer what we once had been, Phillip and I, and forgotten too that there would not be time to start over, to forge something new and bright.

During those months, those holiday-from-life months at home with Phillip, there had been occasions when, running the bath, rinsing a cup, folding a sweater, I had found tears coursing my cheeks. I was not so divorced from my situation. But, if some of those tears had taken me to my knees, my head against porcelain or counter top, if through some of them I had begged God to let me off, to find me a different path, offering up my soul in exchange, these episodes had been as inconsistent as they were unpredictable. And at different times I had considered different things to be at their root: the possibility of death; my husband's infidelity; my repugnance with that event from my past with which I was now constantly assailed, captive to my own memory.

Catherine's visit, however, was unmarked by wretchedness of any sort. I was not, as I had feared, panicked by Phillip's absence, plagued by thoughts of where he might be and with whom, but relieved. I guess the forgetting, the forgiving, had not gone so deep, and he, in the flesh, was at some level a reminder. Catherine, though, like Sonia, but for different reasons, awakens better things in me. I look at her, now necessarily across oceans from this side of my torments, and feel not jealousy or resentment, but admiration instead. Catherine seems to own her life. She has taken hold of it piece by piece in steady increments, her gaze always set clear ahead.

That first night, before the fire had died down to embers, I told her that I did not want to die in Aldenbrook Hospital, did not wish to take my last breaths against the backdrop of distant strangers coughing. She looked at me solidly and sought no clarification, but went ahead, sturdy little tugboat on a threatening sea, and led me through the bare, unadorned facts. Facts that I could make use of at some later date, when the time was right, at a time when she, as a medical professional, would be honor bound to extend life. She talked all the while in language so clean that you could almost forget that the words carried any anguish at all, and then when she was sure, from my understanding nod and sincere thank you, that the topic was done and would require no revisiting, she went on smoothly to talk about giddier plans. The kind people with terminal illnesses make all the time, for the future.

During the remainder of the week we laughed a great deal and amused ourselves by planning a holiday. A perfect holiday, for when I was well again. Phillip and I and Catherine and Dan had holidayed together before, once in a lovely house in Greece. We'd ridden bicycles everywhere on white dusty roads. Sonia had come on that holiday too, with her second husband Chris. No one had taken much to Chris—he was a vague presence and his marriage to Sonia was short-lived—but I remember other things about that fortnight.

It was the year all of us started complaining about our ages, while slightly reveling too in the notion of being forty, or over forty even. Trying it out. We indulged in a lot of talk, sort of mock complaint, about things that we no longer approved of or didn't like, things that younger people liked, delivering these gripes as jokes, tentative practice for the mild grumpiness we felt middle age owed us. The women had some more sincere grievances, though, centered on softening jawlines and thighs and upper arms; suddenly, frighteningly, we could see our mothers in them.

Now, of course, I am caught in a swift and inevitable acceleration of the aging process, and I wish that I could say that all my priorities have changed, but they have not completely. I care very much that Josee is not only younger than me, but also more beautiful.

·   ·   ·

"You passed on the invitation?"

"Yes. They'd love to come."

Maria had almost jumped with pleasure, clasping her soft palms together in a gesture that had reminded me of Hudson. "Tomorrow?" she'd said, confirming. "Por la tarde?"

"Tomorrow evening. Yes," I'd told her.

"Very good," she answered, beaming. "Veeery good."

"Thank you," Sally said now.

I nodded, taking my seat for lunch.

"What will happen to these students of yours when you leave, Frankie?" Patsy asked. Her tone was light enough, but any mention of departure felt vaguely hostile to me. Departure implied a future that I didn't want to think about.

"I'm sure someone will come along," I replied, deliberately matching the casualness of her expression. "There was an American woman teaching here before me. We took over most of her pupils."

"You and . . . your boyfriend?"

I had unwittingly introduced a second unwelcome element into the conversation. "Yes," I hurried on. "There never seems to be a long shortage of English teachers. People arrive and stay for a while—"

"Beats me," Skipper interjected dreamily, "why they want to learn English anyway. Spanish is such a beautiful language."

"Gets you a better class of cleaning job in California." Bee Bee's smile lingered too long after her own joke.

Skipper, pulling herself up, turned so that she was facing Bee Bee. "Bee Bee," she said in a voice that carried, "I am aware that you are a friend of Carl's wife, and that probably accounts for some of your hostility toward me, but I would just like to make it clear that I did not *steal* Carl from Marianne. His marriage was a formality, an unhappy one. He and I, on the other hand, are in love. So perhaps, even if you cannot find it in yourself to like me, you could put aside some of your enmity for the sake of your friendship with Carl. You could be happy for *him*."

Bee Bee's mouth hung slack. Her glass was arrested at chest height.

Carl, next to Skipper, put a gentle, proprietorial hand

on her bare shoulder and said, softly, "She's right, Bee Bee. Marianne and I were . . . it was over. I love Skipper, and I wish you'd accept that."

Bee Bee took a long sip of her drink and set it on the table. Then, reaching for her cigarettes, she gave her shoulders a constricted shrug. "Oh hell," she said, tucking one of the cigarettes between her lips and narrowing her gaze against the flare of her lighter, "I guess I may as well. After all, what's a little adultery between friends?"

The faint sadness in Bee Bee's voice was dismissed by Patsy. "All the world loves a lover . . ." she clowned, "except the spouse."

It might have been Skipper's little speech and Carl's reaction, but I think it was Mason too—his constant attentiveness, his ardor—that set me imagining the unimaginable. Imagining that the end of the vacation needn't necessarily entail a goodbye. That I could go to New York. Mason had an apartment there. He had told me so. An apartment with silk-covered walls the color of my eyes. The silk-covered walls had been Sally's idea; she'd hatched it with some crazy decorator she'd hired. Mason, he'd told me, laughing, had shelled out a fortune for them, and now Sally barely set foot in the place. She spent all her time in their house in Connecticut.

In the dead hour between lunch and cocktails, sunbathing in those gorgeous surroundings in the lazy afternoon heat, any distance I had felt from him as we were leaving my apartment that morning melted away. And I found myself thinking, why not? Why not picture myself there with him? Just the two of us and the silk-covered walls.

F I V E

THE NEXT MORNING, the day that Arturo and Maria
were to come for drinks, I had an early lesson with
Letty. I woke easily, rearranged the pillows, skewed
by some unconscious nocturnal tussle, and got up and
walked to the window. I stood there, naked, looking down
at the pool. On my skin clean white triangles marked out the
shape of my bikini. "You'd be that color all over if you spent
the winter in Connecticut," Mason had teased.

"What's it like?" I'd asked. "Winter in Connecticut."

"Too frosty," he'd replied, cupping one breast and pinching
the rose nipple slightly so that it firmed and darkened, "for
a creature with blood as warm as yours."

Now he was swimming. I stepped forward, leaned my
thighs against the sill and put one hand, tenderly, to the glass.
I hoped he would pause and look up. If he had, I would have

smiled, blown a kiss maybe, but he didn't. I watched him a few seconds longer, then shook my hair and went to take a shower.

I dressed with extra care in an embroidered dress he'd recently admired and, lowering my head to look in the dressing table mirror, added a slick of pastel lipstick. Patsy, I had noticed, always wore it, even at the beach, smoothing the stuff on with an unselfconscious index finger.

Ned caught us as we were leaving. Skimming the outdoor breakfast table he lifted a banana and tossed it from one hand to the other. "Sorry to be a third wheel," he said, grinning, in a tone too friendly to carry meaning, "but I'm afraid it's a necessity."

It was Lesley's birthday, he told us in the car. Bee Bee had opened half an eye, kicked his backside out of bed, and told him to get something organized. Then she'd gone back to sleep. He laughed. "Not that I'm complaining, you understand," he said. "I took 'em on as a package deal."

Ned loved Lesley—that was clear—and she loved him. But I thought about something then that Mason had told when we were whispering soft confidences into each other's hair. Ned had two sons of his own. In Canada. They lived with his ex-wife and her new husband, and Ned hardly ever saw them. It was a shame, I thought. Still, he had Bee Bee and Lesley now. Things had a way of working out.

"I wouldn't mind," Ned was telling Mason, "only Bee Bee didn't remember until this morning. She claims the kid does it on purpose." He winked over his seat back at me.

"Does what?" I asked, catching Mason's smile in the rearview mirror.

"Forgets to remind us."

I laughed.

Sitting across from Letty at the lace-covered table in her mother's kitchen I wondered how easy it would be to forget a child's birthday. A child to whom you had given birth. I could not imagine it. The birthdays of my own youth had been so orderly, cards displayed in neat lines of interlocking Vs on the mantelpiece. Lesley's growing up, though, was very different from what mine had been, I thought. And from Letty's too. Her brown eyes stared at me, expectant.

"When were you born?" I asked her, beginning the lesson. The answer involved a difficult construction, and she closed her eyes, mentally forming it.

Later I met Ned and Mason on the square.

"All done?"

They were laden with shopping.

Mason said, "We bought the town."

"We let 'em keep the post office," Ned said. Flecks of perspiration dampened his hairline as he piled parcels into the backseat. We laughed, looking at the heap; there was barely room for him beside them.

"Listen, I got a responsibility to the kid," Ned said. "It's up to me to provide the kind of life to which she's gonna become accustomed." Mason had told me that Lesley would inherit a steel fortune through her paternal grandfather when she turned twenty-one.

Now, opening the Buick's front door for me, he looked into my eyes and brushed my arm with a tenderness that resonated somewhere below the pit of my stomach. I was sorry about the lack of opportunity for a visit to my apartment, but there was something pleasant nonetheless about Ned's third-party presence. It seemed, in an odd way, to confirm us as a pair.

.   .   .

I have begun writing these recollections because they are so vivid, and it suddenly seems imperative, something I am unable to control. Recording them may impose some order, and perhaps, I hope, blunt them a little. I asked Catherine to buy the notebooks for me, three of them, which she did, unquestioningly, and it was during her stay and Phillip's absence that I first opened one and wrote down a little about Mexico and the Severances, with my own hand inscribing names that I have avoided summoning for many years.

In the writing and the precision it demands I am of course confronted with the parallels between the story that was then and the story that is mine now. It will seem strange, I suppose, that these had not already been obvious to me, but the surface characteristics of life can be very distracting. There I was young; now I am approaching middle age. There the sky was diamond-hard; here even on the hottest days it is tempered by haze. There I played lover, now my role is wife. There I propelled someone toward death, and now I am propelled toward my own.

So, by committing all this to paper I am willingly exposing it, to myself and possibly to others, because I do know that despite my conviction that writing is easier somehow, less inflammatory than affording the words oxygen, stories on pages, unless speedily reduced to ashes, have a far longer and more potent life than any given up to air and others' ears.

Phillip returned from his week in London more attentive and sadder than ever. Was this the proof that my hunch had been accurate, or did I simply impose a conclusion on the evidence? Was I seeing things, hearing things that were not there?

Two mornings after his return, I answered the telephone and silence responded, then, swiftly, a dial tone. I stood with the receiver to my ear listening to that dial tone for several seconds, imagining, on the other end of it, a young woman with her heart drumming in her chest. If Josee was in love with Phillip—and I was in no doubt that she was—how dismal these few months must have been for her. I knew.

I do not think these things have changed so much, despite the liberation women have won, or believe they have. They still hand over their phone numbers, don't they? And wait. They still tie their notions of the future up with men. Live half-lives often enough until a man comes along to fill in the gaps. Do men do that? I don't think so. I think men just keep moving onward, unidirectional, unless they are determinedly sidetracked. And Josee, too, is in that halfway generation, not mine—the last to accept that marriage, children could end a career—but not Chloe's either, which emphatically denies the possibility.

I guessed that Josee had a flat, a nice flat that she had bought with her own money, in a nice area not too far from her office, a flat with a spare bedroom for friends and for keeping the clothes that she wore least often in. I imagined that she had a smart, modern kitchen in which she rarely cooked. I guessed that she had expensive bottles of expensive-smelling things in her bathroom and on her bedside table and that she employed these things in preparing for my husband's visits. I decided that in the times between these visits, now, of necessity, very long times, she probably often sat on a smallish sofa and cried. Just as I had seen her cry that night in her car, as if she would never stop.

I wondered if she had confided in a well-meaning friend who talked her into going to the cinema sometimes, or to one of those wine places London is full of. I am surrounded by people who want to do that sort of thing for me.

Everybody has come, or been in touch. Anna, our neighbor from our first house, the one Phillip had before we were married, drives over often. Carly Bryant has visited too. We talked about our old days, our London days, living together those first two years after I arrived in England, talked about them with great humor and sentimentality, the lack of money, the dull men, the drab food all turning in the talk wildly entertaining. Carly's old boyfriend, Patrick, with whom I have kept up intermittently over the years, telephones often now, and when Tom comes to discuss business with Phillip, usually over lunch at the hotel in Dunstan, Alice arrives with him as often as not and stays here with me while they are gone.

And there are the stalwarts as well, of course, Helen, Chloe, more and more often Ed, Catherine and Dan and their children, Jack and Ben and Ness, my godchild, and Sonia and even her son Ollie, now an angry seventeen, here perhaps only in hopes of seeing Chloe, on whom he has had a lifelong crush, poor child, but here nevertheless.

All of them come, all of them full of love. The house is plump with it, and with the things love brings—kindness, patience, understanding. But what if they knew, these dear hearts? What if I told all, shone a spotlight on myself? And

on Phillip? Would the fat, soft orb of goodwill disintegrate?
I don't know. But I keep writing, understanding the risks.

· · ·

They were not the kind of crowd who needed encouragement
to turn a day, or any ordinary night, into an occasion. The
week before there had been a funeral for a lizard. Howie had
found the thing, claimed it was a scorpion, and chased the girls
with it for a bit, before Jessica, suddenly feeling sorry for the
creature, had realized it was dead and begun to cry. Skipper,
comforting, had donated a small velvet box as a casket, and
then we'd all joined a procession to the garden gate for the
burial. Ned sang "When the Saints Go Marching In" and
Patsy draped her head solemnly with a black silk half-slip.

Nighttime entertainment tended to take a more liquor-
fueled edge. Once Patsy and Bee Bee had clambered onto
a glass-topped table and performed a double-act striptease.
Today a birthday party, which Ned had christened The
Hoopla, was to be held on the beach. Sally, who could set the
house humming with the merest inflection of her perfectly
tapered eyebrows, had already sent the garden men down
there with blankets and umbrellas, and Christina and the
maids were working on a cake.

"I want everybody dressed up. And we're having games,"
Ned announced.

"Okay." Skipper was an easy sell.

Carl, her ally in everything, grinned amiably. "Sure,
great." They were eating muffins on the patio.

"What shall *we* do?" Jenny asked.

"Bring elephants," Ned replied.

The twins stared, then laughed, used to Ned now.

"All right. Forget the elephants," he said. "There's not enough room in the car. Anyway, I have a better idea. But this is a real job. A serious job." The twins nodded. "You up for it?" They nodded again. "Good, 'cause somebody has got to keep Lesley out of the way for an hour, and I think you're just the twosome to do it."

They raced off to stand guard outside Lesley's bedroom in case, with some sudden alteration to the adolescent schedule she had adopted from Paige, she woke up before lunch.

It was a wonderful day. Not too hot and with just enough breeze. I remember thinking, seating myself near Mason on a bamboo beach mat, that this was happiness. That I knew it, right then. That I wouldn't need to look back from some distant future to realize it. I nestled on my elbows and filled up with sunshine as Skipper, a lipstick-cheeked rag doll in a pink dress of Jenny's, announced, "Here beginneth the official birthday celebration hoopla of Miss Lesley Patricia Mulholland Newson." Ned and Lesley grinned at each other at the addition of his last name to hers. And then Skipper led the applause. As she clapped her hands above her head, the hem of her dress skimmed her upper thighs and fell open from a single fastening at the back of her neck, revealing the even trail of her spine and the rear triangle of her bikini.

"I saw this show, I think, Off Broadway," Mason said. Patsy, pulling her T-shirt over her head, laughed with her face obscured.

"Bring on the dancing girls," Bee Bee yelled, hands cupped to her mouth. Tallulah, startled, began to yip madly.

"It's great, isn't it, Dad?" Howie beamed as Ned, hoisting a cardboard megaphone, bellowed, calling for order.

Hudson, from his pastel bouncer under an umbrella, squealed, and Richard, smiling, put a soft arm around one son and lent an index finger to the other. "It's great," he agreed.

"A Feat Of Great Daring Performed By A Person Standing On One Leg," Skipper declared, "to be performed by . . ." Mason mimicked a drumroll as she pulled a paper slip from one of Bee Bee's floppy hats. "Richard," she read.

There were cheers as Richard, loosing himself from his offspring, stood and scratched his head. "Would a feat of great daring standing on two hands do?" he asked.

Ned put it to a vote and pronounced that it would.

Richard flipped his weight forward and walked easily on his hands some ten feet along the beach.

"I married him for that," Patsy said dryly.

Richard righted himself with a little jump, curving neatly in reverse. There were more cheers.

"That," Patsy went on, "and the fact he could ski faster than me." Mason smiled at her. "Whaddya know at twenty?" she said with a laugh.

Soon I was called upon as "A Person Singing A Short Song In Dramatic Fashion." I sang "Boogie Woogie Bugle Boy." It was a party trick from my teen years. I enlisted the twins to shimmy beside me and toot imaginary bugles.

"Bravo," Mason shouted when the three of us took our bows. "Moo-ore." But by then it was lunchtime.

Christina had packed a picnic to match the festivities. In a box, an enormous white frosted cake was already festooned with candles. As Lesley shut her eyes to blow them out, Patsy said softly, "Wish for happiness, honey. Wish for it whenever you can."

Patsy's tone was too poignant for the occasion, but the tiny puncture was overwhelmed by a more marked intrusion—the sound of an unfamiliar engine on the stony roadway at the top of the beach.

The car belonged to a pair of sandy-haired Americans named Beau and Myra. We struck up conversation with them after their swim. It was natural enough that we would; the beach was small, and we had claimed the center of it. They were taking a two-month driving tour around Mexico. It was the sort of thing they did quite often now that their kids were grown. Ned offered them a drink.

"Oh no," Myra protested. "We don't want to intrude." But everyone denied the possibility, and Mason, gentlemanly, offered her one of the director's chairs that Sally had ordered brought down to the beach. She and Bee Bee had been sitting on them, cross-legged and behatted like two old-fashioned movie stars over lunch.

Myra said she'd have a lemonade.

"You sure about that, Myra?" Ned said, with a wink. He had the measure of her. "This is a party."

"I'm not much of a drinker," Myra said, smiling, taking her seat.

"Nor was Frankie," Ned answered, "when we first got her, but she's doing just fine now."

Myra laughed and agreed to a daiquiri, which was what, Ned assured her, all the other ladies were drinking. We were. Flasks had been packed. Three flavors. Myra asked for lime.

"Would you look at that house!" Beau said, accepting a beer, scanning the cliff and whistling softly.

"I'll be," Myra exclaimed, following his eyeline. She drew the air in audibly between her frosted lips when Mason said that it was ours, for the time being anyway.

The children, impatient with the interruption and the adult talk, began clamoring for more entertainment. So Ned and Lesley did a Laurel and Hardy routine, clearly well rehearsed in the past, and Bee Bee and Mason danced a tango, with Howie's snorkel standing for the rose and Ned humming the musical accompaniment. Beau and Myra lent enthusiastic hurrahs. Sitting again, amid the applause, Bee Bee, who was a little breathless, said, "He sure is a mover, that husband of yours."

"Yes," Sally replied disinterestedly, "he sure is." Then she announced, "Our guests will be at the house by six." It was after four.

Reminded of Arturo and Maria's visit, people looked at their watches. Beau and Myra said that they ought to be off, but the children groaned until one last event, a three-legged race, was agreed on.

Ned bent to attach his ankle to Sally's with a linen dishcloth. She smiled, compliant, and lifted her foot gracefully to ease the process. I felt a familiar hand at my waist.

"You up for this, Frankie?" Mason's breath was warm near my ear.

"Why not?"

Patsy, next to us, and alone after the pairings off, pouted, "Heey." She had evidently been heading for Mason. He turned, rotating me with him, our legs tied together at the calf, and shrugged, raising his free hand, palm up, apologetically.

"Be *my* partner, Mommy." Howie began inexpertly attaching his leg to his mother's.

Beau and Myra joined the press at the starting line. Carl had paired off with Bee Bee. Paige and Lesley had a twin each, and Richard was hopping and laughing with his arm around Skipper.

Ned shouted, "On your marks."

Everyone started without waiting for "go." There was a blur of movement and noise until the mass of us reached the driftwood marker ten yards or so along the sand.

"The winners," Ned declared, raising his and Sally's arms and spinning her around. "The champs."

There were yells of dissent. We were all dropping, breathing hard and laughing, onto the sand. Bee Bee and Carl landed with a thump next to Mason and me.

"I think I'll stick to bobbing for olives in the future," Bee Bee said. "Give this amateur stuff a miss."

Carl laughed.

"Oww." Howie had fallen backward while Patsy remained standing, wrenching his foot into the air, though without enough force to do any damage.

Patsy ignored him. She was staring, her features fractionally compressed, at Richard and Skipper, who, alone, had not made it to the finish line. They were lying where they had first fallen, near the start, stretched on the sand, legs intertwined. Richard's chest was heaving. His laughter mingled with Skipper's. One of her braids snaked softly across the base of his throat. She pulled herself up and a little over him, dislodging it. His arm was still folded comfortably around her, the hand at her bare waist obscured by the flap of the pink dress.

Carl, detaching himself from Bee Bee, laughed too. "Want a hand, baby?" he called and, approaching Skipper and Richard with a languid gait, leaned to untie the dishcloth at Skipper's ankle. Then he helped her to her feet, hands tucked gently under her armpits.

"We couldn't get up," she said, turning to him, still smiling. He kissed her forehead and grinned, then extended a hand to Richard, who took it and pulled himself up.

"Hell," Richard said, wiping the faint trace of a laughter tear from his face, "I don't remember the last time I laughed so hard."

Patsy, snapped from her reverie by Howie's clumsy tugs at her ankle, spoke sharply, "Be careful, Howie."

Howie, worn out, began to whimper.

"Oh, for heaven's sake." Patsy deftly unhitched herself from her son, and then, sending up little sprays of sand, turned and flounced back up the beach, pausing to pick up her colored straw basket, but ignoring Hudson, curled in sleep against a striped cushion. She tossed the basket into the jeep and clambered in after it. Then she waited, sullen-faced, in the passenger seat, with her feet on the dash and her arms folded.

Sally turned to Beau and Myra to say goodbye with such an amazingly gracious tilt of her head that I thought for a moment that she was going to invite them to the house, as she had invited me, but she didn't.

"Very nice to have met you," she said, smiling.

Hudson, waking tetchy, began to cry, and the rest of us, party over, began to gather up the gear until Sally said, "Leave that. I'll have them come down for it later."

Pausing, as she spoke, from collecting a ball and bat set of Howie's, something came to me with absolute clarity. Beau and Myra would remember Sally Severance and her remarkable beauty and her charming husband and her crazy friends and the children, and the incredible, enormous house for a long time and probably speak of it all often. Whereas Sally, and Mason, and the others would probably never mention, or even think of, Beau and Myra again. It was a realization that made me feel hollow.

We were only two people extra that evening, but the slight formality of the occasion made it feel like more. The maids, under Christina's icy-eyed supervision, were dipping in and out of the little knots we had formed, offering hors d'oeuvres.

Maria twitched with pleasure. "Beautiful," she said to me, rotating her hand to take in the room and slipping the last of a shrimp-filled pastry case into her mouth.

I followed her gaze. I hadn't been in this room much. None of us had. It was the kind of room a different crowd, in a different climate, might have retired to after dinner for coffee. As it was we usually ended up out by the pool.

Maria was admiring a vast oriental bowl on a mahogany sideboard. She ran a tentative finger gently over its gold rim. A small, neat handbag dangled from her elbow.

"I don't think you've met my children, Señora," said Sally, joining us. Jenny and Jessica were standing with her, in matching, pastel party dresses, each of them holding a hand. The image was, to me, incongruous: mother and daughters. Sally let go of the girls and nudged them forward, palms between their shoulder blades. "These are my two youngest."

"Jessica and Jenny Severance," I said. "Nueve años. They're nine."

Maria beamed.

"Say buenas tardes to Señora Rodriguez," I coaxed.

"Buenas tardes, Señora Rodriguez," they chirruped, pleased with themselves.

"Ayee. Que bonitas." Maria, rapt, reached out and gave Jessica's blonde hair an admiring stroke. "Que bonitas niñas las dos. Veery beautiful," she said to Sally. "Beautiful children." Beautiful was her best word.

"Delphina," Howie announced, interrupting determinedly. He was wearing miniature grown-up clothes, a crisp white shirt and formal navy trousers. "Delphina," he said again loudly at Maria's side. She looked down at him, confused. I told her about the dolphins we'd seen from the boat. Howie had been repeating the word ever since.

"Ahh, sí, delphina," Maria said, beaming.

Howie beamed back.

I guided Maria around the room, while Mason did the same, taking an opposite figure-eight path, with Arturo. Even Paige and Lesley, I noticed, could manage a reasonably sophisticated level of light cocktail party chat.

"You remember Mrs. Luke," I said. "Patsy. And her husband Richard."

Patsy, despite her earlier mood and wordless disappearance to her room when we'd returned from the beach, fell into neat social step beside her husband. "Very nice to see you again, Señora Rodriguez," she said, and Richard, leaning forward slightly, took Maria's hand and echoed Patsy's greeting.

"Very nice," Maria repeated, sending Arturo a swift, nervous glance over her shoulder. She was uncomfortable on such foreign ground, even with me by her side. Arturo was deep in amiable conversation with Sally. I watched as he said something to her and she laughed, tipping her head back but holding the drink in her hand perfectly still. I felt a prick of shock to see how soft her beauty turned under his attention.

One of the maids, just then, brought Hudson in, freshly bathed and doughy in fluffy baby pajamas, to be kissed goodnight. Maria, delighted by the child, put her glass down so as better to clutch at his chubby face.

"A fine boy," said Arturo. Hudson had the whole room's attention.

"Thank you," Richard said. "We think so."

Patsy smiled, gracious in her acceptance of the compliment.

"Delphina," Howie repeated, almost shouting now, to Arturo.

Arturo, understanding, grinned, rubbed Howie's head, and said, "*Two* fine boys."

Shortly afterward, they made an elegant exit, Maria holding my hands in hers for a moment before they left by the front door, standing open for once, and got into the large dark car that was waiting for them there.

"Nice guy," said Ned, coming back inside, refilling his glass, and freshening Bee Bee's.

"He *is* nice," said Richard, dropping into a wicker chair and extending his legs. "In fact, I like them both."

"But then," said Patsy with a small sigh, "Richard is not exactly fussy about who he takes a shine to." She lifted the olive from her martini, put it into her mouth, and sucked at it theatrically for a moment before removing the pit and dropping it into an ashtray. "He's like a little puppy dog," she said. "He'll just wag his tail and rub up against anybody."

· · ·

In October, somewhere past the midpoint of this extraordinary journey that I am now near to completing, it was our anniversary. Phillip took me to the seaside, not half a day's travel from home, though we stretched it to more than that, stopping for coffee on the way.

It was one of those hot days that October in England's south can sometimes deliver—rather cruelly, I think, since November inevitably introduces winter with a snap—and the sun through the windscreen was very warm. Phillip had worn a tweedy jacket and we pulled over so that he could get out and take it off. Standing in the sunshine at the roadside, the middle part of him, blue striped shirt and tan gabardine trousers, was framed in the doorway.

I was struck by the fact that I loved him very much at that moment, loved the way that he gave the jacket a little shake before laying it in the backseat, loved the way that he ran his hand absently over his forehead, tidying his hair against the slight breeze. Strange how it ambushes you like that, love. That's why it is so difficult to defend yourself from it, I suppose. I wanted to reach out just then and touch that blue shirt and feel the soft familiarity of the skin beneath.

He leaned into the car to talk to me, squinting a little. "Are you all right?" he asked. "Comfortable?"

I was.

I knew that Josee and Phillip spoke on the telephone, not so often, but sometimes, at night, the door to Phillip's study pulled closed. I had become sensitive to the click ever since one morning not long after the hanging-up incident, when waking early, I had walked into that room in our house that is most permeated with him, his maleness, his past, his secrets, and, in the gray light, lifted the telephone receiver and pressed redial. Josee's voice had answered, not with the throaty tones of someone roused from sleep, but the brighter, slightly false notes of an answering machine.

I had replaced the receiver instantly and stood fearful for a moment lest she returned the call, but she had not. After that I had wondered, did they write too? Were there love letters tucked in the packages of correspondence bundled up by his office and couriered to him? Did Carla, who had worked for him for six years now, recognize the hand? But I had begun to care not so much less as differently about these things. I was no longer obsessed with the business of my husband's affair in that way that detaches one from reason, but interested in it instead, almost as one might be in a new and absorbing hobby. I felt as though I were discovering something, something important.

It was the beginning of a new phase, the last phase, of our marriage.

We were to spend our anniversary at a hotel that we had visited many times before, often, when Chloe was younger, making the trip just for a day, she and a friend in the backseat, swimsuits under their clothes. The hotel has a pool as well as beach access, and Phillip and I used to have lunch on the terrace so that the children could play in the water, clambering needlessly in and out the way that children do, while we ate. Today, I noticed as we pulled up, the pool was closed, sealed beneath a thick greenish rubber cover. I was pleased. Poolside images are vivid enough for me now.

I wanted, before we went in, to walk a little on the shore.

It took me many years to love the English ocean, and then, when I realized that I did, I could not pinpoint when the affection had begun. But anyway, somewhere along the way, I stopped yearning for the gemstone sparkle, or the breathless calm, or the warm embrace of other seas and fell for this one, with its pebble fringes and grubby little wavelets, only ever whipped to any sort of passion by bad weather. I came to like the salty damp and the slap of wind that so often accompanies beach visits in this country even in summertime and may have even absorbed some of that superiority with which the English turn misery into a challenge, with which they make everything that has an element of difficulty in it somehow better. What use to us are those easy beaches? Ours take work.

At the water's edge, on a beach that was empty but for a lone woman tossing sticks for a happy Labrador, I said, "Bring me here."

I meant my ashes. Phillip put his arms around me and told me that he would.

We ate inside that day, by the window, looking out with that sort of middle-distance gaze that the sea elicits, and after we had ordered, Phillip gave me my present. It was an eternity ring, fashioned to match my engagement and wedding rings, emeralds and diamonds set flush to white gold. I gazed at it, snug in its leather box, for a long moment before he took it back from me and slid it onto the appropriate finger, above the ring his mother had supplied for our brief engagement. He held on to my hand then, and we looked at each other, love and sadness tangible, compressing my chest.

· · ·

"Why is Patsy laughing so loud?" Jenny asked, toying with her spaghetti next to me at dinner.

Patsy's voice had grown, in the two hours since Arturo and Maria had left, steadily brassier. Jenny, giving her plate a bit of a shove away, dropped her fork. Everyone else had finished and Christina had begun to clear the table. Patsy, dipping her delivery to a sugary coo, said, "I'm thinking of becoming a vegetarian and wearing flowers in my hair." She leaned toward Paige and went on in a strident, conspiratorial whisper, "That's the kind of thing men like."

Paige colored and dipped her head.

Patsy turned a defiant shoulder to her husband and snared his eye.

"Isn't it, Richard?" she asked brightly.

Richard stared.

Mason, in the chair next to Patsy, lay a light, restraining hand on her arm.

"Can we have some ice cream?" Jessica asked.

"Can we?" Jenny echoed.

Patsy, ignoring these interruptions, rotated her body pointedly toward Mason and arched her eyebrows. "You're quite partial to a hippyish young thing too, aren't you, Mason?"

Bee Bee, who was tight, said, "Here we go." She was watching Patsy steadily over the rim of her wineglass.

"I scream, you scream, we all scream for ice cream," Ned sang, winking at Howie.

Howie, though, was intent on his father, whose jaw and lip line had taken on an unfamiliar, hard set.

"Will you please just shut up," Richard said in a low, commanding voice.

129

Patsy sprang, sharp and alive, overturning her chair. "Will *I* shut up? That's rich, coming from the giggle king." She laid her hands flat on the table and put her weight on them. "Oooh, baby, let's smoke a little weed," she sang, saccharine.

"*That's enough!*" Richard, standing, upset his glass.

Jessica began to cry.

"Why is everyone yelling?" Jenny said, distressed.

"Come on." I pushed my chair back. "Howie, you too."

Howie did not respond. His little eyes darted, first to one parent, then to the other. I decided that he must have witnessed scenes like this before.

"Go with Frankie, Howie," Mason said.

The child glanced at his father a last time, for direction. None came. Richard, his head down, looked exhausted. I gestured again to Howie and he slipped obediently from his chair. I put one hand on his shoulder and led him, with the twins, out of the room.

The children's rooms were on different corridors. I sent the twins on alone and told them to clean their teeth. Then I took Howie's meek hand. "My room is right above you," I said when we got there. "Do you hear me . . . stomping around?"

He looked at me, mute.

"Where are your pajamas, pet?" I asked, waving off the jokiness and recalling, for a moment, my father, in rare, sweeter circumstances, saying the same thing to me.

Howie tugged a pair of pajamas from under the pillow of one of the room's single beds. They were festooned with cartoon cowboys, Stetsons and lassos flying. I knelt to help him with the buttons of his stiff party shirt. Stripped of it he looked frail. I hugged him quickly, the floor tiles hurting my knees. He stretched his arms obediently, one after the other, for the pajama top, and when I had fastened it, he stood with them flat at his sides. I got up and handed him the bottoms. He clutched them to his chest, shy.

"I'll go and check on those naughty girls and come back in a minute," I suggested, and he nodded, bowing his head then to slip a narrow black belt from his trouser loops.

The girls were easily settled with hugs and reassurance. Tallulah had been slipped, against Christina's rules, into Jenny's bed; I pretended not to notice. They wanted a story, but I said it was late already and it had been an exciting day, reminding them of the fun we'd had earlier at the beach. "What was the best bit?" I asked them from the door, my hand on the light switch.

"Boogie Woogie Bugle Boy," they shouted, shimmying their shoulders.

Under the bedclothes Tallulah wiggled and yipped.

By the time I had checked again on Howie, there was quiet in the dining room. Coffee had been served by the pool. I helped myself to a cup form the tray. For a moment nobody spoke. Then Patsy said quietly, "Oh look, the other little hippie."

I felt myself stiffen, the way an animal does sensing danger.

Richard stood, took his wife firmly by the elbow and tugged her from her chair. She tottered as he forced her inside. Her expression as she passed me was almost gleeful.

I had seen Patsy and Richard argue before, often. But I had never had the sense of either of them being genuinely engaged. It was like a habit with them and almost a performance from her. One night, one of the late nights when the drinking had gone on and on and people had swum naked and lain afterward in the dark singing along to some popular song, a row had erupted from nowhere about the war in Asia. Patsy, jumping up, had shrieked vehemently at Richard that he was a pompous jerk, but even then I'd felt that she was just bouncing off him somehow. No one else seemed to pay much attention to her outbursts either; they faded too fast.

"Big day," Ned said now, as if we were all children, tired from an outing. But his voice was covered by Richard's, plainly audible through an open bedroom window.

"What is it with you?" he yelled.

"With *me*? You're the one who's been all over that brainless little tramp for three days. Humiliating me."

"Humiliating you?"

"What else would you call it? Your tongue's out of your mouth every time that little nympho waggles her tits."

There was a beat of dangerous silence. Then Carl, a protective arm around Skipper's shoulders, said, "I think we'll turn in."

"Good night," people said.

"Good night."

Richard's voice, worn, drifted again above us.

"I wish you wouldn't talk that way, Patsy. It's disgusting." And then with an audible sigh, "Anyway, Skipper's a perfectly nice girl."

It was a mistake.

"*Skipper.*" Patsy's voice was thick with mockery. "Let's see, what would you call her in the sack? Skip? Skippy?"

"For Christ's sake."

At the pool Ned tried again to start a conversation. No one else had the heart.

"Come on, Bee," he said, giving up. "What about hitting the hay?"

Bee Bee was reluctant.

"Come on," Ned repeated. He took the empty brandy glass from her hand and put it on the table. She looked at him for a second, then got up meekly, and they went into the house.

"I think that's enough for me too." Sally stood, still holding her coffee cup. When she put it down, she shifted the tray slightly to a more solid position on the table. "Good night," she said, half turning, smiling at me and then at her husband before walking steadily away.

Alone in the night, Mason and I heard Richard say, "Maybe I just like getting a little attention from a woman for a change. A little *warmth*."

"Oh, don't be pathetic," Patsy spat.

There was a rumble. A chair toppling? Something knocked from the dressing table? Richard's voice came deep and even over it.

"Don't you think I see the way you look at other men? Mason, for instance?"

There was silence. Then a slamming sound—the windows and shutters closing.

Mason did not speak. Neither did I. We were sitting a little distanced from each other, too far to touch. I was aware of the sound of my own breathing and the jangle Richard's words had set off inside me. We remained like that, motionless, for some time. One by one the lights in the house dimmed, and the going-to-bed noises died. After a while Mason stood and took my hand. Wordlessly, he led me around the pool and through the gate at the far end of it. There was a soft click as the latch closed. In the dark he kissed me, the weight of his upper body pressing me to the wall behind. He raised my skirt with quick, insistent hands.

S I X

I SLEPT LATE AND ate breakfast alone except for the younger children playing nearby. I had almost finished when Howie, sitting on the side of the pool with his feet dangling, suddenly looked up warily. Patsy was at the glass doors, holding a coffee cup. She came out and, without encouragement, took the seat opposite me.

"I think I may owe you an apology, Frankie," she said, cradling the coffee in both hands and looking at me directly. She was paler than usual, and the skin under her eyes was thinned by mauve shadows.

I looked at her, not knowing what to say.

Seeming to take my silence for a rebuke, she dropped her head.

"Things have just been rather . . . difficult," she said, "for some time now. For Richard and me."

"I'm sorry." I put my coffee down. There was real sadness in her voice.

"Well, you know . . . marriage." She raised her shoulders and flashed a wan smile. "Actually, I guess you wouldn't, would you?"

"I guess not," I replied, smiling too, though a bit of me resented the remark.

She rested her elbows on the table. Inhaling, she rolled her head sadly from side to side.

"Hudson," she said, "was a mistake."

It was a level of confidence that I wasn't prepared for. Mild shock must have registered on my face, but, if so, she went on anyway, apparently not noticing.

"If there was only Howie, I might have just, well"—she flipped her hand and sighed—"made a decision. I don't know. It's all complicated enough already, without a baby." There was a pause. Then she said, "There are other people involved." She looked up at me, holding my gaze for a long moment, as if I might say something, or know something, of great importance. Then she shook her head, dispelling the idea. "Anyway," she said, with a deliberate lift of tone, "the point is, with all this going on, I say things sometimes, especially on top of a few martinis, that I don't mean. So I'm sorry if—"

"Let's just forget it," I interrupted.

She smiled, and nodded, and got up, and went over to the pool. Howie, tentative, watched as she walked absently toward him.

"Do you want to see me swim, Mom?" he asked in a small voice as she neared.

"Sure," she replied, sitting and letting her feet drop over the mosaic tiles into the tealy blue of the water.

Patsy had a full absolution. Sally, arriving at the pool later that morning in a strapless sunbathing outfit, simply laid her book on the table and said, "Good morning."

"They got off all right, then?" Bee Bee asked, midway through her first cigarette. The hollows under her eyes were more pronounced than Patsy's.

"Oh, yes. I assume so. Mason's briefcase was gone when I woke up." She laughed and looked toward Patsy, who spoke matter-of-factly.

"Uh-huh. I heard them leave."

I was listening with mounting apprehension. Who had left? Sally had referred to Mason's briefcase, but Mason could not have left. Could not possibly have left. Not without talking to me. The sun had begun to turn white, and in the fresh heat a prickly sensation crept across my skin. I could not bear it. I sat up. "Leave?" I asked suddenly, not caring if my voice betrayed me.

"Richard and Mason have gone to L.A. for the day," Sally explained simply. "You know men. If they're away from the cut and thrust of the workplace for too long they lose their ability to function. Mason is like some sort of small animal detached from its natural habitat if he goes more than two weeks without contact with a lawyer or a secretary."

"Worry if he starts dictating when you sit in his lap," Bee Bee said.

They all roared. I shut myself behind the protective screen of my eyelids as Sally settled herself elegantly in the sun and heard them, across the sudden brutal gulf that had arisen between their world—worse, Mason's world—and mine, drifting into pleasant, detached conversation.

It was something I had marveled at in the past, and would

again, the ability of that set to refix the veneer, tug the covers over anything troubling, with their talk. They had a kind of language that united them, a glib clever kind of language that I was impressed by and tried not to copy too obviously. Their talk revealed things about them too, about their lives that I enjoyed my glimpses of. They spoke in familiar terms of politicians and millionaires and artists who I had not yet heard of, but would later. They knew a couple who had had a child kidnapped for ransom, they employed au pairs from Sweden and cooks from Tennessee, and they had close friends who lived in Paris.

That day they talked about the house. There were several things, it seemed, in addition to the yellow sun umbrellas, of which Sally did not approve. She thought the marble in the bathrooms too creamy, she was unhappy with the linen and she regretted not having had her own bedding and towels sent ahead, and she disliked red geraniums.

"Although," she said, "in this kind of setting, in these sorts of hot countries, red is perhaps right."

I was astonished. I had no idea that such a thing could be wrong. I heard laughter as they blamed what they apparently considered lapses, not just in taste, but something deeper, more fundamental, on the owner's wife. I had seen a photograph of her once. It had been pointed out to me, in fuzzy black and white, in one of Richard's newspapers. The husband was a businessman, a tycoon, whose name I knew. I had thought the wife looked rather prim, in pearls and a suit with a short jacket, but nice enough, kind enough. Perhaps I didn't understand anything.

"Daddy used to tell us that money didn't buy breeding," Patsy said.

"Unfortunately, the reverse is also true," Sally replied. And then there was a change in her tone as she said, "Oh. Hello."

I opened my eyes.

Carl and Skipper were standing at the glass doors. Carl was holding two carryalls.

"Hello," Carl replied to Sally quietly.

Skipper just nodded.

Patsy looked at them, then away.

"We thought we might move on today," Carl said. "We'd planned to tour around a bit, you know. Thought we might head off . . . on the next leg."

Skipper was holding a fat guidebook. She waved it pathetically. "It was very good of you to have us," she said to Sally.

"Not at all." Sally stood. "We'll miss you. And I know Mason will be sorry not to have been able to say goodbye."

"We only ever meant to impose on you for a few days," Carl said. "Anyway, I hope we might see you all in California some time." He shifted his gaze to Bee Bee.

"Oh," she said. "Sure."

We all followed them out to their car, Patsy lingering at the back of the group, till she could no longer avoid saying goodbye. She took Carl's hand and looked at him, ducking Skipper's eyes.

"Look . . ." she said "I—"

Carl, cutting her off, hugged her noncommittally and patted her back. She didn't go on.

"Bye," Skipper said, opening the door of the little red car and turning to get in. "Thanks for everything."

We all waved until the crunch of wheels on the gravel had faded and Sally said pleasantly, "Let's have tuna fish salad for lunch."

Things were not as bad as I had thought. When I went to my room before the tuna fish salad, which I didn't think I could face anyway, there was a note. It had been slipped, apparently, through the gap between the door and the floor and had caught there, lodged in the knotted fringe of an Oriental rug. I hadn't noticed it.

Darling, the note said. *One lonely day. Sorry.* A penned heart, the lines not quite meeting in the sweet upper V, signed it. I refolded the stiff buff paper and, elated, slid it into the bottom drawer of the tall bureau near my bed. It nestled there, happily, between a white shirt and a blue swimsuit, ready for later rereadings.

Mason and Richard were to be back in the early evening. They had chartered a small plane for the day, and it would return them to the dusty airstrip north of the town. They'd taken the jeep there at dawn for the trip out and left it parked. I knew the airstrip and imagined the jeep waiting, forlorn as I was without them. Without him.

The afternoon threatened to drag. Patsy had gone to her room to sleep, and Paige and Lesley had taken advantage of a momentary lack of pestering from the twins to escape to the beach on their own. I was glad when Ned suggested a run into town. He and Bee Bee and I decided to take the younger children but Sally cried off with one of those polite little half smiles that didn't quite reach her eyes. She had a headache.

On the way Jessica sat on my lap.

"That cactus looks like a man," she said, pointing.

Ned pulled the car over and got out to dedicate his hat to the illusion.

"Looks better on him," Bee Bee said when he got back in the car.

As we pulled out again Howie said, "If he is a man, then he has to have a name. A man's name," he emphasized. He had never quite gotten over Tallulah's being a girl.

"His name is Roy," Ned said, as if this were a matter of common knowledge, "Cactus Roy."

In the town that day there were mariachis pah-pah-pahing at the sky in honor, it seemed, of the local beauty contest.

"Miss Mexico," Jenny hollered, thrilled.

Both twins were lifted to look. There were crowds in the square. At the far end of it, half a dozen young women tottered on a red-bannered podium wearing high-heeled shoes and old-fashioned bathing suits.

"Who ya for?" Ned nudged me.

"Number three," I said. I knew her slightly.

"Now me, I like number six." He grinned. "Not that I'm looking," he added for Bee Bee's benefit.

"Look all you want, fella. I don't see any of them looking at you," she said.

There was a hush, and then a linen-suited judge, some local dignitary I remembered meeting at the Rodriguez's house, took the podium ponderously and tapped the microphone. It squealed. The musicians stopped playing. A blue Ford that had been circling the square pulled sharply to the curb, and behind us a gang of boys who had climbed onto the bench outside the barber's shop jostled each other, causing one of them to fall. Number six was announced.

Ned cheered. "I could always pick 'em," he said with a wink for his wife.

There was a carnival atmosphere. We ate ice cream and cotton candy from the carts in the streets. Ned danced with Jenny and then Jessica balanced on his feet. Howie, his face tight with concentration, almost waltzed with me. He'd had lessons.

On the way home the children, still excited, yelled "Roooy" with enormous gusto from a hundred yards distant.

"How's the head?" Ned asked.

Sally was rubbing hand cream into her palms. It smelled of almonds. "Worse," she said. She frowned and carefully twisted the cap back onto the hand cream jar. "It's been a long afternoon."

"Da-da-da-da-da dah," Jenny sang. Ned had shown her how to conga.

"Dah dah," Howie shouted, wiggling and grabbing at her.

Sally, one hand to her forehead, called, "Christina."

Christina appeared instantly, as if she had been waiting, hidden somewhere, for just such a summons. "Yes, madam."

"This might be a good time."

"Yes, madam," Christina said, and then commanded, "*Children.*"

Christina proceeded to herd the children, like so many stunned geese, out of the room amid a general subduing of the atmosphere. Something in Sally's tone had suggested more than the words. She sighed when the children had gone and said, "I had to send one of the garden boys into town with that dog. It was sick again, and yowling." She gave her ring finger a last gentle stroke. "I couldn't believe something so small could make so much noise."

Patsy came in, doe-eyed from her afternoon's sleep.

"What noise?"

"That dog yelping. Christina put it in the basement, but it was no good." Sally touched her forehead lightly and stretched her long legs, emphasizing the headache.

"Tallulah's sick?" Bee Bee asked. She looked at me. "Is there a vet or something in the town, Frankie?"

I didn't answer because Sally said, "I told him to have it put down."

There was a silence, which was pierced by the wail of a child. Christina's timing must have matched her mistress's.

"It was a stray," Sally went on calmly. "There wasn't much point in doing anything else."

During the twenty minutes of shouting that followed, Bee Bee called Sally a coldhearted bitch. This got very little in the way of a rise from her. She was apparently unconcerned both with the pathetic demise of the little dog, and with Bee Bee's fury. But at the insult I noticed that Patsy, watching the row from the corner, smiled. Inside I felt oddly satisfied too. I was sad about Tallulah, and I knew that the children must be upset, but Sally's chill distraction had given me reason to genuinely dislike her. I was certain that Mason would feel exactly the same way.

Sally put a fleeting hand on her husband's chest, at lapel level, when she leaned forward to kiss him hello. Their cheeks brushed.

"Well," she asked, "got your fix?"

Mason set his things down by the glass doors. He was foreign to me, and more attractive than ever, in a white shirt, silk tie, and dark trousers. A maid, at a nod from Christina, lifted his briefcase and draped his jacket carefully over her arm.

"I always used to go to meet him," Sally said, sitting, draping an elbow over one of the outdoor chairs. "But then I realized it was easier to wait at home for the call saying that he wasn't coming."

"Aah," Mason said, passing her on his way to fix himself a drink. "No such call today though." He winked at me then. I read oceans of meaning into that.

Switching his glass from hand to hand to undo his cuffs, he leaned, proprietorial, against one of the arbor corner posts and asked, "So what's been going on?" His smile implied that nothing serious could have occurred in his absence.

"The vegetarians skipped off, hand-in-hand, to pastures new, and your wife slaughtered a puppy," Bee Bee said.

Mason's eyes swept the faces of the adults scattered around the pool and lingered on Sally's.

"That little dog got sick," she said calmly. "I had to have it put down. Bee Bee thinks I slit its throat and drank the blood."

The twins, who were hovering near their father, squealed at this and buried their heads in his waist. Paige and Lesley glared. Bee Bee took a hard slug of her drink and tightened her lips. Mason put his glass down and gathered his youngest daughters in by the shoulders.

"Oh for heaven's sake," Sally said. "Let's eat."

Ned sent Bee Bee a beseeching, pacifying look, which she ignored. She spoke steadily into the pall that had fallen over the evening. "You know, Sally," she said, "sometimes I think there's marble where your heart ought to be."

Sally didn't reply.

"Ned?"

Ned raised his eyebrows.

"We're going out," his wife said.

"Dinner's ready," Sally announced smoothly.

"Screw dinner." Bee Bee tucked a hand into Ned's elbow. Lesley got up and took the other one. Ned glanced back, once, over his shoulder as the three of them, united, left.

A moment later Sally stood.

"I'll just let Christina know we're only eight," she said to nobody in particular.

It was a subdued sort of an evening, but it stretched on a while after we ate. The Newsons had not come back. Sally and Patsy and Richard and Mason and I sat outside drinking brandies in the quiet. Everybody was tired. Talk ran out. Eventually Sally said, "Mason?" and got up.

Mason got up too.

"Good night," he said to Patsy and me.

I said good night and smiled. To hide my disappointment. Watching, I saw Mason open the door to the hallway and put his hand on the small of his wife's back as she passed through it.

In bed I switched on a lamp. I felt worn out, but not yet able to sleep. I opened a paperback I'd borrowed from the shelves in the television room. There were lots of them there, scattered amidst the driftwood and gathered shells of other vacations. But I knew, even as I nestled my thumb between the arc of its sepia-edged pages, that I would not settle to the story, a lonely tale of a Chinese girl unsuitably in love. I sighed and gazed up at the dark of the windows, projecting an image there of a different sort of homecoming for Mason.

I fell asleep with the light on, and the book open, and woke bleary, wondering where I was. I turned the corner of my page down and switched off the lamp. When I rolled over, I heard voices, low and murmuring. I couldn't distinguish whose they were. I assumed Bee Bee and Ned's, come back from town. Then I heard a softly throaty laugh. Not Bee Bee's. Patsy's. I got up and crossed the floor to the window. Outside even the underwater pool lights had been switched off. It must have been very late.

I could see the tiny blaze of Patsy's cigarette and made out, against the faint orange glow of a single lamp lit inside the glass doors, another silhouette. Mason's. I blinked, confused. Mason had gone to bed before me, when Sally had.

I strained but I couldn't make out anything, though I could hear that they were talking. They were very close to one another, side by side. Patsy turned and extinguished her cigarette in an ashtray that would be cleared before anyone came down in the morning. Then she faced Mason. She may have said something, her face at his shirt front. He made a sound and drew her to him, resting his chin on the top of her head.

I felt cold and I trembled. But I didn't move. I stood and watched as they walked into the house and Mason slid the glass door shut behind them and stopped to flick off the lamp.

· · ·

Many women before me have decided to ignore the signs, reduce the obvious to explainable trivialities and plough on with their marriages. In some cases this behavior can be considered almost elegant, in others delusional. I cannot claim either of these forks. I was not deluded. I had no doubts that Phillip had been, and was still, in love with Josee. However, nor was I so noble in my lack of confrontation as to remain steadfastly above it. I mentioned her name to him occasionally, unnecessarily, to watch his face.

However, I do know that, whereas I had done this in the past with a dominant mood of mischievousness, of doing something that I ought not to do, like a child scratching, I was by then more motivated by wanting to know. I was opening a door for him, offering him an unhindered route to . . . not confession, discussion. I was worn out with pretense. Secrets, while unseen, are nevertheless burdens, and I did not have the energy to carry mine, or Phillip's, anymore. I wished, sincerely wished that he would just tell me.

One day, not long after our trip to the beach, my eternity ring still new enough to feel odd on waking, I did not come downstairs all day. It was the first of a few days like that. I was exhausted with a new kind of exhaustion, one that is quite familiar to me now. Dr. Griffith was called, and came, but no immediate emergency was declared. I just needed sleep, real sleep, beyond the rest kind I had been relying on up to that point.

So I slept while, outside, Mr. Hardwick took advantage of the last of the good weather to tidy the hedges and mend the wall where it was clipped on the lane side by a tractor. Mr. Hardwick built that wall himself fourteen years ago and now he attended to the damage with skilled, old hands. His labors provided the background sounds for my drifts in and out of consciousness, the sleepy drone of the electric shears, then, later, the singsong tap of metal against stone. These are the sorts of things that mark the passage of time on the poor days, the bedridden ones, when I cannot get up and afford myself the more distinct rituals of daily punctuation.

One afternoon, dreams turning real and reality becoming distant as I dozed, I opened my eyes at some point to see Phillip at my bedside, sitting on the little nursing chair that Helen gave me years ago and that I have been meaning to have re-covered and now never will. He had a book in his lap, but he was not looking at it. Nor, despite his proximity, did he seem aware of me. He was staring instead out the window at the garden, messy with the ragged start of autumn, the asters still in bloom and falling, roses not yet turned to hips. He had that blank look that people have when they are hugely troubled by untold things. And I longed to say to him, "I know." But I did not. Not then.

· · ·

I would have liked to walk crisply into breakfast and demand an explanation. But I was nobody's wife; I could not. So I overslept instead. I felt leaden when I finally got out of bed, and I was slow to shower and dress. Downstairs, Bee Bee and Ned were up with Mason and all the children. Patsy appeared half an hour later with Sally right behind her.

"Good morning," Sally said.

Bee Bee looked at her. Ned looked at Bee Bee. Bee Bee, holding Sally's gaze, sighed and shrugged.

"We've been friends a long time, Bee Bee," Sally said and Bee Bee, with her husband's silent encouragement, smiled, crossing back over the thin crevice of ill will that had split Sally from the rest of us.

I wasn't alone with Mason until much later, on the beach. I wandered off by myself and he contrived to join me, back at our old spot, in the seclusion afforded by the wineglass rock. He had been swimming. Plump drops of seawater clung to his shoulders, and his hands, on my waist, were cold. He turned me to him and kissed me. My mind, though, was still full of brisk questions. I kept a little stiff. He didn't seem to notice. He smiled.

"Did you miss me?" he said, and then maybe he did notice because he said, much more seriously, "I missed you."

But I had been stewing.

"How's Patsy?" I was appalled by the petulant sound of my own voice. It was too late, though, so I tensed, backing myself up and making it uncomfortable for him to keep his arm around me.

"Patsy?" He was taken aback.

"I saw you. Out by the pool," I said, aware as I did that this wasn't the way I had meant things to go. "Last night. After I'd gone to bed. After *you'd* gone to bed."

"Aah," he said, putting a tentative hand to my hip. "Look, darling, that's nothing for you to worry about."

I stared at him. I wanted to worry about it. I did not want to be detached from any aspect of his life.

He sighed and kissed my forehead.

"Look. Patsy and I are friends."

"Kissing friends?" I asked ludicrously.

He chortled at this, the way he might have at something one of the twins said.

"I kissed her at our last Christmas party," he told me, mock earnestly. "It was that kind of party." He was smiling, but then he stopped. "And now I'm kissing you." He did.

I pulled back, although I was beginning to want to be pacified, to start over.

"I couldn't sleep," he said, steadily. "I got up, and I found

Patsy out by the pool. She was pretty miserable, so I stayed with her for a while. Then I went back to bed. That's it, sweetheart." He raised his palms. "That's it."

This explanation, especially in light of Patsy's recent revelations, was horribly logical. I felt ridiculous. I didn't reply.

"Look"—his expression, watching me, was vaguely amused, pleased by my concern—"I was thinking of doing a little supply run, before dinner. Let's go together."

I felt then, all at once, the time that he had been away and the time without him since. I had missed him. I nodded.

"Good." He ran a smooth hand over my lower back, and lower. Burying his head in the hollow of my neck, he said, "I have a little present for you."

It was a bracelet. Small gold links and a fancy clasp, a tiny blue stone in it. I was astonished. I had never been given a present like it before from anyone other than my parents. A watch once for good examination results, a family string of pearls on my twenty-first birthday. I stroked the bracelet after he had fastened it to my wrist.

"I thought it was nice." He reached out and slid the links up my arm, looking at it as if for the first time. "Pretty," he said.

"It's lovely. Thank you." I put my hand on his. We were in a café in town.

He kissed me swiftly, leaning over a bag of limes, and laughed. So did I, his girl again.

That night there was pink champagne, Patsy and Richard behaved as if the air between them had never been bruised, and all the children came to dinner wearing cardboard crowns crayoned purple. Even Hudson had one. He shoved it back from his damp forehead with pudgy hands.

"Someone oughtta make a proper toast," Ned said. "There are some nights when you can't just pick up a drink and down it. Not even an average-to-inferior glass of fizzy foreign firewater."

This remark was greeted with a wave of good humor.

"Here's to nights like this, then," I toasted.

Sally, resplendent in the silver white empire-line dress of a goddess, raised her champagne with an elegant, unhurried gesture and smiled. "Well said, Frankie."

"To nights like this," Bee Bee repeated, "and plenty of 'em."

A stranger would not have picked up a single crosscurrent in the room.

Much later, some time in the thin hours after midnight when Sally and Bee Bee were recementing their friendship in low voices through the soft nimbus of Bee Bee's cigarette smoke, the two of them fell silent and settled four cold eyes, it seemed, for an uncomfortable moment, on me. Just then, though, Richard called my name. Patsy had invented some sort of drinking game that involved forfeits and spelling, and I was challenged to "anaemia," so the moment, the look, if it had happened at all, was immediately swamped by merriment.

I had been asleep for about an hour when I was awoken by a tap at my door. I held still for a moment and listened for it again. When it came, I got up and pulled a cotton robe around me. I could feel my heart beating in my chest.

Mason didn't speak. He opened my robe and put his arms around me and touched his lips to the base of my throat. We stood like that for a long time in the moonlight. He looked up and said quietly, "Your shutters are open."

"I like the light, in the mornings."

He kissed me again. "I like *you*."

There was a great tenderness in him that night, and the frantic edge that had marked some of our lovemaking honeyed, mellowed into something, if not softer, then deeper. It left me utterly passive and, if it were possible, even more open to him than I had been before.

"You are a fabulous girl-woman," he said, his hand on my belly.

"Girl-woman," I repeated, rolling onto my side, propping myself up on an elbow and looking down at him.

"Yes," he said. "This part girl." He touched a finger lightly to my left breast. "The heart of a girl. And this part woman."

I lay back again at the feel of his hand, but he took it away and smiled.

"Sleep now, darling," he said, his breath at my forehead.

We had, to my delight, breakfast alone, except for the younger children, who were occupied with some insect that Howie had found. The girls were squealing, running away from it, then running back to be teased some more. Howie at some point took off after Jenny in earnest, holding the creature with his arm outstretched. She, longer-legged, and faster, kept just ahead of him, shrieking and twisting her head back constantly over her shoulder.

"Make him stop, Daddy," she shouted, passing us.

"You make him stop," Mason called. "You got him started."

Jessica, coming up behind Howie, made a grab for him,

surprising him. He dropped the insect. It landed stiff and brown on the poolside tiles. "It's dead now," he moaned. "You killed it."

"It was already dead," Jessica said.

Howie bent down and gave the insect a poke. It skimmed, lifeless, a few inches over the tiles. Jenny came back to have a look. But she wasn't in a standing-around mood.

"Race you to the front gate," she challenged, and started for it. Jessica and Howie took off after her, Howie soon lagging by a yard. Mason turned to watch them round the corner of the house.

"That kid has no idea what he's up against," he said, turning back to me. "Even miniature women will tie you in knots."

He laughed, more or less to himself, and we sat for a moment, sipping our coffee in the gentle warmth of the sunshine.

"I've been thinking about going to New York," I said. I'd been thinking about it constantly.

Mason smiled. "Could get awful cold in your bikini come fall," he said.

I laughed. "Well, I guess I'll just have to buy a coat."

"That's a look I could learn to like," he said, "a bikini and a coat."

The children's shouts returning to the house were clearly audible as he leaned over and bit my earlobe.

. . .

I realize that the narrative of the more recent chapters of my life is not as orderly as that of those further past. But day-to-day life has that quality, muddy, while you are still in the process of swimming through it. It is the stored accounts that get polished, tossing about all those years inside the mind. Incidents from the last ten months come to me now with no particular chronology—conversations with Chloe; the clematis, especially the Montana, the pink one on the pergola, thriving despite, because of, my lack of attention; and the week, sometime before the end of the summer, when a mix-up with dates led to everybody, Chloe and Ed, Sonia and Ollie, Catherine and Dan and the children, and Tom and Alice, all coming down on the same weekend.

It was the loveliest weekend, though not in terms of the weather, which was muggy and threatened by heavy clouds that in the end delivered only spots of cool rain. At first people were embarrassed and said they'd leave, but I wanted them all, and these days no one refuses me anything.

Joan came over and helped with beds, and Catherine and Dan decamped to the B&B in the village. There was a great deal of food in the house because Helen leaves provisions after all of her visits and Catherine, as usual, had arrived laden. The atmosphere quickly turned festive, with everybody pitching in and Catherine's boys setting up some kind of ball game in the garden. It was all so perfect that for a while I came dangerously close to returning to an earlier state of mind, one in which I was convinced that reprieve was still possible, that everything could still be put back into a dark drawer and locked away for eternity.

That weekend I gave Catherine some of Chloe's old, stored-away things for her daughter Ness, Chloe picking over them first, nodding yes or no. It was after I had sorted the things—a ski jacket, some books, and a long cotton sun frock—and once again closed up the chest that held so many more of Chloe's treasures that I noticed the apricot dress. The apricot dress has hung in my wardrobe for almost five years and goes mostly unnoticed, but that day, Ness's new books in my arms, it caught my eye. I stopped and put the books on a chair and twisted the dress toward me on its hanger, slipping it from its protective plastic. It is a lovely dress.

Chloe, behind me, lumbered with the ski jacket, said, "That's gorgeous. Why don't you wear it more?"

"I've never worn it," I said. I looked at her, confessional. "It cost an arm and a leg."

We laughed. It's a female thing, isn't it? Buying clothes, in this case an expensive silk cocktail dress, and never wearing them.

"I've got shoes to match," I said.

"So have I." Sonia, prelunch drink in her hand, had come looking for us. "Still in the bloody tissue."

We had bought the dress, and the shoes—a pair each—together, on a shopping trip to celebrate my fortieth birthday.

Downstairs in the kitchen Chloe's things met with Ness's steady eleven-year-old gaze and then her approval, largely, I suspect, because they had once belonged to Chloe. Chloe is grown-up enough for Ness to look up to and young enough for her to want to emulate. She took them away solemnly and piled them by the back door so that she would remember them when they went back to the B&B. Then she helped Chloe lay the table for lunch.

All the men and the boy children, in that way that sometimes happens at house parties, had drifted to the garden and were gathered there now, an amiable crew, talking, waving glasses and bottles, taking imaginary swipes at imaginary balls with imaginary sporting equipment. We could hear them, though not what they were saying, and see them through the big window above the sink. And Alice was telling a story about a handbag, prompted by Sonia's rendition of the apricot dress confession. Alice said that she had bought the handbag when she and Tom were first married and money was tight. She had felt so guilty about it that she'd hidden the bag in the back of a wardrobe for two years.

"I used to take it out and look at it sometimes," she said.

Everybody laughed at this, and I was glad because Alice was the outsider in the bunch and I wanted her to feel welcome. I was full of affection for everyone. I think now that that was the beginning of the feeling of floating almost, of wanting everything around me to be happy and gentle and pleasant—all those mild adjectives. I wanted nothing abrasive in my world, nobody hurting. I remember now that Dan had once complained of Catherine being that way during her pregnancies, weeping for the plight of the poor and animals without homes; he had claimed that she was prey for any passing con man, any brush salesman with a sob story.

I still have a very clear picture of the lunch we had that day, although I could not tell you the date of it without the prompt of a calendar and other events for reference. I remember there being bowls of steamed corn and baskets of hot bread, and I remember that the goodwill feeling that I had then seemed to radiate from everyone, even the children, even Ollie, who could be sullen sometimes, especially around his mother.

It was during that lunch that I decided, not just that I wanted more lunches like that, more weekends like that, but that I wanted to have a party. A really thumping proper party with all these people and more. People I hadn't seen and wanted to see. People will come to a party, I thought.

I thought too that if I had a party I could wear my apricot dress. A frivolous notion, wasn't it, for someone in my position, my circumstances? But not entirely without purpose after all, because I had decided that I would be wearing my apricot dress when I spoke to Josee. I would invite her to the party. And she would come.

· · ·

I did wonder sometimes in the gray dawn, after my door had slipped closed behind him and the gentle slope that he had made in the mattress had eased flat again, how it was that Mason managed those nocturnal visits, which, once begun, soon developed a rhythm and had on two separate occasions led to his sleeping briefly beside me while I, afraid to move, did not, lest I wake him and advance his departure. But I chose not to dwell on that mean detail. I had shut my mind early on to all difficulties where he was concerned and allowed myself to become dopey with blind optimism.

Nevertheless, it struck me through this lavender fog one morning that Bee Bee's voice was caustic when she said, "My, we are bright, aren't we? Shiny like a little Christmas bauble." She was speaking to me. I looked at her. I had agreed to play a silly, riotous swimming game with the children. Jenny had invented it. Now, the game finished, I was sitting on the pool edge in my wet bikini, still laughing, my hair dripping over my shoulders.

"Nothin' wrong with a spark of good humor," Ned said, deflecting.

Bee Bee, her eyes still on me, half closed them and put her cigarette to her lips. "This particular good humor just happens to be getting rather noisy," she said. "Some people could do without it." She ran a pampering finger over one eyebrow and adjusted her dark glasses.

Ned smiled. "Are we a little shaky this morning, dear?" he asked.

Bee Bee spun her head to him and tightened her lips. "It's not a hangover that's bothering me if that's your implication, my sweet. Hangovers never bother me," she said, with a matter-of-fact expression, looking in my direction again. "I know how to handle them. They run in the family."

Ned laughed, but I felt my nervousness escalate.

"Sorry . . . we did get a bit loud." I shushed the children, or tried to.

"Oh," she purred, "I'm not against people having fun. It's just that I think they ought to be aware when they're having fun at someone else's expense."

I snapped my eyes to her.

She smiled under her glasses, laid her cigarette in the beaten indent of a copper ashtray, and said neutrally, "I don't know what's gone wrong with the barman today. A person could die of thirst."

Ned hopped up.

"Apologies, ma'am," he said, scooping up her empty glass and heading off to refill it.

Left then, the only other adult, alone with her, I looked back down at the children splashing in the water and waited for the next blow. But she just said, "It's going to be hot this afternoon."

The prediction was accurate. The sky turned hard blue and the sun burned. It was too hot to walk down to the beach, though the children were keen on the idea after lunch. We took the cars instead, loaded with gear as usual. Even with the umbrellas up, though, and the light breeze off the water, it was too hot to just lie on the sand. We all headed for the sea. Bee Bee and Sally kept their sunglasses and hats on. I watched as they waded through the soft frill of waves to the calm beyond, where they sat in the water, floating with their toes poking out, talking.

Ned had found a rubber raft in the basement and excited the children by showing it to them. Now he was attempting to inflate it. His cheeks strained at the small plastic valve. He signaled to Richard, trying to palm off the job.

"Nuh-uh," Richard responded, laughing. "You found it, you blow it up."

Ned rolled his eyes. Richard grinned and walked farther into the water. Eventually he let himself fall forward and swam off.

"You need a bicycle pump," Mason suggested when Ned, heaving, quit blowing for a second.

"Nobody likes a know-it-all," Ned said.

The three of us, me and Mason and Patsy, began to wade deeper. Ned, curls of froth rising up his calves and the twins and Howie tugging at his elbows, looked up for a second and yelled, "Well, thanks, fellas."

"You're welcome," Mason called and lifted his arm without looking back.

The water was warm. Too warm to be much use for cooling purposes, but we lay in it anyway, enervated. The raft, blown up at last, had a pinprick puncture in one of the seams and needed reinflating at regular intervals. Richard, swimming back in and regaining his breath, took a turn with the puffing. Then he helped Howie to wriggle on top.

"How far'd you go?" Patsy's asked.

Richard lifted one dripping arm and pointed to the curve of land beyond where the house sat, at the wineglass rock end of the beach. "Past that funny rock and out. You can see right along the coast."

Patsy looked at Mason. "Up for it?" she asked.

Richard looked at Mason too. Then, as if shaking away some thought, he gave his head a flick, dislodging water, and sniffed.

"The sea's cooler out there," he said. "Feels good." He turned toward us, lifted his feet from the bottom, and began treading water.

Mason and Patsy struck out rhythmically. Richard looked at me for a second, questioning.

"I'm not much of a swimmer," I said. We were both watching the flutter of Patsy's and Mason's feet on the sea surface. It felt, just for a second, as though we were the spare pair on a double date.

"You caught the sun, Richard," Sally said at the pool over drinks.

Richard, freshly showered, his complexion as shiny as his children's, touched his nose, which was pink. "I guess I did," he said. "I can feel it. You kept your hat on, didn't you?"

"Yes," she answered, putting her glass down.

"My mother always wears a hat," Patsy said. "Never goes out of doors without one."

"Your mother is a Southern belle," Richard offered.

"Well, yes," Patsy went on, "but I think it has to do with age too. You know, women of a certain era wear hats. Especially as they get older."

Sally was looking at Patsy and running her index finger idly up and down her glass. The movement cleared a line in the condensation.

"Touché, dear," she said and lifted her drink with a small superior smile.

Patsy, not letting go, giggled rather childishly. "Well, if the hat fits."

Bee Bee, sitting near Patsy on a slatted chair at one of the round tables, uncrossed her legs and turned to her. "Don't fool yourself for one second, baby face, that youth is a match for wisdom in any sort of fight that matters." She had fixed Patsy with an extraordinarily hard look.

"Who was it," Richard asked, "who said that youth was wasted on the young?" It wasn't clear whether he was attempting to dispel the tension or was simply unaware of it.

"It's a song," I answered, relieved. It seemed Bee Bee's barbs were not reserved for me.

"It is too," Ned confirmed. "Sammy Cahn wrote it. 'Love, like youth, is wasted on the young,'" he said, quoting.

"Ain't that the truth." Bee Bee settled back in her chair.

"You're a real mine of information, aren't you, Frankie?" Sally said.

I shrugged.

Mason, who had been quietly sipping his drink in the

corner, detached from developments, said, "Now there's a worrying possibility, people who are smart *and* young."

I smiled at him, and Patsy toasted in his direction.

"To smart and young." She grinned. It was a grin tinged with triumph.

That night, when I heard his tap, I got up straightaway. I'd been waiting for it. Hopeful. I went to the door without putting on my robe.

"My," he said, low-voiced, "what a little sex kitten I have for a mistress."

I did not like his use of the expression, but I forgot about it in the forty minutes that followed.

Then, after a sweet silent time, I said, "You don't think Bee Bee knows, do you?"

"Knows?" Mason asked, turning his head on the pillow beside me. "Oh, you mean about this?" He ducked to kiss my breast. "Or do you think she suspects *this*?" He ducked his head further, lifting the sheet, kissing me again.

It always set me a bit on edge when he got like that, teasing. I didn't respond.

He sighed. "Darling, I've told you before about trying to understand everything."

"It was just that she was strange to me, at the pool this morning. Made some comment about people having fun at other people's expense, and I wasn't sure exactly what she meant."

"Nothing, probably. It's just Bee Bee. You've seen how she is."

"Yes," I said, looking at the ceiling for a minute. The fan was clearly visible against it in the moonlight. "But what I thought was if Bee Bee knew then Sally would know, wouldn't she? Bee Bee would tell her if she thought . . ." I didn't finish. I didn't really want to talk about Sally. I had just been wondering about the Bee Bee business, and that had set me . . . fishing, I suppose, testing what his reaction might be to Sally knowing about us. I had lost momentum, though. I didn't want to go on. I turned my face to his, and he smiled. Then he rolled onto his back and looked at the ceiling himself.

"Sally and I have been married for sixteen years. I figure she knows pretty much everything."

I was shocked. It was one thing for me to make suppositions. It was another for him to state things as if they were plain truth.

"What do you mean?" I asked, in a voice that, though quiet, threatened shrillness.

"Mean, mean, mean." He turned, smiling, back at me. "Darling girl, always looking for what things mean. I don't mean anything. Nothing means anything. Except this."

I wanted very much to keep him there. I did not stop him with more talk.

SEVEN

A SERIES OF LAZY days followed. More than lazy—liquid, vast, and endless at times as the ocean below us. Events, occasional obstacles, looming as they did above the otherwise limpid surface of the sleepy flow, took on unnatural proportions. Once, an argument about a dead president ran for five hours before it flagged, though no one remembered how it had started or why. And one blue afternoon, a trifling scatter of children's shoes, toe-to-toe, some partnerless, one flipped unaccountably into the swimming pool, set off a storm.

Bee Bee had tripped, scuffing a small pink sandal in the second before her shaded eyes adjusted from the patio glare to the relative gloom of the arbor. A dull streak of cigarette ash atop a slick of whatever had been in the glass she was holding in the other hand marked the spot till a maid was summoned with a mop. Richard, amid gales of wailed innocence, gave all the children a round telling-off and a stern reminder regarding poolside safety while Christina tsked agreement in the background. All the shoes were scooped up after that and tidied away by little, unwilling hands

The next morning a pair of apparently ownerless sneakers materialized, and thereafter made several mysterious appearances, under pillows, perched on umbrella spikes, then, fabulously, inside a hollowed-out breakfast melon. Ned, through all this, shrugged his uninvolvement.

"Shoe fairies," he said to Jessica as she stared wonder-eyed at the navy canvas toes poking up from the melon half. Hudson was hoisted to look.

Another day, in the otherwise languid after-lunch hours there was an expedition to find a puncture-repair kit for the inflatable raft. Mason, and Howie, and the twins, and me. We found one piled in a teetering stack in the hardware store. Mason showed the slim metal container to Howie.

"I remember them being in tins like that when I was a kid," he said.

"Me too." I smiled, fingering the smooth surface.

Small shared things. We were new enough that they seemed poignant.

By then the road between the house and the town, once featureless, was full of landmarks. There was Roy, still wearing Ned's hat, and a bit farther along, a spot I had marked for myself. The place where Mason had first pulled over to kiss me. A small stone monument stood nearby with a wooden cross on it. Somebody must have been killed there in a car accident; recently I had begun to wonder who. After that there was a rock called Jailhouse, for no reason other than that it was bigger than the other rocks and a regular twenty-minute drive with children needs attractions.

That day, traveling these markers in reverse, Jessica said, "This is my favorite part," as we drove past the trash dump.

I twisted to smile at her. "Why?"

"Because of that boy." She inclined her head toward a boy, about Howie's age, sitting on the front doorstep of a little house nearby. Next to him pink blooms tumbled from a rusty paint can. "He's always there," Jessica said. "He waves."

She waved to the boy and the boy waved back. But then a small bicker flared, the twins versus Howie, about why the rock was called Jailhouse. Taking advantage of their distraction Mason removed one hand from the steering wheel and laid it on mine. Between us the puncture-repair kit, a loaf of market bread, and two newspapers slid on the smooth leather seat. It was lovely, the simplicity of it.

"I had a dream," Mason said, quietly, the children's prattle as background.

Something in his tone made me look at him, but his face, turned to the road, gave nothing particular away.

"Four black birds were carrying me away." He did flick his eyes then, quickly in my direction. "What do you make of that?"

Behind us the children, the girls anyway, had started singing "Jailhouse Rock." Ned had taught it to them. I turned toward Mason, who was intent on driving again, and I felt sure, seeing the curious set of his mouth profiled against the bright side window, that this wasn't a casual inquiry. That he was genuinely in search of interpretation. I suspected that he had already come to some conclusion of his own and that my answer would be tested against it.

"I guess it has to do with freedom," I proffered. "Flying away, it suggests some kind of release, don't you think?"

"I don't know," he answered softly.

"*Roooy*," the children cried, roaring in unison behind us.

"It made *me* think of death," Mason said.

His hand on mine quit its caress. Roy stood only five minutes from the house. The gates were clearly visible. I had got it wrong. And there would be no chance, now, for redress. In my head an already familiar routine, of replaying the exchange over and over till it was mangled and pitiful, began.

I was still in the grip of the feeling that I had failed to please him when Sally, in the glaring outdoors, in front of everyone, slid her fingers suggestively down my lover's arm and looped her fingers through his.

"We might take a nap," she said, an indelicate flush on her cheeks.

I was appalled. The lunch table was barely cleared. Patsy stared at her, then lifted her hand and, with an exact, faintly mocking imitation of Sally, ran it down her husband's arm. "So might we," she said.

Richard reddened, but stood with her. She led him off.

"Lambs to the slaughter," Bee Bee remarked, not quite under her breath.

I watched mutely as Mason's back disappeared after Sally's. On the way to their bedroom. I remembered seeing that bedroom once, in another life, when the children had taken me on a tour of the house the day after my arrival. Jenny had pushed the door open, exposing a large bed with a fluttering muslin canopy.

"And this is where Mommy and Daddy sleep," she'd announced.

It had meant nothing to me then. I remember Christina was in the room, busy looping something pale and expensive and feminine-looking onto a padded hanger. She had shooed us off. As the door was closing I had seen her hold the hanger up and brush her hand lovingly over the front of the garment. It was a nightdress. I thought of that nightdress now. Its thin straps. I felt sick. A little dizzy, and sick.

"Did that girl of ours ever come back from the beach?" Ned asked sleepily.

Bee Bee, sitting, looking at me as she reached for a cigarette, answered, "Guess not."

"Lack of discipline," Ned said, settling behind the close straw weave of a hat with a tan ribbon. "I blame the parents."

Bee Bee laughed and I offered, quickly, in a voice that I didn't recognize, to walk down to the beach to check on Paige and Lesley. They had taken to spending whole days down there, a gaudy tangle of towels, and magazines, and bottles of Coke in their rucksacks. I left before Bee Bee or Ned could reply, desperate to get myself as far as possible from the house.

The beach path curved downward. It wasn't impossibly steep, but we had learned to watch our footing on the way down. Patches of dry dirt would give way under heels. I walked carefully, and my tennis shoes didn't make any noise in the dust as I approached the lower stretch where the view opened up. I saw Paige and Lesley before I heard them, but it was clear they were talking, sitting on their towels, arms around their knees, backs to me.

"I think he likes me quite a lot really," Paige's voice was saying as I approached.

"He is married, though, Paige," Lesley answered.

"Oh," Paige said with a shrug, "married isn't anything. Married men screw other people all the time."

Lesley spun her head to Paige, then, as if not wanting to betray any shock, relaxed back again, eyes to the sea.

"Yeah, I know," she said, casually. "My father screwed somebody else. So did my last stepfather."

There was a pause before Paige replied, "Dad screwed someone too."

I stopped, just above them, not breathing.

"Who?" Lesley asked. "Christina?"

"*Nooo.* Of course not."

"Well"—Lesley's tone was wounded—"my stepdad, before Ned, screwed Julia who looked after me." She added, as confirmation, "Mom threw them both out."

Paige was silent for a second. "I dunno who it was. But I heard them fighting about it."

"Oh," Lesley said. "I don't think Ned will."

"No." Paige shook her head. "Ned won't. He's too old."

I walked back up the hill a little way and mustered my voice to call out to them.

Richard came down to dinner with a smile so bright that you could have cooked on it. Ned made some comment to that effect, but Richard, unembarrassed, continued to beam, handing a glass tenderly to Patsy. Her returned expression, I noticed, was distinctly frailer.

Sally, arriving soon afterward, acompanied by her husband, beamed too and then announced, as if she were drawing a raffle, that she and Mason had decided it would be great fun to have a moonlight picnic on the beach.

"Wouldn't that be cute?" she said, the word, in her mouth, not only inappropriate, but somehow crude. "Wouldn't that be fun?" she pressed, looking at me.

. . .

It was during the lazy part of Sunday on that weekend when everyone visited—the part when people are avoiding thinking about packing cars, when someone is about to suggest some last, stalling repast, inevitably unnecessary given the amount that everybody has already eaten and drunk— that I announced my intention to throw a party. They were all dozing and reading and doing the things that people do when they only have half an hour and want to make it seem like forever.

Sonia looked at me, faintly comical in her half-moon glasses. "Hear hear," she said.

"A goodbye party," I added.

Chloe burst into tears. Ed, I was pleased to see, moved immediately to her side and placed a reassuring hand on her arm. I was sorry then, but I had given the toboggan a push, and it was a long steep slope.

I reached out to Chloe and raised her dear chin. "I don't mean it in a maudlin way, darling. I just want to know that I'll have all the people I love around me at least one more time in an atmosphere like this. A happy atmosphere."

Chloe calmed a little, and Sonia, bless her, said, "If it's a party you want, hon, it's a party you'll get."

"Not for a while, though," I answered.

Everyone was pleased at this. The tension broke.

"Not for a bleeding age," Dan said, putting his arm around Catherine, who looked as if she might cry too, and I thought how unfair it is, that aspect of this experience, that you have to watch people who you care about suffer. Even if I deserve to hurt like this, they do not.

The party was, of course, forgotten in the weeks that followed. There was our anniversary, and then a few days of poor health, and then another stay at Aldenbrook. When I got back, it was November. The sky was slate. My health rallied. We all readjusted again, let our breath out. It wouldn't be yet. Not just yet. But I knew that it was coming, that death was waiting for me quietly and steadily, in a way that I had not known it before.

The thing is that, much as I loathe my hospital stays, loathe the squat brick buildings and the sticky asphalt in the car park, loathe the scraggy half-dead plants and the constant, permeating smell of canned soup, there is, from time to time, in that detached unreal atmosphere, a sense almost of relief, a sense that things are in someone else's hands. I never have that feeling at home, not completely. And so it isn't such a surprise that it was while I was at Aldenbrook that I came to truly accept the fact of my imminent death.

Naturally I had thought about it, talked about it too, to Phillip, to Chloe even, though she is distressed more by such allusions, but still the absoluteness of the thing hadn't been clear. It had been forming, not in a cleanly progressive sort of way, but with differing levels of violence, little eruptions, until at last there it was, complete and unconquerable, a mountain with me in its shadow. I knew that I was going to die, and although I do not believe as some people do that life hands out justice in fair measure, that suffering is related to one's past sins, it did seem logical, understandable that I should not live a long life.

I had been home for almost a week and had just eaten lunch with Phillip in the kitchen, Joan's fish pie and green beans. Our plates were cleared but we were still sitting opposite each other, Phillip finishing the glass of wine he'd poured to go with his pie. It was warm in the kitchen, warmer than anywhere else in the house, and a gentle voice, my voice, said, "I want Josee to come to my party."

Phillip looked very shocked, but he did not speak. After a while he drained the last of the wine and asked simply, "Are you sure?"

I was relieved, relieved that he was not going to skate away, skim the issue or lie about it.

"I think so," I said, "although it is probably fair to assume that I am not at all sure about a lot of things just now. But I have thought about this, and I know that I want to see her and speak to her. And I want to do it at a time when I feel . . . supported. In control, I suppose. I want to feel that I am on my own ground."

Phillip nodded, very slowly. I felt that he understood my point of view even if he didn't know how to come to terms with it. He got up and walked across the kitchen with his empty glass in his hand. He rinsed it in the sink, and then he turned and leaned against the cupboard where I keep the dishwashing liquid and the furniture polish with his arms crossed over his chest.

"How long have you known?" he asked.

"A long time," I said.

His expression was stricken. For a moment all the strain of the past year threatened to spill from him, but he staunched it, one hand rising and cupping his mouth and chin for a second. Then he left the room.

· · ·

The thing that was striking about the moonlight picnic was the precision with which it had been planned. At the beach a low bonfire already burned, sending stripes of light bouncing off the sea. There were rugs spread on the pink sand, and baskets of cold meat and salads, and peach pies, and bottles of chilled wine. We arrived to all this and more. We could hear over the noise of squealing children, delighted to the extreme by the proximity of the fire, music.

There were musicians, cloistered in the shadows beyond the base of the dirt cliff path. I watched as Sally, barefoot, pulled her husband to dance. I sat a good way back from the revealing flare of the firelight, and took a glass gratefully from someone and drank, wanting to be dulled against the events and pace of a day that I could no longer keep up with.

I kept drinking until I was tipsy and my legs, dancing hopelessly later with Richard, felt numb.

"Sorry, Frankie," he said, goofily cheerful, standing on my foot.

I nodded, attempting to smile forgiveness. The music wasn't really dancing music anyway. Guitars playing marshmallow love songs. None of us would have danced at all if Sally hadn't started it, I thought. I gripped Richard's hand too tightly in mine, worried suddenly about the possibility of being knocked over by his heavy shuffle. In my head Paige's words, *Daddy screwed someone else*, continued to repeat.

I had not considered the possibility that Mason might have had other affairs. At twenty-two I'd had so little experience of marriage. My parents and their friends were my models for it. Of course I realized that married people could be unfaithful, but those that were, it seemed to me then, separated and got divorced. The kind of marriage that accepts infidelities, adds them, like so many bricks, to the fortress that shields the pair within, was alien to me. But then, when the music stopped, and the sound of the sea interceded, and Richard stood back and grinned, it struck me suddenly that if Mason had had other affairs—Paige was just a child after all, and prone to showing off—but if he had, wasn't that just another indication that his marriage was unhappy? I wanted that night, more than any other night, to believe wholeheartedly that his marriage was unhappy.

The children were heavily asleep by the time we got back, draped over shoulders like so many sandy rag dolls. At the house Mason and I carried the twins to their room. They woke when he switched on the light and they stared at us blearily. We undressed them and slid them into their beds, dragging the sheets up to their chins.

"We didn't brush our teeth," Jessica said, croakily, over hers.

"If they fall out in the night, I'll buy you some new ones," Mason whispered.

Jessica, drifting again already, giggled softly into her pillow.

In the hallway, he turned to me and said, without preamble, "It's married people's stuff, not like us."

I stared, dumb from drink and tiredness, exhausted by the spiking effort of loving him, the impossibility of the circumstances. Fighting the realization that I had let my whole life, in that pastless, futureless, rose-tinted bell jar, become him. A man I hardly knew, someone else's husband, who was putting his hands on my shoulders now and talking to me about spending the afternoon in bed with his wife.

"Not like us," he repeated.

I nodded slowly.

"We'll get away for a bit tomorrow," he promised.

Sometimes there's no going back, and anyway, what did I have to go back to? The next day in my apartment, that had, shut up between visits, begun to smell of us, of love, I thought, he lifted his lips from mine and said my name. Just as I had imagined he would all through Maria's lesson, all through the constant firing of her fascinated inquiry about the Severances, and the Lukes, and the Newsons, but particularly about Sally. Where did she buy her clothes? What foods did she serve most often? How many maids did she employ all together?

I smiled now and simply kissed him back, a girl in love with a man who loved her, and I thought, as I often had, that the other lovers I had known paled next to him. Then, confident in the grip of this happy moment, I leaned into his neck and said, "Have you done this before?"

Mason tipped my head back to look at my face, but he made no attempt to avoid the question. That was one of the things I admired about him; even at times when I didn't particularly welcome it, he was candid with me.

"Sally and I have had our problems," he answered

thoughtfully, his gaze moving, fixing on some distant space above my head. He raised my chin and looked at me and said, "But with you it's special."

I saw myself, in the moment before he bent to kiss me again, reflected in his eyes.

My face must still have been gleaming with love when Mason said casually to his wife, "Look. Pineapples." He had bought them when I was with Maria. "The ingredient that will force Mr. Newson to concede on the best rum punch recipe."

Sally, answering with a noncommittal hum, looked at me steadily over her sunglasses, her book, her golden knees. Next to her Bee Bee seemed to stare too. I didn't care. I didn't care about anything. I was just glad that the mood of capricious flirtatiousness that had marked Sally's behavior the day before seemed to have dimmed.

It was Patsy who suggested we go back to La Roseleda. She felt like dancing, she said to me later, out by the pool, and reminded me what a lot of fun we'd had that first night, my first night, when we'd gone there. She smiled that gorgeous smile of hers directly at me. "Do you want to go?" she asked, as if it was somehow my decision. As if I was central to her plans.

Since her confession to me, that morning after the row, she'd treated me like that quite often, like a special pal. Like the sort of inseparable sidekick girls have at school. Patsy was the sort of girl I'd wanted to be at school, pretty, and petulant, and popular. She jumped up and swiveled her hips a little and announced her desire to go dancing to the spread of sunbathers. Richard got up and threw one arm around her shoulders and swung his hip awkwardly to bump hers.

"God, I hope it's not contagious," Bee Bee said, as the movement knocked them both off balance. The recovery was jerky.

Richard, though, continued good-spiritedly, "Just warming up my samba, Bee Bee." He jived toward her a little, with prematurely middle-aged knees.

"Well, you don't seem to be lighting any fires," she retorted, backing up from his advance. "Still," she went on, lowering herself into a tapestry-covered chair, "that's not your fault, darlin'. You gotta rub *two* sticks together to get a spark."

Bee Bee laughed and so did Sally. Patsy did not.

Richard, uncomprehending, grinned, snapped his fingers jauntily, and opened his mouth to speak, but Patsy stopped him: "Shut up."

Sally, still smiling, looked up from the intense business of fastening the clasp of a fat silver bracelet.

"What's all the hilarity in aid of?" Ned asked from the door.

"I was just—" Richard began.

"Stop!" Patsy commanded. Richard turned to her. "You're letting them make a fool out of you," she said, "fools out of both of us."

Behind Ned, Mason stood watching. Patsy squeezed her eyes closed for a second and seemed to forcibly control herself. She sighed. "Look . . . sorry . . . Just forget it." She raised a palm, then smiled a small apologetic smile.

"I always get cranky when I'm inappropriately dressed," she said. She still had on her white tennis outfit, an intricate affair of sewn-together daisies. She and Ned had played before lunch. She turned and walked off, ostensibly to change.

Richard, meek, followed her.

"Terribly highly strung," Sally commented dryly to Bee Bee.

"Distinct touch of the Scarletts," Bee Bee agreed.

I turned away, uncomfortable with the subtlety of their mockery and, worse, the hint of truth in it. Patsy could be hysterical. But I thought of her as a friend. And, recently, more than that, an ally.

Ned applauded that night, in the square, beneath the twinkling night-lights, when Sally parked the Chevrolet. "Hats off to Mrs. Severance," he said as the stately tail of the staff's big sedan slipped easily between the Buick and the jeep. Sally had volunteered to drive so that we could take three cars.

"The thing's a tank to handle," Ned had warned.

"But we won't have to cram," she had said. "I hate to cram."

"Never underestimate Mrs. Severance," Bee Bee told us now with a wry look.

"Any friend of yours, my dear . . ." Ned grinned, taking her arm for the short walk.

The hinged windows at La Roseleda were angled open toward the sea and a light breeze blew the cigarette smoke generated by two men at the bar toward the barman who was wiping glasses behind it. It was quiet. The musicians, playing rather listlessly for a lone couple on the dance floor, perked up a little at our entrance and the beat brightened as we took our table. When Patsy, standing, shrugged off her knee-length jacket, baring her back to a point below her waist, one of the men at the bar whistled and we all laughed. Then, seated, we fell momentarily silent, the atmosphere between us suddenly flat and a little self-conscious.

"Hell, I've seen wakes more lively," Ned challenged.

Richard, spurred, got up and invited Patsy to dance. As she stood, he held her chair and watched her with the expression of a boy who has caught a butterfly in a jar.

"Frankie?" Mason asked as they moved off.

I was surprised and pleased at his boldness. In his arms, my chin at his shoulder, I remembered something. Myself. However many hours, or days, or weeks ago it was, dancing with him here before. What was it that had changed so? Everything. I shut my eyes for a minute and pretended we were alone.

"Hello." Patsy turned, her arms open to us, and peeled off with Mason.

Richard flashed his eyebrows. "Take me on, Frankie?" he said, leaning toward my ear.

"Sure," I answered, disarmed, as he placed one hand carefully on my waist and extended the other, cautiously crooked, for me to hold.

I got to dance with Mason again later. The table shuffled, once, twice. Everybody danced with everybody. I flirted with all the men, even the waiter, in the way that a woman who is crazy in love with one man does.

"Do you think you'll buy the house?" I asked alone with him at the table. Richard had escorted Sally to the dance floor, Ned was dancing with Patsy, and in his absence Bee Bee had wandered to the bar. She was propped there now, happily absorbed with the barman, smoking a slow cigarette.

Mason shook his head over the noise. A lively group of young people had come in. "No."

I smiled at him. What did I care? In the bright new future

his love promised, a lot of things would be wonderfully unimportant.

Ned said maybe we ought to make tracks. Bee Bee, heading vaguely for the ladies' room, had lost her bearings and ended up in the street. Ned had had to bolt down the narrow staircase to fetch her.

"I'd be happy to," Sally replied. She gave her chair a short, rigid push backward. "Perhaps someone could alert Fred and Ginger."

Richard, who was as drunk that night as Bee Bee, got up messily and padded to the dance floor. At the edge of it he lifted his thumb and indicated the door. I watched as his wife, noticing him, turned her face from Mason's shirt front. Her expression tightened angrily.

Ned slid Bee Bee into the Buick's backseat, behind Mason and me, but she just grinned and kept on sliding and hauled herself out the door on the other side. She tottered toward the Chevrolet. Sally had got in to drive it.

"She's all on her lonesome," Bee Bee called back, her voice loud in the quiet street.

There was a slam, then the purr of an engine, and Sally pulled out. I saw Patsy put the jeep into gear as Richard, in the passenger seat, gave his head a little shake, fighting sleep. Ned's presence prevented Mason from reaching for my hand as we moved off, but I was glad, anyway, to be sitting beside him. We exchanged a smile. In the back Ned was humming.

Just past the turnoff to my apartment some men were smoking together under a streetlamp. One of them turned as we passed and looked at me and touched his hand to his head. Dizzy from the lovely day and the dancing, and Mason's proximity, I waved childishly, fluttering my fingers, and then I shut my eyes for a while.

That was all I could remember later. The men. The wave. Ned's leisurely hum behind me. Then the crack, the slap of Mason's arm across my ribcage as I hurtled forward toward the dashboard.

I screamed, shocked, involuntary air forcing my voice, but by the time I had lurched back against my seat, I was aware that I had heard the violent exploding sound of buckling metal. It wasn't us. We hadn't hit anything, though the jeep's taillights loomed directly in front of us.

"What the . . ." Ned had been jerked forward off his seat.

I flicked my head toward Mason, who had already flung his door open. He sprang and was gone. Ned and I, slower, dazed, watched stunned for a moment in the faint flicker of the interior light. Then we were out too. Running behind Mason through the chaotic, crisscrossing beams of headlights.

We were near the trash dump. People were coming out of the little houses, shouting. I recognized among them the little boy that Jessica had waved to, sleepy in an undershirt and cotton Y-front briefs. But I kept running, like everyone else, toward Sally's car and the sound we'd heard. And something else—the plaintive echo of a locked car horn.

Richard tugged the Chevrolet's passenger door open and began pulling Bee Bee out, his solid torso bending to her frail one. She emerged, papery, his solid grip on her upper arms, one of her hands faltering slackly ahead of her. Patsy, on the other side, was leaning in, talking to Sally, asking her something. Mason, reaching them, grabbed Patsy's waist and flung her so forcefully out of the way that she stumbled.

"Sally," he shouted. "Sally?"

The car was at a forty-five-degree angle to the road, the long hood jammed against a thick wooden post. Sally's head was on the steering wheel, and one arm, bent at the elbow, was pinned between the wheel and her chest.

"Darling?" Mason squatted at the open door beside her, and Sally slowly raised her head. She lifted one hand, tentatively, as if it did not belong to her, and pushed her hair back from her face.

"Something ran out," she said, quietly.

I looked around. There was no sign of a carcass. Whatever it was had escaped.

"There's nothing here," I said.

Mason was lifting his wife carefully from the vehicle. One of the women from the houses offered to help. "Ayee. La pobre," she said, seeing Sally, shaky at the car side.

Sally leaned on her husband for support, dropping her head to his shoulder. Mason, looking down at her, reached up and stroked the back of her neck.

"It's all right," he crooned. "It's all right."

Bee Bee was fine. Ned, his arms around her, called out, "Nothing broken."

"Are you okay?" I asked Patsy. She was bent over rubbing her shin.

"Yes," she answered, "I just scraped it jumping out."

Richard, joining us, said, "I must have fallen asleep. I didn't see what happened."

Patsy, looking over at Mason and Sally standing still entwined at the car side, said nothing.

"Me neither," I said.

"Do you think we should take Sally to a hospital? Is there a hospital?" Richard asked.

"There is, a small one, on the other side of town. You would have passed the road where it is on the way back from the airstrip."

"Right," he said. "What do you think, then? Should we go?"

"I don't know."

Mason looked up. "I'm worried about concussion," he said, tipping Sally away from him to look at her.

She raised her head like a doll. "I'm all right. I think."

"Really?" Mason took her face in both of his hands.

"Yes." She pulled herself upright.

"What about the car?" Ned asked.

"Could someone get me a cigarette before we start fussing about the wretched car?" Bee Bee muttered.

Patsy fetched cigarettes from the jeep and lit one each for her and Bee Bee. Ned left them smoking together and wandered around the car. It had attracted quite an audience of locals by then. One of them, a man with a belly protruding appleish over the sagging elastic of his shorts, spoke to Ned.

"Sorry, bud," Ned said, shrugging, and gestured to me.

"The police will impound the car," I translated.

"Sí," the man said, nodding knowingly, running a thumb inside his waistband, "policia." He gave me a shrewd look.

"If a car has been in an accident," I explained to Ned and Richard, who had come up behind me, "the police can impound it. Plus they can fine you or jail you," I said. "Things can get complicated, especially for foreigners."

Ned nodded. "I don't want to mess with any Mexican jail," he said.

It crossed my mind that this was the sort of situation that Arturo Rodriguez could fix, but it was very late, and, anyway, the police could arrive at any moment.

"No," I answered. "The smartest thing might be to just ditch the car."

"What do you think?" Ned called to Mason. "Do we care about the car?"

"We don't give a damn about the car," he said. His arm was around Sally's waist. "I just want to get Sally home."

She gave him a wan smile.

"And Bee Bee," Bee Bee said, dropping her cigarette and grinding it out. "Bee Bee might be in need of a little lovin' care too, doncha think?"

"Come on." Patsy took Bee Bee's elbow and helped her into the Buick.

Ned said to me, "What do you think?"

"If we don't care about the car, we can leave it to these guys. My guess is they'll have it off the road pretty quickly."

"And the plates changed pretty quickly after that," Ned said, grinning a bit.

"Probably."

"Come on then. Let's go."

I explained to the local men that we were in a hurry and worried about the ladies.

"Sí," the fat man agreed gravely. He was worried about the ladies too.

So they ought to just do whatever was necessary with the

car. We all understood each other. The fat man took his hand from his shorts and shook mine.

"Buenas noches."

"Buenas noches."

Patsy did not want to drive anymore. Richard took over at the wheel of the jeep and I got in with them, leaving the others the comfort of the Buick. As we drove around the wrecked Chevrolet, four men were heaving the front of it back from the pole.

"I don't think it's too badly damaged, actually," Richard said. "Jus' the hood and the grill. Prob'ly looks worse than it is."

He was, I realized, still pretty unsteady. He drove cautiously, bending his arms unnaturally and concentrating his attention on the five yards of road directly ahead of us.

"Did you say you didn't see what happened?" Patsy asked. It wasn't clear who she was speaking to. Richard answered.

"No . . . nodded off I think."

"Right," she said, taking a cigarette and lighting it with her head dipped and her hand cupped over the flame. Her eyes narrowed against the flare.

"Did you?" I asked. "See anything? Sally said something ran out."

Patsy turned to face the front again. I leaned forward, resting my elbows on the back of Richard's seat. In profile she shook her head.

E I G H T

CHRISTINA HAD BEEN in bed. Her hair was coming slightly loose from a long thick plait and the high neckline of a white nightdress showed above her dressing gown. Mason had shouted her name once when we arrived and she had materialized instantly from wherever it was that she slept. Tightening the dressing gown around her now, she attended to Sally.

"Really, Christina," Sally said, "go back to bed."

But Christina would have none of it. Mason, kneeling at Sally's side, looked up at her. "What do you think, Christina? About Madam's arm. Should she see a doctor?"

"Yes, sir. I think so."

"Now, now, you two." Sally turned her head from her husband to her housekeeper and back again. "I won't have you conspiring. I've said I'm fine and I am. No more fuss."

She frowned prettily and then flinched as Christina made one more nimble inspection of her right arm. "I mean it," she insisted. "I just need some sleep."

Ned had poured brandies. Mason took Sally's and held it to his lips. As if, I thought, she were dying.

"Please, Christina, we've disturbed you enough. Do go back to bed."

Christina, reluctant, finally turned away.

When she'd gone, Sally pulled herself up a little and said to Mason, "We'll have to arrange something about another car for her, I suppose."

"Don't you worry about that," Mason replied, consoling.

"All right," she said, looking into his eyes.

He reached forward and lay a hand on her knee.

He did not come to my room and I suppose I had not expected him to, but I was disappointed nonetheless. Not immediately, because I fell asleep quickly, worn out by the evening and lulled by the brandy, but later, when I woke up and twisted the little clock on my chest of drawers to see what time it was. I flicked the lamp on and blinked. Five a.m. I knew he would not come.

I switched the lamp off again and lay back in the dark. Thinking. I had been surprised by the way Mason had acted toward Sally after the accident. I probably shouldn't have been. She might, after all, have been seriously hurt. But I was. He had been so . . . affectionate. I punched a light depression in a downy pillow, knowing that this was a petty kind of jealousy. I felt it nevertheless, needling.

. . .

Is it acceptable to demand love? To be angry with those who withhold it from us? We behave as if it were, don't we? We rear up on righteous hind legs and howl when our loved ones do not love us back. Like infants squalling for survival. I think that is what I would have done if the drama that was playing out in our home had been set only a year earlier. I would have demanded and then, in that hideous progression that so often comes when demanding is the start point, fallen to asking and then to begging. I'd have bayed for my husband's affections, and my husband would probably have left me.

Phillip waited three days to pick up again on our short conversation about his affair, and I knew when he was about to do it, saw, in the seconds before he spoke, a slow readjustment of his features. Saw him summon the words and the courage he needed.

"I love you, Frances," he said.

And then, as if exhausted by this declaration, he said nothing more for a moment and I thought, in that distant way I am capable of now, watching the actress in the movie of my life, what an ill-defined term *love* is.

My parents, I am sure, loved me and certainly would have said so. They would have cited, I suspect, concern for my welfare, their desire to pass on to me the tools that they thought life called for, as evidence. And yet for many years I felt no such emotion from them, did not consider, even after I had married Phillip and found myself relying on the things my mother, in her tutorly way, had taught me—how to cook chickens, how to hang curtains, how to hem skirts—that this connection represented love. I did not realize through those years I spent packing lunches for Chloe that the skills that had gained me the life I wanted were the legacy of a child-hood I had considered barren. And I am not sure that, even when we took Chloe to Singapore after my father's retirement and watched them with her, formal, but kind and proud, too, of their sweet proxy grandchild and my role as wife and mother, I understood the kind of love they were offering.

Phillip finally lifted his head and looked at me, presenting his version of love, but I did not feel the need to say I know, or I love you too, not out loud. We were sitting in my day-room, though it was evening, and Phillip was wearing a green sweater that accentuated the color of his eyes and a pair of faded corduroys. He had a tumbler of whiskey in his hand. He looked so comfortable, so husbandly.

"I did not stop loving you, no matter what you might think."

Again I had no desire or energy for response, and anyway, none was sought. He seemed to need to speak, to unroll all before me, and I understood that, that craving for confession.

"But even when it began, with Josee"—he had hesitated, I felt, over her name, but he went on—"it seemed like something very different. I can't explain it exactly. It was something that I didn't expect and God knows wasn't looking for. It was not like anything I had experienced before."

He looked up suddenly, pained, guilty, conscious perhaps that he had said too much. It must have struck him that he was telling these things, things that he had probably wanted to tell somebody for quite some time, to his wife, his wronged, betrayed wife.

"What I mean is," he said, steadying himself, his compo-sure only slightly off-kilter, "it's not like I met somebody and replaced you. It wasn't like that at all. I really did try to make sense of it, and I know that I have hurt you, and I know that that is unforgivable, and I also know that it is trite and unreasonable to say that none of this is what I wanted, but really, *really*, it is true. I just wish you hadn't ever . . ." He trailed off then, because we both knew that what was implied here was that it would have been better if I had died without knowing.

I looked at him, feeling like I was weeping, but in fact I was not.

"I need to make sense of it too," I said.

"I'm so sorry—"

"Look," I cut him off, "I can't explain very clearly how I feel about this. I just know it's different from the way I felt a while ago. There are other things now that seem much more important." Briefly, in that confessional air I did consider telling him what these things were, but I did not. "I think I want to feel that I have some sort of control over the future. Chloe's future, really."

He looked stung at the mention of Chloe's name, as if it had never occurred to him before that she might be affected by all of this, and I was angry with him for that.

"If you and Josee are going to be a couple, Phillip, I want to meet her again." He made no denials at this point, but looked, simply, crushed. "I want to have a party, and I want Josee to come."

"I'll ask her," he said, resigned, but with no promise in his voice.

. . .

No one was eating breakfast when I came down, though the table was laid, and next to it Hudson, in a wooden playpen, was squealing with a toy in each hand. I had slept badly and woken grumpy, and there was no sign of Mason. I had a headache.

"Leave him," I said to Christina as she went to take Hudson away.

She righted herself slowly. It was not my place to instruct her, and especially not in so brusque a manner. We both knew it. I regretted the exchange immediately.

"As you like," she replied as a small metal train engine flew from the playpen and crashed at my feet. I winced, bending to pick it up.

"Sorry," Patsy said, appearing suddenly. "Is he being a pest?" She looked at the child and sighed.

I was relieved to see her. "No. It's not him. I just have a headache."

"Hold on," she said.

She was back a few minutes later with two red and white caplets.

"Thanks."

"That's okay. I never leave home without a well-rounded supply of the miracles of modern pharmacology."

I swallowed the pills.

She raised her eyebrows cheerfully over the coffee Christina had brought. "After all, if you've got to leave your shrink behind . . ."

She was talking about a life I didn't know. Her life. She laughed. Then, abruptly, sobered.

"Did you say you hadn't seen what happened? Last night."

"You mean the accident?"

"Uh-huh."

"No. We were behind you. We didn't see anything. The first I knew was when Mason braked."

She lifted her cup again. There was a faint trace of pink on the rim of it. "You don't drive, do you?"

"No," I answered, dropping my voice a little. I couldn't drive then and it was something I was embarrassed about. Especially around people like Patsy, who could do everything.

"Still," she said, contemplating, "if something ran in front of you—imagine you're driving." She put her cup back down without drinking from it and lifted both hands, as if to a steering wheel. "Something runs in front of you. What do you do?"

"Brake, I suppose. I don't know. Swerve. Isn't that what happened?"

"Maybe," she said. She looked like someone who hasn't completely figured out an equation, but is working on it.

The trip to the hospital was Mason's idea. Sally's arm, he said, had swollen in the night and looked rather bruised in daylight. He was concerned. Patsy and I, quitting our talk, stared at him for a moment over the remains of our coffee. Mason did not seem to notice the abrupt cut in our conversation.

"Would you come with us, Frankie?"

"Well, yes, but I could call Arturo if you like. He could certainly arrange for a doctor to come here, to the house."

"I think we may as well go to the hospital. She's going to need an X-ray, and it will save time to go straight there." A deep, sincere crease distorted his brow.

"All right."

The hospital was a low whitewashed building with a flat

roof just out of town. It was less than a year old and had been opened, officially, by Maria. I had watched the ceremony, standing with the doctor's wives and a small assembly of other town dignitaries on the gray pavement while Maria cut the blue ribbon with a pair of plastic-handled scissors. The scattery applause, as the severed ends fluttered, had been swallowed quickly by the cloudless morning. I had only been back once since then, not long afterward, with Adam. He had dislocated a finger tugging out a chest of drawers to get at a pen that had fallen behind. I noticed that the bougainvillea in the front had grown since then.

The hospital was always busy, and that day it was bedlam. People were sitting on the floor. Babies were crying. A receptionist peered at us from behind a sliding glass panel before opening it tentatively and passing over a form on a clipboard. She indicated, with a beleaguered look, that we would have to wait. Like everybody else. We waited for an hour before Ned and Bee Bee, who had come with us on Ned's insistence that Bee Bee ought to get looked over too, decided to give up.

"A body could keel over just sitting in this place," Ned said. They took the car into town, fixing a time to come back for us.

Mason was fidgety, pacing. "Find out how much longer, would you?"

It was a bark, and I stared, shocked.

"Please," he said, softening.

I got up, sighed, and glanced at Sally, sitting serenely on the orange plastic chair that a smiling man in a farmer's hat had graciously given up for her. A child had been whisked from the one next to it for me. Sally had sat ever since, calm and uncomplaining, with her hurt wrist nestled tenderly against her breasts. I wanted to slap her.

"Please," Mason said again.

The receptionist slid her protective screen back again reluctantly at my tap. We both knew what I was going to ask, and we both knew what she was going to answer.

"Dios sabe," I said a moment later, repeating her reply verbatim, with a slight edge of spite, to Mason.

He looked at me. Lost, I thought, like a child separated from its mother.

"God knows," I translated wearily.

A sad-looking woman, with a baby on her lap and a toddler at her knee, had taken my chair.

"I'm going outside for a bit. They'll call you."

The automatic doors slid back on their trundling mechanism and released me to the sunshine. I went down the steps and wandered vaguely left, glad to be outside, away. Away from Sally and Mason and their disturbing double act. I had become convinced during the course of the morning that Sally's wrist was not at all seriously injured, and yet Mason had persisted with his panicky reaction. I couldn't understand it. I closed my eyes for a moment and breathed in and out, slowly. When I opened them again, he was standing beside me.

"Don't be cross. I just feel bad, about Sally." He reached out a hand and held the side of my neck.

I saw, in his tired eyes, love and guilt. Love for me, and guilt for Sally. It was guilt, I rationalized, that was motivating this unusual behavior of his.

"Go on back," I said, smiling at him. "I'll be there in a minute."

He lifted my fingers and kissed them swiftly, reassuringly, before taking the steps two at a time.

I waited for a moment, plucking a leaf from a bush, before turning to follow him. At the curb Bee Bee was leaning against the car, while Ned, still inside, bent over, putting something in the glove box. I had not, through the stream of people arriving and leaving, heard them pull up. Bee Bee looked in my direction but offered no greeting. She seemed to stare for a moment before twisting toward Ned, who had spoken to her as he pushed his door open, getting out too. I assumed that she had not seen me.

A man in a doctor's white coat was bent over Sally. He turned and shook my hand. I knew him a little. His son had been a student of Adam's. I asked after the boy. Then, sensing Mason's impatience rising again, I explained about the arm without going into too much detail about the accident. A bump, I said, a bang, in the car. The doctor, though, was not interested in the car. He motioned for Sally to follow him and for me to come too. Mason he discouraged.

"It's a small hospital," I explained. "They try to keep the working areas quiet."

Sally's arm was delicately turned and lifted and inspected, then X-rayed, laid tender and disembodied on the cold metal plate. There was no break. Just some swelling and a few bruises. This news, delivered by the doctor as if it were the miraculous and unexpected outcome of an arduous procedure, cheered me enormously. The guilt that Mason and I had just discussed, without discussing it, could subside. Things would get back to normal.

"Just a little rest," the doctor instructed. And then, in English, "Take it easy."

I laughed, and Sally said thank you with a ladylike nod of her head.

As we made our way along the corridor that led back to the reception area, I said, "Well, that is good news," with inappropriate enthusiasm.

Sally, her shoes clicking softly on the yellow linoleum, turned her head to me without breaking her stride and gave me a look of pure and absolute disdain.

"I did tell you," Sally teased Mason a moment later, "that there was no need for so much fuss. It's just a sprain."

"Great," he said with a grin. "Let's get a drink to celebrate."

We went to the Blue Moon for beers and fried chicken. Sally had Mason slice hers into neat triangles, so that she could manage not too awkwardly with her left hand.

"I saw you all here," I said in response to a flashed smile of Mason's as he passed Sally's plate back to her, "one night just before I met you."

"I know." Sally indicated the corner table with a nod over her glass. "You were just over there."

I felt deflated. It had seemed till then that I had a secret, something of my own, over them. I'd thought, telling it, that I was letting them in on something. Happily, Mason, surprised, asked, "Did you?"

But it was just then that I remembered I should have been at a lesson with Letty. "What time is it?" I asked, pointlessly, knowing it made no difference now. "I should have been teaching this morning," I explained. "I forgot."

"Aah," said Mason sweetly. "And there we were, dragging you to the hospital. Sorry."

I smiled. "Don't worry," I said, speaking only to him. "I'll walk over now and explain. I'll meet you back here. In twenty-five minutes or so."

As I stood to go, Sally asked smoothly, "You have an apartment nearby, don't you, Frankie? So you wouldn't be stuck if we left."

I was shocked. I held motionless for a second, too unnerved to reply. Was Sally throwing me out? It struck me, suddenly and thunderously, that she could. My eyes twitched to Mason, but he didn't catch them.

"No need for that," Ned said pleasantly. "You guys have another drink, and I'll drive Frankie. We'll be back in a shake."

I looked at him, and my heart fluttered with a rush of gratitude.

Letty came to the door and I explained about the American lady who had hurt her wrist and needed to go to hospital.

"Poor American lady," she said.

I felt uncomfortable, standing there while she held the screen door back, her face all sympathy, the porch wood spongy under my feet. I cut her off, declining her offer of a cold drink and quickly rescheduling the lesson, inclining my head to indicate Ned waiting for me in the car.

"All hunky-dory?" he asked when I got back in beside him.

"Yes, thanks."

He started the engine and then he looked at me as if he might begin one of his fatherly chats.

"Home, James," I said jokily, avoiding it.

At the Blue Moon Sally stood as soon as she saw us, though Bee Bee's glass was still half full.

"I'm really very tired," she said. "Let's go back to what's left of the day."

I felt, inexplicably, as if all the disruption so far had been my fault. In the car I was quiet. Everybody was. When we passed Cactus Roy, Bee Bee said, "Somebody ought to buy that guy a decent hat." That, at least, got a laugh.

. . .

I think I have already said that the house that Phillip and I live in now is quite big, rambling even. We bought from a fellow who had made a lot of money in bonds. I had no idea what that meant at the time. I still don't really. Anyway, the bond-money man had invested in country life, but it hadn't suited him, and he was keen to feel pavement under his feet again, so we'd got a better deal than we'd hoped. I remember having the feeling when we first saw it, that feeling people often say they get when they look at a house, that it would be ours, even though the original price, before the negotiation, had been out of our reach.

We both wanted it. I knew that before we'd even been upstairs, before we'd met the bond-money man's children, who came rushing down them just as we were about to go up, a cheerful gaggle of tumble-haired blondes. Passing us, they shouted hello, one after the other, as if they knew us, as if they knew everyone in the world. I realize now that those children reminded me of other children, but the past was too recent then for me to want to recognize that.

The bond-money man's wife had sat in the kitchen while

we looked around, smoking cigarettes and talking to another woman who looked just like her, same clothes, same hair. A sister, perhaps, although women friends are like that sometimes too. They grow similar. Sonia and I, after all, own the same shoes, and Catherine's green cast iron cookware matches mine exactly, and we all like the same films. It's part of how we learn, how we become what we become, that mimicry of other women. We are not like men, who so often leave school and preserve their hairstyles and nicknames intact for life. Instead we dart from fad to fad. I tried to dress like Sonia, to lay a table the way Catherine did; I copied hairstyles from magazines. All foolishness, all innocence. I long for that now.

Before we lived here, before I owned any green cast iron cookware, we lived in Phillip's first house, nearer to his parents. Before that he'd lived in a flat on a busy road in London, where Chloe had been born. This house, though, is the one that marked her childhood. This is the house where the brown felt owl she made at Saturday Club is still stuck on the inside of the pantry door; this is the house with her paddling pool in the shed; this is the house where we buried the spaniel and she planted the cross on the spot, "Beezle" painted across it in wobbly blue letters. Josee will not want to live here. I wonder, will Phillip sell?

The fact of the house's size and the comfortable spread of the downstairs rooms meant that I was not limited in terms of numbers for my party. It sounds rather childish, doesn't it? My party. But that is what it was. I cannot think of a more sophisticated term, or a more appropriate one. It wasn't a celebration really, and it was more than a gathering. A lot more. It became—and this will sound melodramatic, but it is no less true for that—my reason for living. It gave me a point on the horizon to head for, and I did so with all the strength I could muster. Which, it turned out, was a good deal.

When you are ill, everything is taken from you. I don't just mean the full stop that inevitably halts this kind of illness, my kind. I am referring to the control over day-to-day life that slips from your grasp as the illness progresses. I had not cooked a meal in my own home for months; the party gave me something to take charge of. Something that was mine again.

Carla, Phillip's P.A., helped me a lot with things like getting the invitations printed, and I liked her friendly but impersonal way of dealing with me. She was helpful, but businesslike, rather than desperate to please me, which was the tone that had begun to characterize some of my interactions with people who are closer to me. It was Carla who found the jazz band. She had a friend, she said, a saxophonist who played with some other musicians quite regularly. Would I like them for our party? I would, I said, very much.

I suggested to Phillip that we ought to send Carla flowers or something for all the extra work she was doing, a thank you. I was conscious that her duties had probably expanded with Phillip not in the office anyway, and now here I was on the telephone with her every day, more than once usually. He laughed.

"I pay her enough to take three foreign holidays a year as it is," he said. "She lives like a duchess; she can take on a bit of extra work without a standing ovation."

I laughed too. "Let's send something anyway."

We did. We made one of those joint phone calls where one person dials while the other calls out the number, and then the caller consults constantly with the second person over his shoulder so that the conversation becomes three-way and immensely irritating for the stranger on the line, but amusing, unifying, for the conspiring pair. You have those light moments no matter what, don't you? It's how you recognize the dark ones.

"Roses?" Phillip asked me, mouthpiece at his chin.

I agreed. "White," I said, thinking that they would be from a hothouse at that time of year and have no scent.

Carla was very pleased with the roses and called to say so as soon as they were delivered. She was the envy of the office, she assured us, and then she told me that they would do to stir her boyfriend up a bit too if she didn't tell him who they were from. He needed a bit of a nudge now and then, she claimed, a bit of a kick in the behind. And I thought, rather sadly, that women, young women especially, will go to all sorts of lengths to complicate their relationships with men, as if life will not hand them enough complications all by itself in time.

With Carla's help I planned that party with the kind of precision that some women, particularly nowadays, reserve for their weddings. I had not had a wedding that required the hiring of caterers. Phillip and I had been married at the Register Office in Grantham and had lunch in the private room at the Carpenter's Arms afterward with ten of our friends. I'd invited all of those friends to the party, even Mandy and Todd, who had gotten divorced five years later and with whom we'd lost touch soon after that. I'd invited them both.

The only part of the party plan that had not gone well was the apricot dress. I tried it on, with Chloe's help, two Saturdays in advance, and we had both agreed that it wasn't right. I don't know what Chloe's reasons were, but I thought it made me look jaundiced. I had begun to imagine that I looked jaundiced a lot of the time. I didn't, not then, but I knew what looking jaundiced signified for somebody in my condition, and fear can make you see things.

Chloe said, "Would you like something new?"

I wanted to answer, No, what was the point of something new when I was unlikely to see the crocuses? Because the failure of the apricot dress was a blow, and I had felt deflated just then. But I knew that Chloe could not take it. Her face warned off all talk of endings, or last times, so I said that perhaps I would.

Chloe drove me, carefully, into Grantham in her father's car; it was too big for her, but comfortable for me. We parked just outside a little shop that a woman named Judith runs off the high street. Judith is overly tanned and talkative to match, and she has run that shop for the whole eighteen years that we've lived here. It is the kind of ladies' dress shop that most English market towns offer, lots of good cloth skirts and too-floaty outfits for more formal occasions—nieces' weddings, say. I didn't hold out much hope. But the universe can smile in the smallest and most surprising corners, can't it? Judith produced, with a flourish, of course, and a flush of advice, a dove gray sheath dress with three-quarter sleeves and a funnel neck.

"It would look lovely with your pearls," Chloe said.

Pearls for tears, I thought. My mother used to say that. My mother who'd had so many more tears in her life than pearls, but so many more pearls, I reflected, than she'd ever acknowledged.

I looked at Chloe, so eager, so keen for our little excursion to be a success, and back at the beaming Judith, who was holding the gray dress by the hanger, spread across her other arm like a tablecloth.

It was a very nice dress. We bought it. Then, pleased with ourselves, we went into the coffee shop in the alley. The coffee shop in the alley suffers from lack of passing trade and changes hands on a regular basis. It was under new management again, judging by the fresh décor, which seemed to be an attempt at a Caribbean theme, uncomfortably laid over the Olde English oaky style of the previous incarnation. But I was ready to sit down so we went in anyway and ordered muffins and coffee from the new young owner, whose enthusiasm for the muffins was painful and all the more poignant given that we were the only customers.

The muffins, though, like the dress, turned out to be a surprise and did taste of banana. I was about to comment on this to Chloe when she said, "Ed has asked me to marry him."

I looked at her. She was not looking at me but fussing with her paper napkin. It was pink, candy pink like a child's bridesmaid's dress.

"Do you want to marry Ed?" I asked.

"I hadn't really thought about it very much before he asked me," she said, meeting my eyes then, "but now I think maybe I do. I don't know. I mean, is there a way that you know? I don't mean all that daft stuff about wanting a wedding and having a husband and everything. I can see the appeal of all that, and I do . . . I really do love Ed; he's a wonderful man, but it is big, isn't it? It's a big thing to do, and I don't want to make a mistake. I suppose I always thought I would just know, and there'd be no doubts."

"And it would all be happily ever after," I said.

She nodded, smiling at herself.

"It won't matter who you marry, sweetheart. You'll have doubts. At some point you'll have doubts."

She seemed a bit surprised, and perhaps my tone had been overly sober, lacking in the reassuring tenor that has been a constant in my dealings with her. Her father and I have always gone to such lengths to protect her from things. Our own arguments, petty as they seem now, were always kept at a distance. We have presented her with a terribly hopeful picture of marriage. Perhaps we shouldn't have.

I reached over and laid a hand on hers on the small table, amongst the tinkly array of coffee-shop paraphernalia.

"It won't be perfect, Chloe. No marriage can ever be perfect because no two people are perfect. You just have to do your best and hope that you choose someone who will do theirs. There isn't a magic formula or a magic time. You have to decide if this is what you want and what Ed wants and then you just have to keep putting one foot in front of the other. I wish I could give you something better, some sort of universal golden rule, but I can't."

She didn't reply for a moment, just watched me, and then she said, "You like Ed, don't you?"

"Yes," I said. It was true. I liked Ed very much. "And Ed might make a wonderful husband, but I don't want you to marry because of me."

She understood what I meant, and did not hedge it, though she avoided direct reference to the obvious—that I would not be around to meet the next man she fell in love with.

"I know, and I don't think it would be because of you exactly, but I do like that he knows you. And you know him."

I squeezed her hand and she turned it palm upward to mine.

"I like that too," I said.

Ed came to the party, of course, and played the young man about the place in a very charming way, refreshing ladies' drinks, dancing with Catherine and Sonia, being helpful to Phillip and attentive to me, like a son-in-law in the making. And why not? He is thirty-one, after all, and well educated and steadily employed. Why shouldn't he marry? And why wouldn't he want Chloe for his bride? Darling Chloe, wondrously lovely that night in a delicate dress that defied the season.

I won't detail who else came because the names as a body carry meaning only for me, but there were seventy-two affirmative RSVPs and seventy-two of those came. Plus one more.

It was all just as I imagined it would be, just as I had planned: musicians in the conservatory, barmen serving champagne, pleasant women circulating with silver trays full of all the delicious things that Catherine had recommended. The furniture had been rearranged so that there was a natural passage between rooms and enough places for people to stand and to sit, and in the kitchen there was pheasant casserole and mashed potatoes to be served at ten thirty. I felt, as it all began, and the liquor oiled the voices and the music struck up, not happy, because that can convey an element of deliriousness, more like content. I felt that everything was in its place.

We had had parties before of course, and I thought of many of them that night and in the weeks leading up to it. Parties and dinners and whole weekends full of guests that had left us with a litter of partially empty glasses and overflowing ashtrays and new sets of inexplicable marks on the carpet. We had sat in that sort of debris often enough, Phillip and I, dissecting an evening's events, the talk, the jokes, the arguments, and more than once in those talks, from that safe distance, we had analyzed the state of other people's marriages.

Had other people been analyzing ours? Were there signs? Perhaps there had been a turning point that I'd missed during the years when the parties grew smaller, when the same faces always appeared at them, and the same jokes and arguments reared. The years when Phillip and I no longer automatically took the opportunity to make love in the mornings afterward before we fetched Chloe from Emily's or Joan's. Perhaps it was then that whatever had seemed to me so robust had begun to crumble.

People had started to dance, and the noise had risen to that bubbly level that signals the true beginning of a party when Chloe wandered past me and smiled and kissed my cheek, and I thought, if there were signs, she did not see them, does not still. And then watching her walk away again, back into the thickness of the crowd, and seeing her settle on the arm of a chair that Ed was sitting in, I felt very deeply that all my losses were bound up in her. In the beginning I had thought often of things that I wished I had done, places I had not seen, experiences I had missed and would never have, but Chloe was the only thing now that represented an unfulfilled future to me. Chloe was all.

Catherine, my protector, perhaps concerned by my dream-like state, took my arm and asked quietly if I was all right. I did not reply, because through the double arch that leads from the room where I was standing to the one that opens onto the front hallway, I saw Josee.

N I N E

THERE WERE TWO or three days then that were the last days. The end of things, though I didn't know it at the time. Still, looking back, that's how they seemed. A little autumnal despite the heat. I remember that we ate cold soup one night, thick and creamy green as Patsy's eye shadow, and that the children organized a relay race around the perimeter of the house, using rolled-up magazines for batons. But what I remember most is the shift in the players. Sally, who had until then, apart from her one stab of girlishness the day of the moonlight picnic, been more or less a background figure, at least as far as I was concerned, was now firmly established at the center of everything.

Christina was fashioning a protection cover, with plastic wrap and tape, for Sally's bandage.

"Does it hurt, Mommy?" Jessica asked.

"A little."

Christina tsked, tender in her ministrations. Sally acknowledged her concern with a small smile.

"Is it smashed?" Howie enthused.

"No, dear." Patsy's voice came unexpectedly, lightly from the glass doors. "Nothing so serious as that."

When the bandage was covered, Christina tucked in the neat ends of tape.

"Couldn't you just take it off?" Patsy suggested dryly. "It isn't as if it's really *doing* anything, is it?"

Sally slipped her arm into the gold-patterned silk scarf that Christina was tying at her neck, like a sling.

"Thank you, Christina," she said, smiling. Then, gingerly nestling her damaged wrist into its stylish cradle, she said to Patsy, "I think it's best to keep it on," as if there had been no interval between question and reply.

"You'd think she was really hurt, wouldn't you?" Patsy said to me in a low voice later. Sally had persevered all day with a fragile-eyed weariness, gasping stagily at one point when Howie had bounced a ball too near to where she was sitting on a carefully arranged beach mat. Now Christina would not quit her fussing. I was beginning to find the whole business irksome, not least because Mason, despite the hospital's assurance regarding the minor nature of Sally's injury, remained extremely attentive to his wife.

I watched, horrified, as he lifted a candied cherry from a drink and held it to her lips. I turned my eyes decisively back to Patsy, and giggled, pleased, when she took the cherry from her own drink and sucked at it with an exaggerated pout.

If Mason became rather attentive to his wife, he offset this behavior with his pronounced ardor toward me. He was, by then, exceptionally opportunistic. He cornered me in hallways, shadows, and once, determinedly, in a downstairs bathroom. These bold exertions lit in me a shivery state of constant desire. I was, like any addict, hostage to it.

That morning he whisked an orange juice from my hand and swept me, with a flexed arm, into the brief seclusion offered by the corner of the house. There he leaned me against the Buick's sun-warmed bonnet and pressed his hips to mine. I kissed him, my hands on his face, enveloped by my own emotions and the peaceful tremble of insect song.

A little later, Patsy and Richard and I were settled on the patio when Mason, host again, nobody's frenzied lover, came to the door and asked mildly if we'd seen Sally. The name might have passed over me, so much feathery nothingness, had I not noticed, behind him, Christina's dark eyes, stirred with alarm.

"I took the tray, sir," she said.

"And she's not in the bath?" Mason asked.

"No, sir. I am worried," Christina replied.

Mason spoke placatingly, "I'm sure we'll find her."

"She always waits for me to come with the tray, sir," Christina insisted as he followed her into the house. "*Always.*"

I watched them go. The contrasting dark of the indoors swallowed them.

"Looks like Mrs. Severance has got another little show planned," Patsy said.

I hoped not. I had to leave soon for the makeup lesson with Letty and I wanted Mason to come with me. But Sally wasn't in the house. The search gathered momentum. The children's rooms were checked. Bee Bee and Ned's door was knocked on. Maids were enlisted. Mason reappeared at the glass doors with Ned, fastening the tie of his polka dot dressing gown, behind him.

"She must have gone for a walk," Ned said.

"*Sally?*" Mason answered.

Ned shrugged.

"Sally is not the go-for-a-walk type," Mason went on. His voice, I realized with a lurch of disappointment, had suddenly taken on the same feeble taint it had had at the hospital. "Anyway," he continued, "her arm."

"It's bruised, sprained at best," Patsy said. She was wearing a full-skirted yellow dress. It suited her. Her appearance, together with the shiny jut of her lower lip as she tipped the last of her orange juice to it, added a tinge of bright offhandedness to her comment.

"Are both cars there?" Richard asked sensibly.

Ned went to check. I already knew.

"Yes," Ned confirmed, returning.

"Anyway," Mason said, looking at Patsy, "she certainly wouldn't be able to drive with that arm."

Patsy, holding his gaze in the sunshine, replied, "Oh, I'd say she could do whatever she wanted, when she wanted, that wife of yours."

I had never seen Mason angry before, but he was angry then.

"Back off, Patsy. Just back right off!" His face, leaning close to hers, was livid.

I stared. Patsy's cocky expression dissolved. She was shaken; she looked, momentarily, as if she might cry. Richard, next to me, was on his feet and Ned took a step forward.

I got up too. "If she *has* walked, she'll have gone down the hill to the beach," I said, the words coming fast and stern. I was trying to take hold of the situation, to restore some sort of normal boundaries. Mason was frightening me.

"I suppose she could have," he said, grasping at this, spinning his attention from Patsy to me.

"Yes." I was relieved. For a steady half second I thought the matter was concluded. I thought Mason would relax again, apologize to Patsy, calm down, and drive me into town.

Mason nodded once and headed hurriedly for the gate that led to the beach path. It swung shut behind him with a bang. We all watched. The latch didn't quite engage and the gate rebounded and clacked again. Patsy, across from me, was still clearly shaken by his outburst.

"Everyone's been thrown off by that accident," Ned said in a pacifying tone.

"Yes," Richard agreed, getting up, offering to fetch fresh coffee.

When he had gone, I turned to Patsy and said, "He didn't mean it," meaning Mason.

She knew who I meant.

"Oh, *you* don't think so?" she replied.

Taken aback, I picked up a fork from an unused plate setting and began to toy with the prongs.

"Sorry," she said then.

I put the fork down and smiled. "Forget it." We were becoming very good friends.

Richard came back with the coffee. Patsy poured some and asked, "Are you going into town, Frankie?"

"Yes, I have a lesson at eleven thirty."

She fingered the crocodile strap on her slim wrist, checking her watch. "I'll take you if you like."

I hesitated.

"That's a good idea," Richard encouraged. "You girls have a run into town. Pick me up something fresh to read." He dropped his paper, with a little flap, onto the ground beside him.

"I need to get my things," I answered. I was thinking, I'll take my time, give Mason a chance to get back.

From my room I watched the corner where the gate was, expecting him. He didn't come. I looked at my little clock. I would have to go.

"Let's take the Buick," Patsy suggested.

"I thought you liked driving the jeep."

"Just for a change." The keys were dangling from her fingers.

During the drive in she was quiet. She smiled when I told her what Bee Bee had said about Cactus Roy's hat, but she didn't seem to think it very funny. Then she asked, "What do you make of her? Bee Bee?"

Her tone made me wary. "You know her better than I do."

"Not that much better," she answered. "We're all the same, you know, social set I guess you'd call it. We meet at parties and things."

I was surprised. I had assumed that they were all closer than that. That perhaps they had all been away together before.

"I think they're both pretty . . . tough," she said thoughtfully after a while, "Bee Bee and Sally. Same mold."

Patsy dropped me off and I told her I'd walk down to the square to meet her an hour or so later.

"We can have lunch," she suggested.

"Don't you think they'll be expecting us?" I said. I had it in mind to hurry back in case Mason, fretful as I was at the lost opportunity, had conjured some new plan.

"I don't care if they are," Patsy replied.

And I decided, watching her put her dark glasses on, not to argue. Recently there had been a hint of hysteria about her.

"What is a slut?" Letty asked at the end of the lesson.

I stared. "Where did you hear that word?"

"I read it," she said. "In a book."

She was such an innocent-looking girl, fawnlike, hopeful.

"Show me the book."

It was an American paperback. I recognized it. There had been several copies in the store on the square the previous week. I tried not to smile. I had recommended to Letty that she try to read some English-language books.

"In Spanish," I told her, "there are some words that are not . . . polite." She nodded, earnest. "This is an English word like that. This book"—I lifted it—"is full of words like that." Letty blushed, pink under the gold of her skin. "I think perhaps I'll take this book and find you a better one."

"Thank you, Frances," she said, dropping her eyes.

I told this story to Patsy over lunch. I hoped she would laugh, and she did, but with no heart.

"Funny things," she said, "words. You say them and other people say them, but half the time you mean different things."

We were drinking beer. I sipped mine. She was fingering her bottle.

"A couple of days ago," she said, "I told Richard that I loved him."

I didn't think she expected me to answer. "It meant nothing," she continued, "not to me anyway. It was just one of those things you say sometimes before you realize it, because you've said them before. Habit, I guess. I don't know. It's all such a mess."

I understood what she meant, but noted more the bone-deep unhappiness that weighted her words.

On the way home she hit the horn hard two hundred yards before the trash dump and revved the engine. The usual gang of children cleared the road. Then, with the coast clear, she jerked the car violently to the left. The hood missed the pole that Sally had hit by inches. On the ground, tiny shreds of glass glinted in the sunlight, remnants from that earlier encounter. I had been thrown forward, but I hadn't hit the dash. Patsy lurched back into her seat.

"*Patsy.*" My heart was thumping. "What are you doing?"

She didn't reply. She knew that I knew what she was doing.

People had come out to look. People who had been bent, scavenging on the trash heap, righted themselves, and the children were shouting. One of them called out "Locos" and shook his head.

Patsy did look a little crazy.

The boy who I thought of as Jessica's boy was on his perch on the steps of one of the shambly houses, surrounded as usual with bright flowers. As I caught my breath he put his hand up and waved.

Patsy reversed the car sharply and took off at speed. At Jailhouse Rock she said, "She did it on purpose." Then, with horrible deliberation, she banged her wrist against the steering wheel. After a pause, during which we both watched the weal rise red and angry on her skin, she said, "Calculating bitch," and laughed too loudly. I began to feel concerned for her.

Sally was out by the pool with a cushion under her elbow when we returned. Her forearm lay across it like an offering. She smiled as we came around the corner.

"I assume you've eaten," she said. "We've just finished, but Christina will fix you something if not."

Mason, reading at Sally's side, looked up calmly and smiled too.

Patsy stared. I feared a scene. She would come off the worse.

"We had something in town," I said. "Thank you."

Paige, dripping, just out of the pool, flapped a little hello. I sent one back. The other children were busy with a ball and a floating hoop. The pool water heaved and splashed; puddles glistened on the patio tiles.

"Where were you this morning?" Patsy asked Sally pointedly.

Sally adjusted her sunglasses. "Oh, I just took it into my head to walk to the beach. I don't know why. I gather I caused a bit of a flap."

Bee Bee, who I'd assumed was asleep, lying on a half-shaded lounger nearby, said huskily, "I wasn't worried."

Sally smiled.

"Neither was I," Patsy added. "You can look after yourself, can't you, Sally?"

"Most of the time," Sally replied, looking at her.

Inside, helping herself to wine at the sideboard, Patsy said to me, "Don't say anything, Frankie."

I took the glass she held out.

"About the accident," she said, glancing swiftly outdoors toward the others.

"All right," I agreed. I hadn't planned to. I thought her theory absurd.

Throughout the rest of the day and the evening Mason's manner toward me was not cold, worse, the opposite, too friendly. At dinner he grinned and offered to fill my glass, waving the bottle cheerily, as if I were some newly introduced acquaintance at a Christmas party. So it was a surprise to wake later in bed to his weight on top of me. He made love to me with a fierce urgency that left me with rose-petal bruises. Afterward, his breath steadying, he curled against me, suddenly fetal, his head on my chest.

"I thought she was dead," he said.

My hand settled, lifeless, near his elbow.

"In the car," his voice came again, weak at my breast, "when she was lying there. Just for a second I thought she was dead."

I stroked his arm once, mechanically, before he got up and left.

The next afternoon, returning from a late newspaper run, Richard appeared at the otherwise sleepy poolside in neat khakis and a white open-necked shirt. "You'll never guess what I saw," he said.

"What?" Jenny and Jessica asked. They were lying head-to-head near the pool wearing red plastic sunglasses.

Bee Bee, smoking nearby at one of the wooden tables, looked up, bemused. "He really expects us to guess, God love him."

"For heaven's sake, Richard," Patsy said, "of course we can't guess—"

"What did you see?" Sally encouraged, her voice interrupting Patsy's. For a moment the two women locked eyes.

"The car," Richard exclaimed.

Jenny and Jessica sat up and looked at each other as if this wasn't much of an announcement.

Howie, though, playing at the poolside, perked up. "The smashed one?" he wanted to know.

"Our car?" Patsy asked, sitting sharply forward.

"It wasn't really our car," Paige said. She was sunbathing on her stomach with Lesley at the pool's edge, one arm dangling in the water.

Richard seemed to sense that things were getting away from him. "Yes. Well, Sally's car. Whatever."

"New plates I bet," Ned said.

"Maybe. Anyway, there was barely any damage. I did say that at the time." Richard sat then and lay his newspaper, folded, next to Bee Bee's ashtray. "I had a good walk around it," he went on. "It was parked, on the square, and it looked pretty much okay. It was a shame, really, just to ditch it like that. Perfectly good car."

"Just dented then?" Patsy's voice had taken on an edge.

"Well, dented and, you know, headlights smashed, that sort of thing. Driveable though, clearly."

Howie improvised a car crash with two of the toys he had been playing with.

"*Smaash!*" he shouted.

Ned laughed.

Patsy looked at Mason. "Perhaps we did all overreact a bit," she said steadily, closing her eyes, wiggling to get a little more comfortable in the sun.

"Oh. And there was this." Richard stood and walked to Sally, fishing awkwardly in his back pocket.

It was a postcard. From Skipper and Carl.

"The post office guy called out to me," Richard said, taking his seat again.

Sally looked at the postcard, flipping it in her lap with a bland expression. Then she tossed it nonchalantly onto the table beside her. It landed against a pile of magazines, read too many times, their cover corners beginning to curl. For the rest of the day nobody looked at the postcard, or even leaned to inspect the photograph of blue-tinged dolphins on the front more closely. It was just too hard to imagine that Carl and Skipper had ever been there.

I'd had, all day, a slight hangover of unease. *I thought she was dead.* The words, remembered, replayed, took on a tone that unsettled me. But unsettled was something that I had become used to being. I brushed the feeling aside as Mason touched my arm, secretly saying good night.

In my room I tipped some lotion into my palm from the open bottle on the dressing table and sat and caressed my legs with it before standing to check my reflection in the hinged mirror that sent back three of me. I fanned my hair with my fingers. Then I got into bed. To wait.

I was woken by the steady bang of the garden gate. Someone had left it off the latch. My room was nearer to it than the rooms of any of the other adults, at the corner of the house, but Howie slept directly beneath me. The noise might wake him. I looked at my clock, picking it up and turning the face to the moonlight; then I switched on the lamp. Two thirty. Not too late. Mason might still come.

I made my way through the dark house with subdued nighttime steps and quietly slipped the catch to release the glass doors. The gate banged once more, louder, echoey. A flare of wind snatched my robe, flapping it open as I negotiated my way across the tiles and through the outdoor furniture. I folded one arm, pinning the thin cotton, and reached for the looped black metal of the gate handle with the other. But the wind gusted and swelled again so that my hair flooded my eyes and the wayward gate rushed sharply in the opposite direction. I grabbed and pulled, dipping my head at the same time against a flurry of dust. In the dirt, on the untended ground just beyond the wall, something glinted silver. I crouched, letting my robe unreel with a snap behind me. It was Patsy's lighter. The wind sent the gate crashing back toward me. I caught it, scooping up the lighter and dropping it into my pocket, and fixed the latch. Then I hurried back to my room in case Mason was waiting.

I got up twice more that night, once to refasten a shutter that had loosened in the wind and once to get a drink of water. After that I slept.

The wind did not let up. The rattle of it woke me earlier in the morning than I'd have liked. I got up and looked out. The garden furniture was lying on its side against the fence in a neat line; the umbrellas had been taken down and stowed somewhere, probably by the gardening men at dawn. The surface of the normally glassy pool was fractured. Mason was not swimming. I decided to dress anyway in the hope of breakfast with him. But downstairs the house was quiet and, with the whistle of the wind, a little ghostly. Christina was in the kitchen with another maid.

"Good morning," they both said.

I wondered where to have breakfast. The kitchen table was laid, but I was wary of being too close to Christina by myself. It was strange that she was the only one of all those people who consistently made me feel that I did not really belong. She, with the clarity of someone used to the underbellies of grand houses, had recognized me immediately as someone unused to the surface of them. Richard came in, though, just then and said yes to the maid's offer of eggs. So I sat and broke a thick slice of bread from the fresh round loaf in the basket and began to butter it.

"This wind's something, isn't it?" Richard said pleasantly. "Do you often get it like this down here?"

"From time to time," I answered, picking up my bread and biting it. The butter tasted faintly rancid.

Much later in the morning, after everyone had come down, I gave Patsy her lighter. We were all in the big poolside room, except the children, who were racing wildly up and down the hallways. Patsy was sitting beside me in one of the boxy wicker chairs, toying with a paperback book, not really reading it. I slipped the lighter from my pocket and held it out to her silently, opening my palm flat so that she saw it lying there.

"Where'd you find it?" she asked casually.

I fixed her eyes and watched them as I said, "On the other side of the pool gate."

"Oh," she answered. "Thanks." She took the lighter and dropped it into the ashtray on the low table beside her.

After lunch Ned and Mason and Richard and I walked to the front gate as a wind test. It was fierce by then, slapping our clothes to us, pasting the men's shirts to their chests. At the tennis courts I was nearly toppled by it. My whipping hair stung my face. At the bottom of the driveway, we all had to squint against the flying eddies of desert dust.

"Which direction's it coming from?" Richard shouted.

Ned licked his finger and held it up, frowning. "Every damn where," he yelled.

"It's a norther, I think." Mason put his arm around me, supporting me.

"There's a gent," Ned said with a grin. The roar took his voice.

When we reached the corner of the house that rounded onto the pool, Mason gave my shoulder a squeeze before he let it go. As the glass doors were hauled open, he dropped his head and said quickly, and without looking at me, "Sorry I couldn't make it last night."

"Gale force," he announced then, stepping inside.

Everyone was waiting for a report.

"Hurricane level," Richard told Howie, who was pestering him to be allowed to see for himself. Richard picked him up and said, "Just to the tennis court, then." But they were back quicker; something had blown into Howie's eye.

While Howie was attended to, the rest of us sat back down. There was a forlorn feeling in the room. The twins, bored, began to drag from one adult to another, nagging, hopelessly, for something to do. We were all prisoners to the wind. The windows and shutters rattled. It was an unpleasant, nerve-wracking sound. Ned tipped his head back and howled. Howie, coming back from the bathroom with the maid who had bathed his eye, joined in, but the noise upset Hudson, so they were both shushed, and the baby was taken away.

Christina came in with a tray of iced tea. We all sipped for a while, listlessly, looking out at the closed-up garden. The pool looked cold and unfriendly.

"It feels like the end of summer," Paige said.

. . .

To my mind, Chloe was the loveliest woman at the party, but to unbiased eyes Josee may have been, though it is strange to acknowledge that with no thud to the stomach. She looked very beautiful with her hair pulled back, almost severely, and her slim figure outlined to the knees by a sober black dress. Of course, hers was the one entrance that I was most attentively watching for, and so when she did arrive I picked her out immediately through the crush of two rooms. She was just then, for me, the only person in the house.

Phillip was caught between us, literally, halfway between where I stood and where she did, looking at me. He remained fixed for a moment, not knowing whose direction he ought to walk in. Josee solved his dilemma by heading determinedly toward me. Little knots of people parted to let her through.

Phillip followed meekly in her wake, and I thought, in those few seconds, of something that he had told me during that second conversation. The conversation that had confirmed for me his relationship with her as a fact, an actuality, and not something I had concocted, not something that I could ever dismiss, even in desperate moments, as slight or imagined. He had said, with immense if unintended cruelty, "It was that week, that week when you wouldn't come to London with me. That week when you went to Madrid."

That was when it had started. By which people mean that that is when they first went to bed together, don't they? As if there were no point before that when the signposts were clear, when the intention was writ large. Had I asked him to supply me with this detail? I don't think so. But in the owning up, it had all tumbled out. He had told me, sitting in that dayroom in his everyday clothes, in his ordinary voice, everything. More than I had wanted to know.

The week in Madrid had been organized by Sonia. She had been blue—her word, "blue"—and had asked me to come on a trip with her, a break, at the last moment. I am sure that Phillip agreed to the idea, encouraged it even, despite a plan we'd had to spend the week in London together. It had been a loose sort of a plan, with no particular highlights or distinctions, as I recall. The week in Madrid had—blueness notwithstanding—been wonderful. But Phillip had taken that from me now. Tarnished a happy memory at a time when I was particularly keen to store such things. He had also, of course, succeeded in implanting guilt. If I had been there, if I had been at his side in my wifely place, who knows?

"Hello, Frances," Josee said.

"Hello," I replied. I felt completely calm. As still inside as a dry ravine, granite to eternity.

Phillip, joining us, looked terrified. Clearly he had never thought that she would come. I had posted an invitation to her office. I wondered if he had even mentioned the party to her. It didn't matter now.

People had fallen away, as they had all evening with each new arrival's approach, and I asked Josee to follow me. I led her to the stairwell and, when we had mounted to the first floor, I turned to Phillip, still trailing, submissive and distressed, and asked him to leave us. There must have been authority in my voice because he did. He turned without catching his lover's eye and, shoulders dipped, walked away. I wondered if Josee's heart went out to him. Surprisingly, mine did.

Once, in the days when Chloe's drawings were still routinely stuck to the refrigerator, when my unique knowledge of her likes and dislikes, her progress at swimming, had made me central to her day-to-day life and therefore, no matter what, to Phillip's, I would have kept a good hold on my husband, whether I wanted him or not. I'd have fought my corner to win. But this was not then.

Since my past had begun to reveal itself to me in all its hideous vibrancy, since my acceptance that my life was over had taken the sting from all small things, my conscious brain had become aware of what the buried part had known all along—none of it was mine. Not Phillip, not Chloe, not the affection nor the social acceptance I had come to enjoy. I had no right to it. It had not been my due.

I showed Josee into a guest bedroom that we don't use very often and closed the door behind her. When she turned to me, braced, I said, "Chloe doesn't like it when Phillip teases her about her legs."

Her face registered surprise. She had no doubt been readied for the wronged wife's onslaught.

"He doesn't realize, though, or doesn't believe it. I don't know, he thinks she's not serious when she gets upset about it.

But she really is sensitive about her legs. Some girl at school used to call her 'stick insect.' I wanted you to know that."

"Yes," Josee said.

"I want you to understand it."

"I think I do."

I thought that she did too. I don't know why.

"Frances, I want—"

I stopped her.

"There is no point in apologizing. An apology would be too feeble under the circumstances. Don't you think?"

She nodded slowly, on the back foot again, a little cowed.

There were twin beds in the room. The sun had faded their bedspreads in patches over the years; if you lifted the pillows there would be darker spots where the cloth had been covered. I sat on the end of one of the beds, and Josee lowered herself onto a chair near the dressing table. She sat right on the edge, perched for flight.

"There was a time, Josee, when I felt very angry toward you, violently so. And I cannot say that has completely evaporated. You are . . . perhaps not the cause, but a central element in a situation which has brought a great deal of pain into this house."

I knew then that she felt shame. It burned at the base of her neck, started a little flush that crept to her jawline. I realized that I had no sincere desire to prolong it.

"But now I am more concerned about the future," I said. I don't know if she relaxed, but she was attentive at least. "Chloe," I went on, and then held still for a moment because tears threatened. I looked down, determinedly focused on the gray lap of my dress, on my own knees, not willing to lose control, not willing to give her that. "Chloe," I said again, firmly, "is Phillip's child. She is the most important thing in his life."

"Well, yes," she said, as if she understood this. But I don't think she did really. It is the kind of thing people pay lip service to.

"I realize that she is an adult now and that you are not much more than ten years older than her. I am not suggesting that she needs a mother. I don't really want her to have another mother, and, anyway, the woman who gave birth to her is downstairs." She was, dancing with some friend of Ed's, her skinny rear clamped in a pair of black satin trousers. "But if you are going to marry Phillip, you have to care for Chloe, and you have to allow Phillip to love her."

I'm not sure if she had really thought about marrying Phillip before. I guessed that she had, but in that shimmery, mirage sort of way that women are prone to, not the brass-tacks practical way that includes mortgages, and sick kids, and no hot water. Not in the way that marriage actually demands. And maybe she thought about it again then in that new light while I was thinking, with the harder part of me, could I have done it? Could I have let a man love an adult child, a fully formed adult child, rather than the embryonic little being that Chloe had been and that I had been able to influence, to cleave to so? How often had we been the team, Chloe and I? *Silly Daddy.*

"I don't really know Chloe," Josee said.

I was brought back then, struck by the "really." Struck hard. I stared at her for a second with the air sucked out of me, imagining that she and Chloe had been introduced. That Chloe was already involved at a level I had not and did not wish to contemplate.

She seemed to read this.

"I only met her that one time when you came to the office. She was with you."

She had been. I remembered. Chloe had liked Josee's skirt, had commented on it. They were almost contemporaries, after all.

"I am sorry, Frances," Josee said. She had needed to say it. I suppose it made her feel better.

When we went back down to the party, Phillip was of course watching for us, and this time he did look at her, at Josee, though only briefly, cautiously. Perhaps, I thought, she is a little diminished in his eyes in this setting, but that thinking was probably wishful and certainly worthless. I dismissed it.

Chloe, seeing us too, came toward me, a little puzzled.

"I was looking for you," she said.

"Well, here I am. Get me a drink of water, would you, darling?"

"Sure," she said, turning to go, and then, casually, she nodded to Josee. "Oh, hello."

Phillip was still watching but had not approached, and Josee, making his decision for him for the second time that evening, said, "Goodbye, Frances," and turned on a smart heel and left before he could.

T E N

I N THE RATHER grand room where we had entertained Maria and Arturo and where tonight, on account of the inclement weather, we had retired for coffee, Patsy wandered around restlessly, drumming her fingers on the mantel, against the backs of chairs.

"Patsy, do sit down," Sally said.

Patsy stiffened, straightened, and looked hard at Sally. "Sit down?" she repeated.

"Please," Sally replied. "There's enough irritation with the wind."

Richard, who had been making a futile attempt to stem a persistent rattle in the French doors with the torn-off back cover of a matchbook, opened them briefly and closed them again with a slam. The wind squealed and faded behind the glass.

"Can't fix it," he said absently, abandoning the matchbook

cover and giving the door handles a last pointless tug before returning to his chair. Passing Sally, he bumped the edge of an inlaid occasional table that had been moved to accommodate somebody's drink, and, stepping back from it, gave her elbow a slight jog. She winced.

"Oh, sorry," he said, turning clumsily. "I'm sorry . . . I—"

Sally raised her hand. "It's fine." She frowned again, though, as she touched her fingers lovingly to the affronted arm. She had, at last, quit her sling, but she continued to wear the wrist wrapped, like something precious. Tonight it was swathed in moss green silk.

"Hermès, no less," Bee Bee had remarked earlier, laughing.

Mason crossed the room and knelt at Sally's side. "All right, sweet?" he asked.

I recognized the lidded quality that alcohol gave his eyes. I had always rather liked it before. But suddenly, looking at him looking at his wife, his mouth slightly ajar with the tipped-up angle of his face, his expression just seemed weak, beseeching.

Sally nodded, and closed her hand over his for a long, painful second.

Patsy, toward whom I averted my gaze, had drunk a great deal at dinner. I noticed that her cheeks were flushed and her eyes almost feverish. I was worried about her before she laughed, but then, when she did, it was terrible.

"Don't you see?" she said in a tight voice as the awful, jeering sound died. "Don't you see what she's doing?"

"Patsy." Richard's voice was too surprised to carry any authority.

Patsy ignored it. "The whole *accident*. The nonsense with the hurt arm. She faked it."

"Patsy!" Richard said again.

"It's a trick," his wife screamed over him. "One of her endless scheming tricks to keep her husband where she wants him."

Shock settled, clammy, about the room.

"Well, they don't work," Patsy went on, weighting each syllable and leaning toward Sally. "He still looks elsewhere."

I froze.

"Your wife is drunk," Sally said coldly, calmly, to Richard.

Richard, looking apologetic, stood and took two steps toward Patsy, but she held up her palm, warning him off. Suddenly her face, which had been malicious, melted, and the other, girlish Patsy emerged. With her arm still extended, she turned her gaze to Mason, who was, by then, on his feet, staring at her.

"It's because she guessed about us," Patsy said to him feebly. "She wanted to get your attention, because she guessed about us."

My head shot from Patsy to Mason and back again. Then the words began to creep through my veins, and as they did, I knew that what I was feeling was not horror at some unimagined revelation, but dread sickness at the confirmation of something already long suspected. And determinedly rejected. I looked again at Mason, who did not look at me, and pictured Patsy and him embracing by the pool in the moonlight.

Mason began to say something but was cut off abruptly by Sally.

"Us?" she asked Patsy, in a tone of disdainful indifference.

Patsy lowered her arm and turned quickly to Richard,

who had remained frozen an arm's length from her. "I am sorry," she said, looking at him, tears coming to her eyes. "I know that I shouldn't tell you this way, but, in the end, what difference will it make? I want a divorce." And then, half to Sally, she said, "Mason and I are in love." She exhaled, as if the making of this announcement had afforded her great relief. She closed her eyes for a second and then opened them again. Freed.

"But Patsy," I heard Sally's dry voice say, distant through the thoughts that were rioting in my head, "Mason is having an affair with Frankie."

I was sure that someone laughed. I felt myself panicking, but I sat nevertheless, absolutely motionless.

"Well, not an affair exactly," Sally went on. "More of a fling. A vacation fling, I suppose."

No one seemed yet to have caught the pace. Patsy was watching Sally, and everyone else was watching Patsy.

Sally continued in a savage tone of false sympathy, "So you see, don't you, dear, that my husband's commitment to you might not be such that you'd want to break up your happy home for it."

Patsy let out a short inhuman howl and launched herself at me. Ned, swift to his feet, intervened and caught her by the shoulders. I leapt up too, some instinct for self-protection finally sparking my legs into motion. We stood, staring at each other, Patsy and I, with Ned between us, both trembling, both breathing hard.

Patsy twisted her head to Mason. "You swore," she screamed. "You absolutely *swore*. You said she was nothing."

I realized she was talking about me. I was the "she." The nothing. She heaved an arm loose from Ned and extracted from the side pocket of her black evening trousers a crumpled sheet of buff paper. I recognized the paper. For an addled second I thought it was Mason's note to me. Patsy, a look of intense concentration on her face, was unfolding it. Her hands were shaking. "Darling girl . . ." she said feebly. Then a sob took her voice.

It was not Mason's note to me. It was a note from Mason to Patsy. She was going to read it. She inhaled with a shiver, pushed her shoulders back, and held the thing at her chest like a schoolgirl about to begin a recitation. "Darling girl," she repeated in a presentation voice.

Sally interrupted. "You *really* didn't know?"

Patsy's determination wavered. The hand with the note in it drooped.

"I thought *everybody* knew." Sally swiveled toward us, and we, involuntarily, all turned to her, the star performer. She crossed her legs. "Bee Bee knew, didn't you, Bee Bee?"

Patsy spun her head to Bee Bee, confusion blurring her features, her mouth hanging slack.

"If you can't stand the heat . . ." Bee Bee said quietly. She lifted her drink and sipped it.

Sally's voice, clear and even, picked up again. "Oh, I can imagine that Frankie didn't realize about *you*. She's such a little innocent, aren't you, Frankie? Except when it comes to other people's husbands."

The prick of this brought me back sharply to real time. I snapped my eyes to Mason, who, it dawned on me, incredibly, had said nothing. Nothing at all since the beginning of this murderous stampede. He was staring steadily down at his wife.

"Sally," he said at last.

"You see," she went on as if he hadn't spoken, "Mason is a marvelous husband but for this one tiny fault. He simply cannot resist a pretty face." She was reveling. Mason shut his eyes tightly, as though in physical pain. "Like Maisy O'Dea's. You know Maisy, I think, Patsy. She played tennis with the same group as you last summer at the club. *She* had a pretty face, although I always thought her nose rather prominent."

"Sally," Mason said again. His tone had gathered some insistence, but he still could not gain a real hold on the situation.

"And Dolly Matheson's," Sally sang. "You might have come across her once or twice. She and her husband are often at the Jeffreys' parties."

"Sally!" Mason commanded, without looking at her. He wheeled his eyes instead, wide and cold, around the room. They caught mine for a flat second, and I did not recognize them. "This is ridiculous," he went on quietly, turning to face his wife, reasoning with her.

Sally, though, seeming to sense the imminent collapse of her moment, raced ahead. "There was Caroline Milford too, of course, Senator Milford's daughter, but she's graduated now, I believe, and moved to California or somewhere."

A sound, rage, exploded from Mason. Scowling heavily, he raised both his hands and strode out of the room.

Patsy shrieked his name, but he did not look back.

"I think you should go to bed, Frankie."

I heard the words, but for an instant did not relate them to myself.

"Go to bed, Frankie." It was Ned who had spoken, in a voice devoid of affection.

Patsy broke free of Ned's grip and rushed after Mason. We all watched the door swing in her wake. Nobody moved to follow her. Sally revolved her head slowly to face me. "Yes, Frankie. Go to bed."

I looked at her.

"We've finished with you," she said.

I nodded, but continued to stand there, wanting, wishing for someone to come and put an arm around me. Eventually I turned, as if through molasses, to go. I was afraid that my legs would not hold me as far as the door. Just then Mason came back through it.

"I'm sorry to have to ask you this, Richard," he said, "but do you think you could persuade Patsy to go to bed? She's in our room."

Richard lifted his chin and looked at Mason. "She can rot there," he said expressionlessly. "You can both rot there." He went out through the French doors.

A moment later I heard the wooden gate bang. That's when I realized that the wind had dropped.

"Good night, Frankie," Sally said firmly.

Mason sat back down in a wingback chair, sighing and dropping his hands over the sides.

Leaving, I could not feel my limbs.

I went to my room and sat on the bed. I lowered my head to let the tears come, but they would not. I felt instead a rush of shivery desperation. Desperation to speak to Mason. I wanted to shout at him and beat on his chest with my fists until he had explained everything to me. And begged my forgiveness. And made it all go away.

As I stared at the floor beyond my knees, the idea began to form in my head that he would want to talk to me too. That he would come to my room, just as soon as he could, so I got up and fixed my hair a little. Then I waited at the dressing table, moving my hairbrush about absently and busying my mind practicing the things that I would say to him.

After a while I got up and looked down at the familiar, night-lit view from my window. I could not imagine what I would do if I had to face the morning without having spoken to him first.

I opened my door and closed it softly behind me. In the hallway I stood and listened to the silence and my own heart-beat for a breathless moment. Then I took my shoes off and began to walk.

When I got to the drinks room, I held still briefly before going in. It was dark. I made my way past the familiar shadowy shapes of the daybed, and the big sideboard, and the wicker chairs, and I opened the glass doors and went outside. The air was very still. I moved, with precise thief's steps, along the wall toward the long drift of yellow light spilling from that other room, the room where we all had been. The room where they still were. I heard voices: Mason's, Bee Bee's.

I shut my eyes, concentrating, but I could not make out what they were saying. All the windows had been sealed ear-lier because of the wind. I edged nearer, my hands flat against the cool of the stucco. Mason had just begun to speak again when another voice, at my back, startled me so much that I screamed. It was Christina. She was sitting, spectre-ish in her black dress, on one of the slatted outdoor chairs. "Good evening," she said. That was all.

Then she stood up slowly, her eyes on mine, as, behind me, the French doors rattled and opened. I turned and ran as fast as I could, my bare feet skimming the ground. I slammed the door of my room shut and leaned against it, panting, for several minutes. Waiting. For phantoms. No footsteps echoed in my wake. No commanding knock sounded. Nobody had followed me. I felt, at the realization of this, utterly, ridiculously abandoned. Eventually I peeled myself from the door and lifted the clock from my bureau. I stared at it for a moment. After three.

In the morning I heard him swimming. It was a sound that I had listened for, half-conscious, many times. My ears were practiced at alerting me to it. I woke and could not believe at first that he would be doing anything so ordinary. Swimming. Then, filled with an absolute and driving resolve to confront him, I got up and rushed down to the pool.

Christina, holding a coffeepot, stood blocking my way for a second at the patio doors, but I was too demented with mission and lack of sleep to be put off. I pushed her aside and stepped past.

Mason lifted his wet head and took me in, my unkempt hair and my slept-in dress. He crawled evenly to the pool edge, hauled himself from the water, and picked up a towel. He gave Christina a nod that sent her away, although she turned a last reluctant glance in my direction from the door. Beginning to dry himself, he looked at me as a stranger might have.

"Mason?" My voice broke.

He sighed and rubbed roughly at his head. "I did warn you."

I stared, uncomprehending.

"I *told* you. Not to try to understand everything."

I felt like a child. A child who has touched something hot when it is old enough to know better. I tried to speak but couldn't.

Mason's hand on his head left off rubbing. He lowered the towel, his hair still damp and boyishly messy. Something in him softened. The set of his arms relaxed. The towel trailed on the ground. I thought, for one raw moment, that the conversation would begin, at last, take the begging coaxing turn I had anticipated.

"Listen, Frankie," he said, sighing a little, "you've had an affair with a married man. You *would* have had an affair with a married man whether I'd come along or not. You're the type, the explorer type. In the end you'll probably just chalk me up to another one of your gypsy adventures." He smiled then, quite cheerfully.

I was astonished. "And Patsy?" I asked in a small, adolescent voice.

His pally expression faded. "Let's not get into that," he said curtly, flipping the towel briskly over a chair back.

I felt my face crease at the harshness of his tone. I was exhausted. I could no longer fight the tears.

"Look," he said quietly, "just because you feel something for one person, it doesn't mean you can't feel anything for anybody else."

I was shaking. None of my imaginings had prepared me for a scene as colorless, as unfeeling as this. He was watching me. The few inches between us were furlongs. I became acutely aware of his persistent, shrinking withdrawal. Raising my eyes to his, I was filled with a sudden urge to run my nails down his cheek, to see blood. To make him real. I lunged and he caught my wrists.

"I am not going to discuss it," he said, looking steadily into my eyes.

"You're in love with her, and I was just a . . ."

I was flailing. It was ghastly. He kept his grip firm for a second on my wrists, then, as the strength seeped from me and I dropped my eyes again, he let go. I had lost control, and I knew somewhere inside that my doing so had made it easier for him and that I would regret it later. But I didn't care then. I wanted so badly to hold on to the conversation, to make it go on at least until I had extracted something from it, from him, that made sense to me.

"And New York?" I asked, hopelessly. It was all so shadowy.

He looked mildly surprised. As if something had dawned on him. He reached out and put a gentle hand on my shoulder. The warmth of it was painful. "You'll be fine, darling, really," he said. "You're a survivor."

He squeezed my upper arm, lifted his towel again, and wrapped it around his waist. I was dismissed. I was supposed to know that it was over, to go, but I could not move. He looked at me for a second longer, then sighed and walked away.

I was still staring glassily at the surface of the pool when I heard the shout. I put my hands to my head, shocked alert from paralysis.

"Frankie!" Richard yelled from the pool door. "For Christ's sake, call a doctor."

He was, I noticed, unshaven and dressed like me, in the clothes he had worn the evening before. He turned and ran, and I ran too, not toward the telephone, but after him, along the hallway. Doors were banging.

Richard stopped running at the door of the room he shared with Patsy. I saw Christina, as he went in, sitting on their bed with Patsy's head cradled in her arms. "Llama el médico!" she ordered.

I turned and raced for the phone.

In the little vestibule, in the warm dark air, I hesitated. I was breathing fast and hard. I could hear voices, woken children. I picked up the receiver and dialed Arturo Rodriguez's number.

Richard's shouts, which had lost definition and merged into a kind of incessant bellow by the time I finished speaking with Arturo, peaked, and I made out the word "ambulance." Then his dominant insistence quieted suddenly, and in its place came the twittering high-pitched concern of children.

"What's going on?" Paige asked, looking from me to Mason. We had met unexpectedly when I returned from the telephone. I was uncomfortable, both with his proximity and with Paige's unwitting casting of us as conspirators.

"Nothing, sweetheart," he answered, and I felt a small, bitter twinge at the endearment, at the idea that he could reserve his coldness so cleanly for me.

Richard came to the door, distraught. "Where the hell is that ambulance? I'm gonna drive her to the hospital." He looked around, panicky, searching for something. Car keys.

Ned had come into the room. He laid a hand on Richard's shoulder. "Give it a few minutes." He looked at Richard, steadying him with his eyes. "If it's not here in five minutes, we'll go."

Richard seemed to accept this.

"Who's sick?" Jenny asked.

Howie looked at his father. "Who's sick?" he repeated.

No one answered.

"*Who's sick!*" Howie yelled with his head thrown back.

Richard stared at his son for a moment, then he turned and

left the room. He didn't seem to see Bee Bee, who passed him coming in, wrapped in a Chinese silk robe. She flattened her collar as she whipped her head to Richard's back and then, questioningly, to Ned.

Howie began to cry.

Ned picked him up. "It's all right, son," he said. "Mommy's a bit sick, and Daddy is busy looking after her, and the doctor is coming soon. Isn't he, Frankie?"

They were all looking at me. I was responsible. "Yes," I replied firmly. "The doctor is coming."

The doctor arrived in Arturo's sleek, dark car and Sally appeared suddenly, a point of stability in the ether, dressed and clear-eyed, just as the doorbell chimed. She indicated, with a kindly inclination of her head and a gentle palm, that she would take things from here. No one challenged her smooth efficiency. I watched as she guided the doctor along the hall toward Richard and Patsy's bedroom.

When they'd gone, I went outside and sat at the long wooden table where, so far that morning, no one had eaten breakfast. Paige followed me, and Lesley followed her.

"Do you think that you two could take the little ones down to the beach?" I asked.

Paige looked at me for a minute. I made no attempt to undo the seriousness of my expression.

"All right," she said.

Grasping some need for speed, Paige tossed swimsuits and towels and sodas into a basket that had been deserted, half unpacked from a previous excursion, in a cupboard in the hall. When she left with the other children, a small centipede of ascending height, she turned her head briefly over her shoulder to look at me before the gate closed again, obscuring her from sight.

When Sally came back with the doctor, neither of them spoke. I looked at the doctor and the doctor looked at me, and he saw in my eyes that I already understood that Patsy was dead.

The doctor took me aside and spoke with careful urgency in rapid Spanish. We agreed that he would speak with Arturo immediately. Arturo, he was sure, would be able to assist with all the necessary arrangements. I was sure of this too. As I shook his hand, I heard the steady murmur of Sally's voice break off. She left Mason and Bee Bee and Ned and joined us. She thanked the doctor graciously and saw him out. Turning away I saw Mason, stricken, in the doorway.

I gazed at my sallow reflection and went through it all in my head. I had come to my room, to be alone and, finally, to wash and dress. Outside there were no sounds of laughter or play or conversation. The house was blanketed with the muffled hush of shock. Patsy had taken an overdose of sleeping pills. She had stopped breathing some time in the early hours of the morning. Her advanced state of intoxication, it was thought, had hastened the process.

Richard had spent much of the night walking on the beach. Then, later, he had fallen asleep on the sofa with the yellow-fringed cushions in the room where the whole horrible scene had unfolded the evening before. A maid had found him there when she'd gone in first thing to clean. She had started at the sight of him, and he had opened his eyes. He had left her to her work and made his way back to his bedroom. His and Patsy's bedroom. Where Patsy was sleeping. At first he had noticed nothing in particular wrong. At least, so many things were wrong that he had not been aware of any freshly jarring aspect. He had sat, for long a while, on the bed, staring at the curved outline of his wife under the cocoon of white linen. Thinking. Thinking about losing her, about losing everything. And eventually these thoughts, retraced so many times in the previous hours, had begun to spark and burn in his brain, and he had reached out to shake her awake, to assail her with them.

After Christina had heard the first shout and come running, he had found the note. Before that he had clung to what he knew now was impossibly frail hope. The note was scrawled and in parts illegible, but she said that she was sorry. It was written on a sheet of yellow legal pad, lying, trivially, on top of a pile of his work papers, mostly files, connected to a dull corporate tax case. If it hadn't been for the note, Richard would have sworn that the whole thing had been a mistake. That she hadn't really meant to do it. But a note made it all pretty clear. She had. She had intended to leave him one way or another. And the boys too. Her own children.

The toneless voice in which Richard had related all this broke at this point and he wept. We responded with silence, just as we had when he had first appeared, ashen, and sat down before any of us had trawled the collective mayhem of our thoughts sufficiently to unearth something appropriate to say.

It was Christina who took Richard by the elbow and led him away. A few minutes later she reported to Sally that she had administered one of the tranquilizers the doctor had left. He would sleep for several hours. In my room, staring into the mirror at my own ravaged eyes, I pitied him his awakening.

It had been decided that nothing should be said yet to the children. By whom, I couldn't remember. The entire morning, reviewed, had a vague, underwater quality. Downstairs, maids and Christina were doing whatever it was people did to corpses. Patsy had been moved to an unused bedroom on the ground floor. I had peered into that room once, leaning around a half-open door. It had a view from the end of the house toward the sea.

I had already spoken again to Arturo. He had called as soon as the doctor had passed on the terrible news, and arrangements were being made, smoothly, with none of the delays or obstructions that tended to mar these kinds of things for other people in this part of the world. Arturo would make sure that the grieving family was not disturbed by gruesome detail or meddlesome questioning. Undertakers would come. Patsy would be flown back to the United States. In a coffin, I supposed. I could not imagine it. Any of it. When I tried, I felt light-headed.

I rubbed my temples and looked out of my window. At the long table under the bougainvillea, a maid was laying things for lunch. No one had eaten breakfast. The children would come back and perhaps people would want to eat. Did people eat in the presence of death?

I saw Sally come out and speak to the maid. Then she turned her head and looked up. Too slow to react, I did not draw back, and we held each other's eyes for a second before she swiveled neatly and went back into the house. I stepped away from the window and began to wonder what I should do. I seemed to have performed all the duties required of me. I had no strength, though, and was far from clearheaded enough for cogent planning. So I just sat down on a wooden chair with a rush mat seat that I had never sat on before, in the corner of the room in which I had lived so fully for so many weeks, and waited.

When the tap at my door came, I was too tired and too befuddled to be startled or even to anticipate who it might be. It was Paige.

"Something's happened, hasn't it?" she asked, coming in and sitting, as she often had, uninvited on my bed.

"Yes." I took up my corner position again. So much had happened.

"Something serious," she said. The sun was on her face. She lifted her hand, briefly shading her eyes, then decided to lean, instead, on her elbow. The shadow from the window frame halved her neck.

"Yes," I said again.

"Something you don't tell children, I suppose." She curled her lip unattractively and might have descended into a sulk, but for the gravity which even I could detect in my voice.

"You will be told, Paige. It's just that I am not the person to tell you."

She looked at me levelly. "You're the only person who ever tells me anything."

I was surprised.

"You treat me"—she gazed at the bedspread, rubbing her fingers lightly back and forth over it—"not like a kid."

"I don't think you are a kid," I said. Then I shut my eyes very tight. Because I liked her so much at that moment that I was afraid my heart would break, and the fragile edifice of my composure would crack, and every tear in me would escape and drown us both.

"Is it something very bad?" she asked quietly.

"Yes, Paige. It is something very bad."

We were called to lunch by Christina. It was not clear whether she had intended to include me in her summons, but Paige, standing, had gently and definitely taken my hand, and I had let her. Christina voiced no protest, and so I found myself, minutes later, seated once again at the same table as Mason and Sally Severance.

Richard was not awake yet; the rest of us, it seemed, were to keep up appearances for the sake of the still ignorant children. Sally gave discreet orders to staff, and Ned poured wine steadily. My eyes, from old habit, were drawn several times to Mason, and the images I caught of him in those glances assured me that he was broken. Felled and immobile.

"Christ," Bee Bee said, "I still can't get it into my head." She picked up her glass as Ned shushed her with a look shot in Howie's direction.

Hudson, poignantly, had been brought to the table in his high chair. He began to bang at it with his spoon. Sally signaled for someone to take him to the kitchen.

"I could feed him," Lesley offered when the maid came to take the child away.

"No, princess," Ned said, his voice subdued almost to nothing, "you just take care of yourself." He leaned and kissed her very tenderly on top of her head.

"Where's Dad?" Howie asked, looking up then, his fork aloft with a too-large piece of ham speared on it. "And Mom?" The expression on his small face was tinged with suspicion.

"Taking a nap," Sally responded crisply, without looking at him.

"Christ," Bee Bee said again.

Very little had been eaten, but a great deal drunk, by the time the plates were cleared. Ned summoned the energy to invent some fort-building game for the younger children and sent them to play on the emerald grass at the front of the house, and Paige and Lesley were encouraged to retreat to the deep indoors with magazines. When they had gone, the adults sat a while longer, still, sad shadows under a vivid riot of bougainvillea.

At some point we stood, the five of us, as if on command, and left the table and moved without purpose around the chairs and tables and tubs of scarlet blooms and sat down again. The cruel afternoon wore on and none of us spoke, or bothered to look at one another. Ned poured Scotch until we began to simply pass the bottle, and then a second, from one seemingly ownerless hand to the next.

No shaving of coconut, or finely sliced lime, or rattle of ice against the smooth sides of a silver shaker dressed up our drinking that day. It was just plain liquor in plain glasses, and yet, I did not manage to reach the lack of consciousness I desired. I was still hypnotized by the inner round and round of my own petty thoughts and miseries when Richard's big, boy athlete's frame filled the patio doors.

"Where's Howie?" he asked.

"He's—" Ned stood, palms on the table, just as Howie, though he could not have heard the inquiry, came racing around the corner of the house. He stopped abruptly at the sight of his father, almost losing his balance, and his grin faded. Richard looked grim. Perhaps Howie anticipated a telling-off for running on the poolside tiles; he had been scolded for it many times before. He scowled.

"Come here, son," Richard said, reaching his broad hand toward the boy's shoulder.

For the second time, we stood on an unspoken order and drifted, this time in different directions. Ned and I walked, devoid of intention, to the front of the house. The others must have gone inside.

"It's great, isn't it, Frankie?" Jenny asked.

There was a sort of hut made of towels and vegetable crates on the grass. It had a flap door. Jessica demonstrated how it worked for Ned and me. "Do you want to go in?" she asked. "It's sort of hot in there though."

Ned said, "Maybe later, cookie."

Jenny and Jessica stood in their checked frocks in front of us. Their faces were questioning.

"Is Howie going to bring Dad to see our fort?" Jessica asked.

"I don't think so, kid," Ned answered. Then he took the girls by a hand each and, gravely, led the three of us back to the house.

We walked past Richard and Howie. Richard's eyes were closed and both his arms were clasped rigid around the child on his knee, whose head was buried in his father's chest. Richard seemed to be holding him there with some force. I had a fleeting concern for the boy's ability to breathe. I did not act on it.

Inside, it was a moment before I could see properly, and the short walk seemed to have sent the drink at last to my legs. I was unsteady and sat heavily on one of the wicker chairs. Mason was in the other one, his head drooping. At the sideboard, Sally stood next to Bee Bee, who was tilting precariously. Paige and Lesley were there too, silent and curled against each other on the daybed. Magazines lay, unread, in their laps. They were both watching the adults with dark, worried eyes.

"Ned," Sally said after a moment. "Would you?" She inclined her head neatly to take in all the children and raised her eyebrows, then turned to leave the room.

Bee Bee shot Ned a grateful, drunken, half-faced smile and followed Sally. And while I sat staring after them with breathless amazement, Mason, with the assistance of two palms on the arms of his chair, got up and left as well, slinking without a backward glance to his wife's side.

"*Tell us!*" Paige ordered, her mother's command in her voice.

The twins, by some instinct, nestled themselves on my knee. The chair was wide and they just fit. I stroked the fine, soft skin on their arms.

I cannot recall the exact words that Ned used, but I know that he did not fall back on any of the euphemisms that people generally do when they tell these sorts of things to children. The twins began to cry. I lowered my head to theirs and I cried too.

Eventually, the children drew together and huddled, forlornly comforting each other. I would have been superfluous then if it weren't for the arrival of the undertaker, who had been given my name by Arturo. He shook my hand solemnly at the front door and assured me with deep gravity that Señor Rodriguez had everything in hand. Not a worry, not the slightest concern should I trouble myself with. Christina led the undertaker and his assistant, without me, to the room where Patsy lay and apparently escorted them and their sad cargo, by some prethought plan, out via a servants' route, unknown to those who most needed sparing from the sight.

Richard and Howie did not move from their position at the poolside until, just as the crackle of the undertaker's car wheels started on the driveway, Howie broke free with a howling flap and ran. Not toward the front of the house and the vehicle that bore his mother away, but across the terrace and through the wooden gate to the beach path. Ned flew after him, while Richard let his arms drop lifelessly to his sides.

Paige, separating herself from the twins, who had worn themselves out with tears, walked out through the glass doors, into the fading sunlight. Her back to us, she stood behind Richard and, without hesitating, laid one soft hand on his shoulder. I watched as, still staring ahead, he lifted his arm and slowly closed his fingers over hers.

ELEVEN

STOOD, NO USE any longer to anybody, and went to my room. There, in the center of the floor, I found my canvas bag. Packed. And a note, written in a hand that I did not recognize, asking me to be ready to leave at eight o'clock in the morning.

When I woke for the last time in that house, I told myself that it was the last time, and did not believe it. It was before dawn. The sky outside was still tinted with dark. I tugged a pillow to me and held it, feeling sick, hungover. After a while I got up to get a glass of water and drank it staring blankly out at the pool. I watched as the sun rose, rich and gorgeous and golden over it, just as if nothing had happened.

By seven thirty I was dressed and standing next to my unmade bed, staring at the luggage that I had not packed. I had been instructed to be ready by eight. That left a yawning half hour. In the face of it I felt ill again.

The sickness combined with the precision of the instructions robbed me of all initiative, though I thought briefly about going downstairs and telephoning for a taxi. I assumed, I think, that a taxi had already been organized. That at eight o'clock exactly, some prearranged, unfamiliar vehicle would bear me at last away. The driver would smile and light a cigarette and ask me a lot of questions about the house.

Outside it was quiet. More than quiet, silent. I sat and watched the clock for twelve and a half minutes, and then I stood, resolute, and hoisted my bag by two worn handles and walked out of the beautiful room for the final time, through the cool hallways, and down the airy stairwell.

"Good morning."

I came to a sudden petrified halt, one hand stiff on the door handle.

Sally was waiting in the room where we had gathered all those nights for cocktails, in the room where the children had played so often and so noisily, in the room where Mason had once taken advantage of a brief absence of hers to kiss me. She was standing in the center of it, perfectly poised, in linen trousers, a rope of gold chain at her neck. The keys to the Buick were looped around her fingers and, eyes on mine, mine on hers, she lifted her dark glasses at a sauntering pace and put them on.

I was astonished. But I said nothing and followed her.

In front of the house she opened the car's passenger door, as if to emphasize that I was supposed to get in, and left it gaping while she walked around the hood and slid behind the wheel. I dropped my things first, behind my seat, then sat and tugged the door closed after me. We stared, both of us, stonily dead ahead, as she started the engine and that great sturdy ship of a vehicle crept to the gate and onward.

The wind had taken Cactus Roy's hat. He seemed bereft. Looking at him I thought sadly of the twins. I would have liked to have said goodbye. But the twins, I knew, belonged to a life from which I was already disconnected, severed, so I quit the thought and set my gaze ahead again, glassily divorced from the whole world, till we reached the rubbish dump and I found myself searching, hoping, for Jessica's boy. I wanted to wave to him as her proxy. He wasn't there.

Sally had had to slow her uniform pace because of the usual gang of ballplayers, and I thought of the day that Patsy had demonstrated her version of the accident.

"Patsy said you'd faked it," I said, my voice coming from some unknown, faraway part of me. For a second I wasn't sure if I had spoken out loud, but there was a tiny contraction of her features at the mention of Patsy's name and it spurred me on. "The accident. In fact," I said, "she showed me how you'd done it."

"What of it?" Her eyebrow arched casually.

"You might have hurt Bee Bee . . . or someone else," I replied, less confident now. Her composure had set me back.

"Bee Bee was so drunk she'd have bounced off a brick wall, and no one else was around. It was the middle of the night." She was completely calm.

"You did that, just to get"—I could not say Mason's name, lest my voice break, so I said—"your husband's attention."

She glanced sideways. "Mason needs reminding from time

to time just how much he depends on me." I felt like a moth on a pin. She smiled. "Bee Bee was in on it," she said patiently, as if explaining something obvious to a rather dull child.

Sally and I did not speak again until she pulled up outside the sorry stone of my apartment block. We both looked at it, she as if from a great distance. Then she cut the engine and nestled back a little in her seat, angled toward me, as if prolonging a pleasant day out. I didn't move. Even the chill rain of her company seemed at that moment preferable to the terrible emptiness that I knew would follow.

She removed her dark glasses and tapped them, rhythmically, two, three, four times against her knee. I realized, perhaps for the first time, that she had a right to be angry with me. That I had it coming. I braced myself, dully, to take it.

"I don't usually get the chance to confront one of you," she said. I knew what she meant and wished that I didn't. "The opportunity doesn't arise," she went on. "I just have to tolerate it. Women at parties, women in department stores, women at tennis tournaments. All those women who think they have something over me because they've slept with my husband."

There was a pause, brief and tortured, between us.

"Because, you see, when men say, 'It meant nothing,' which is exactly what he'll say about you"—I shut my eyes at that and sailed, screaming, from an imaginary cliff top—"it's true. But that's not what the woman thinks, is it? The dizzy Delilah. That's not what *you* think, is it? You persist, just like all the silly, pointless others, wed to some smug notion that something *happened* between you and my husband."

I avoided looking at her. She was right. Despite everything, she was right.

"It didn't," she announced flatly.

I turned then. There was something so distinct, so knowing in her tone. There was more.

"I set you up."

And still more, I knew. I waited, mute.

"You still haven't figured it out, have you? The whole thing was my idea. Think," she urged. "Who invited you to the house? Who suggested that you stay? Who sent you off on all those cozy little twosome jaunts into town, along the beach?"

Sally, my brain answered. Sally had. A feeling like ice dripping began to make its way down my spine.

"So you see, there was nothing particularly special about *you*. You were just a . . . pawn is rather corny. You were bait. I needed you to get him away from Patsy."

It was as if I had been slapped.

Sally's face, for the first time, betrayed something real, a flash of pain, or fear, or hurt. She turned away, gazing ahead over the steering wheel and ran a finger along the lower curve of it.

"You recognize it when it finally comes along, the genuine threat." She straightened against the car door. "Patsy Luke very nearly had him."

Suddenly, inhaling, she smiled and engaged my eye line. "But then I saw you. Little Frances. Just the kind of light entertainment that Mason can never resist. And would *never* leave home for."

Ridiculously, this hurt.

"Well, you needn't look so affronted," Sally said. "You've just been caught screwing a married man."

The grimy smallness of the thing. A holiday fling with

a habitual philanderer. It was the stuff of jokes and cheap paperbacks. I didn't want to hear any more.

"Look," she said then, almost softly, "here's something for free. By the time you can take a man from a woman like me, you won't want Mason."

Her tone had caught me. "Why do *you*?" I asked.

She held my eyes. "We're a team," she replied.

She leaned sharply across me and flipped my door latch. "Don't waste your time trying to think of an appropriate goodbye," she said. "I don't want to hear it." She turned her perfect profile to me, lifted her dark glasses from the dashboard, and slid them up her nose. "My husband is going to be wondering where I am," she said.

On cotton legs I got out and opened the rear door to retrieve my bag. Then I shut both doors. Twin thuds.

Sally Severance pulled the car deftly from the curb and drove away without looking back. I watched, transfixed, until the tail of the car had disappeared in the distance. Then I turned slowly toward the apartment block. Music from several open doorways competed for space in the courtyard.

"Hola," somebody called.

I didn't call back.

At my door I paused, fishing for the single brass key. It was only as I twisted it in the lock that I realized that Sally had not asked for directions.

By the morning the rush of tears was spent, but, sitting half dressed on the messy bed in the airless apartment, I felt the sour prick of self-pity in my throat. I hated them all, I hated my life, and I had a new eye for the cramped unattractiveness of my surroundings. I dropped my legs, sulkily, over the bed edge, and then, for a beat, held still. I could smell him. Through the thin, unreal atmosphere of weariness and defeat, I could smell him in the warm dust of the tiny apartment. I shut my eyes and caught the scent of cloves at the base of his neck.

Eventually I showered and dressed, taking something that I had not worn during those weeks of thrilling elation from the bureau drawer. I walked the eleven milling blocks to Letty's house and stood on her green porch amid the screaming parrot-bright press of flowering plants and told her mother that I was leaving Mexico. It seemed that these were the first solid words to have come out of my own mouth for a long time. Letty's mother took my hands and said she was sorry and invited me in, but I declined, and turned, and walked, in that curious bleak state between misery and exhaustion, back to the apartment and shut the door behind me.

At some point during the afternoon of that veiled day, a burst of reasonless, lunatic hope sent me responding to a knock at the door with my heart crashing in my chest. I smoothed my hair with automatic hands before I answered it.

Maria had come. Her cherub features were drawn with sadness. She lifted her arms so that her creamy wrists spilled from the heavy sleeves of her dress, and she hugged me. At her motherly, comforting touch I cried.

"Tu amiga," she crooned soothingly. "Tu bonita amiga . . . y los bambinos." She shook her head with the great weight of her pain for the death of my pretty friend and the terrible loss for the baby boys.

I was ashamed. I wiped my eyes quickly and invited her in. When she was settled I told her that I would go away. To my parents. She thought this most appropriate and nodded gravely. For a moment I considered, in the face of her simple sincerity, telling her everything. Just to tell it. My side. As Sally had told her side to me. But I let her leave, instead, with her image of me intact.

Alone again, I began to pack up the apartment with a kind of manic fervor, emptying drawers and laying busy little piles of belongings about the place, as if they meant something. I lifted the canvas bag that had been packed two nights before by unknown hands, placed it on the bed, and removed a soft wedge of folded clothes. The bracelet that Mason had given me fell from them and landed with a rickety clatter on the floor.

I looked at the bracelet for a second, then lay the clothes down to pick it up. I put it on, twisting my wrist to clasp it, then dropping it again so that the line of gold links fell tenderly against the outward curve of my hand. I remembered him giving it to me. I didn't imagine all of it, I thought. I didn't.

When I finished packing, I made a parcel of things that I could not carry and black-inked my parent's address on the front of it. Then I went to sleep and dreamed, as I would for many years, of Patsy.

In the morning I did not have to walk to the bus station because Maria arrived early with Arturo's car. On the way to town she held my hand in her warmer one and assured me that she would see that my parcel was posted. She laid her free palm squarely on the string to confirm this.

Maria watched as the driver took my luggage from the trunk and then stood importantly next to it while I bought my ticket. When I turned again from the glassed ticket window, pocketing my change, I saw Letty. She was standing, neat and small, under the arch that led to the wide stretch of pavement where the buses pulled up. Drivers paced there, shouting destinations, and children sold chewing gum from trays at their waists. I walked over to her.

"You will write to me?" she asked in her precise English.

"Yes, Letty. I will."

She handed me a small packet. Taped red tissue paper.

"For you," she said. "A goodbye gift."

"Thank you, Letty." I took the present. It felt soft in my hands.

"Open it later," she said.

My bags were hurried into the bus's dark underbelly and the driver called for tickets. Maria kissed my cheek and Letty began, silently, to cry. I held her for a moment, and then I took off Mason's bracelet, which was still clasped to my wrist, and slipped it onto hers.

E P I L O G U E

I KNOW NOW THAT whimper or fanfare at the end of a romance is no indicator of its legacy, but I didn't know it then. I imagined my pain would linger dramatically, scar even. And so I was surprised when, almost twelve months later in London, I opened a letter, readdressed and dutifully sent on by my mother, and felt nothing. The letter was from Mason. His name, signed simply at the bottom of the single white sheet, failed to elicit any identifiable emotion in me. I did recall, with no rushing heart, telling him once about the part of Singapore where my parents were based. I imagined that a secretary had been charged with tracking down the details.

The letter was devoid of clear intention. He was just finding out, I suppose, whether I was still there. I was rather pleased to discover that I was not. I crumpled the thing and dropped it into a wastepaper basket. In the end, he had left no trace.

Perhaps I had not been aware of the totality of the fading because I often thought about the children, coaxing current images of them, a little older than they had been. I found myself wondering, too, from time to time, about Richard, or remembering, always sweetly, something about Ned. But it was none of these vague reminiscings, I knew, that had convinced me that my time in that grand house had carved something deep. It was Sally. Sally, who I could muster with absolute clarity at the close of my eyes. And it was Sally that the small, stiff knot at the bottom of the wastepaper basket made me think of now. I lifted the letter again, set it in the dark Victorian grate, and burned it. To be rid of her.

In casting Sally as villain I had not ignored my own crime, which is what it was. I did not think that my sins made Sally any less culpable. Accountability doesn't work that way. We like to think that it does; we like to imagine that because someone somewhere has committed a transgression equal to or worse than ours, that we are in some way, at least partially, absolved. But we are not. We are alone when the reckoning comes and measured against nobody but ourselves. Just as I am alone now, as alone as anyone can be.

These past weeks, since the party, my health has deteriorated markedly and will go on doing so. I am in pain, but it is not release from that particular distress I seek. Rather, I have decided that there is no advantage for Chloe in drawing this out. So I will begin the process tomorrow of finishing it. I have a store of suitable drugs, stockpiled over the months, and I understand how to administer them gradually to myself in order to maximize the chances of a swift and effective outcome. I will die by my own hand, just as Patsy did. But unlike Patsy, I will ensure that there is no one to witness the grisly particulars of my passing.

·   ·   ·

That night, the night that Sally raised the curtain so deftly on all the repugnant shenanigans, I ran back to my room after Christina had caught me out by the pool and stood, as I have said, with my blood pumping in my ears, trembling for fear of being followed. It is true that I was not followed; it is not true, as I have implied, that I climbed then, worn out and wretched, into my bed. That version comes easily to me, or did for a very long time, because it is the one that I wanted to be true.

Instead, while I waited for the sound of someone coming after me, the silence turned terrifying, and soon it came to me that the person to find, to talk to, was Patsy. If I could talk to Patsy, I could straighten a few things out. Get them clear in my head for later when I spoke to Mason. I still thought that I would be speaking to Mason. I still thought that speaking to Mason would make everything all right. I needed to believe it because at that moment I had no future without him; my life was a wasteland without him in it. It became urgent that I speak to Patsy. Patsy, once my friend and now suddenly, horribly, my rival. And so I went out again, into the empty corridor.

A few, blind moments later I knocked on the door to Patsy's and Richard's bedroom. There was no response, but I thought I heard her inside and I went in anyway. The room was even bigger than mine, with windows facing the sea as well as the poolside. The shutters were drawn, though, and the only light was cast by a single bedside lamp. Patsy was on the bed, her feet toward me and her head turned away.

"Patsy," I said, though I do not know where my voice came from.

She ignored me.

"Patsy," I repeated, with more vigor this time. I had come that far and I wanted it out. I did not believe, anyway, that she was really sleeping. Who could be in the midst of all that? But then, pathetically, it crossed my mind that if she had indeed gone to bed and fallen asleep despite the evening's events, well, she could not have been terribly affected by them. That would have been just like Patsy, to squeeze a drama from something that in fact meant very little to her. She had been drunk too. She was capable of anything when she was drunk. Noting now the way she was sprawled on the bed, one arm hanging adrift from the single sheet, I remembered the drunkenness. Maybe she had just been playing along with some grotesque game of Sally's. I think, for a few moments, this line of reasoning began to make some sense. I could see a whole new way of looking at things, a way that held a flicker of hope for me. I was keen to turn that flicker into a flame.

I approached the bed and called her name for the third time. That is when I saw the bottles. They were not bottles, in fact, but those small containers that prescription medicines come in. They were both empty, and next to them there was an empty tumbler lying on its side. The tumbler smelled of brandy. On the floor, beside the bed, some tablets had fallen and scattered. I leaned down and scooped them up. Then I righted the tumbler and picked up the containers and put them in a wastepaper bin in the corner of the room. I do not think I had a single coherent thought during this process. Maybe hysteria had given way to shock. Or something else.

As I say, at first I had no conscious understanding that Patsy had tried to kill herself. Nor did I make any attempt to ascertain whether or not she had succeeded. But slowly the idea began to dawn on me and I sat on a chair that was an exact replica of one I had in my room, and I thought about it. And what I thought was that, if Patsy died, Mason would naturally turn to me.

Can it be love that makes such dangerous fools of us? Does love descend like a lead bell and cut us off bluntly from the call of reason, of right? Or do we wantonly, selfishly give ourselves over to this delusion in order to avoid the tougher decisions demanded by dull decency?

I sat and watched Patsy, her sleek hair in a tangled mass on the pillow, her one bare shoulder very tanned against the white of the linen; I was watching her die. A fact that only truly came to me, only reached out and grabbed me by the throat and shook me when she actually did.

Some time close to dawn, after I had sat in that room for an hour or more, stupefied by my ludicrous musings, my pitiful longings, Patsy convulsed. And if I had thought I had known fear before that moment, I had not. Bile lurched to my throat as the body on the bed shuddered, electrified. A noise came from it that was part gargle and part animal cry, and Patsy's face twisted toward me, its color changing horribly, violet to blue. Eventually—after how long?—this unspeakable racking violence stopped and she seemed to collapse, to exhale, her soul releasing with a rattling sound. And then she was dead.

I do not think that I screamed, although perhaps I did. Certainly I leapt to my feet, but I just stood, rigid and immobile, rooted to the spot on which my limbs had planted me. By the time it was over I was shaking, shivering all over, like a small bird does before it dies in your hand. Then, appalled, terrified, I switched off Patsy's bedside light as if she were sleeping, which in fact she looked as if she was. Just as she had when I had first come in.

I left after that. And I ran, for the second time in eight hours, without stopping, without breathing.

For many years I expected the battering at the door that would signal exposure. But it did not come. Until now. And in a very different form from the one I had anticipated. Nevertheless, it is real enough, this call, this demand to lay bare my part in that death, my failure to act to prevent it. My willing of it. Could I have helped her? I can't be sure. What matters is that I did not try. I was the man on the bank offering not even a twig hopelessly stretched out to the drowning boy. And now the truth of that, the sin and burden of it, is all here, preserved in my sloping hand, in these three notebooks. They are the school exercise type, flimsy with thin cardboard covers. And at my back the fire rages.